Mind-drive:

I stand apart from the ship in my analog web, looking down at the ball of light webbed from a network of power and energy, sparked with arrows of mental light, a hundred mental waves turning in on themselves, waves on a muddy shore, churning up soot and soil, foaming in coils of power. Central to that silent storm is the prism of the Cork's mind-field, which seems to draw the darkness in a whirpool even as we generate it, funneling the black richness of our emotions through the Engineer and out of the ship in a beam that shoves the *Charter* through the Back Region, a helix blue and white behind us.

Behind the ship are the stars. Ahead, the golden glow of hyperspace. We move through . . . and in.

Like a golden bird, we fly.

MINDSHIP

Gerard F. Conway

DAW BOOKS, INC.
DONALD A. WOLLHEIM, PUBLISHER

1301 Avenue of the Americas
New York, N. Y. 10019

Published by
THE NEW AMERICAN LIBRARY
OF CANADA LIMITED

Cover art by Kelly Freas

For my mother and father:

A brief note of thanks

First Printing, February 1974

1 2 3 4 5 6 7 8 9

PRINTED IN CANADA
COVER PRINTED IN U.S.A.

Prologue: "Valve"

We were three weeks out from Centauri when our Cork blew.

He was a thin man, as Sensitives go, quite gaunt, with lines and hints of age wrinkling the paper-weight thinness of his skin; but for all of that, he was a young man, and it showed in the way he moved—easily, sliding along with that forward shove affected by men new to space, the lop-sided tumble that bumps you off walls and cracks your head against low hatches, gives you a hundred bruises and cuts on your first trip out. Like a fly on water spinning on gauze wings—he moved like that. He was a quiet man for a mindship Cork; usually the burden of draining the emotions of a crew makes a man want to talk, but not him. Occasionally he would smile, but when he did, the smile would rest only a moment on his lips, as though it were unsure, waiting to be blown away. I suppose if I were to chose a word to describe him, a single word, it would be young.

Like all Corks he was a Sensitive. You could see it in his hands, the way they fluttered over his lap when he sat in the lounge, the way they touched and lighted on the arms of his chair, rested on his knees, or moved on to trap themselves under his elbows. His fingers were long, tapered candles lit from within, always sallow and drained, pink at the tips where the nails used to be. When he spoke, his hands would jump and dive, winding tapestries in the smoke-stained air of the lounge where we sometimes slouched about, chatting and listening carefully to the worn tales. When he spoke, his voice was quiet and unobtrusive. When he spoke, he looked down, watching his hands. Sometimes he stared at them as though they were apart from him, flesh-tinted birds nestling in his lap. I know that look.

Three weeks out from our third port, he blew. We were lucky to get back to Endrim. Lucky for us. *His* luck ran out the day he shipped aboard the *Charter*.

A man can't think of himself objectively, at least that's the way it is with me. I can't judge my actions; it's too easy to relax the more temperate aspects of one's personality and take hell out on oneself for the mistakes of one's past. Too easy. We all tend to mark ourselves as martyrs.

I was captaining the *Charter* when we first limped in to Endrim. Half the crew had been blown away by our last jump into the Back Region; our previous Captain had been among the first to go, and because I was his First Mate, I took us up and carried us through and brought us down and kept us Out. I did all the right things, all the smart things . . . and we still lost half our crew.

By the time we touched down on Endrim we were a crippled mass of mindship. Even the Engineer was on the verge of being blown. Somewhere back during the early moments of the disaster our Cork—this one an old man way past his third 'juve, a crumpled wreck who'd managed to stick it through six runs aboard the *Charter* with only minor emotional adjustments; the contrast between him and the Cork we picked up on Endrim was startling—had cracked up and had begun fingering the pod controls in his bay section. Somehow he punched a lifecraft node and ejected himself into hyperspace. Never found him. At that point, we were all too busy trying to stay alive to go looking for a senile Sensitive. Perhaps we should have sent out a pod, though—after he blew, everything seemed to crumble at the edges, eating toward our middle like acid rust on a sheet of cheap tin. It was then that the Engineer began to complain of stress along the lateral line; it was then that half the crew snapped and went screaming into madness. Perhaps we *should* have tried to save him, after all.

A Cork is a useful thing on a mindship. Without one, crews have a tendency to dissolve in their own insanity. It's the nature of the game: we need emotion to pass into the Back Region, and we need a Cork to keep us alive.

That's why I made finding one first priority when we finally touched port on Endrim. Some things can't wait on formality.

In a port, any port, whether it's on the dark side of the Spiral or the light, you'll find three types of districts: the pleasure center, where the less discriminating Physicals congregate; the livers—local residents only; and the communes. It's the last area you look for when you're seeking a Sensitive.

That's where I found the new Cork.

I was with the Cook. He pushed through the screen ahead of me, twisting around to hold back the strands and let me through. I ducked under the low hangings and came up into a wreath of sweet smoke tainted by an under odor of dust, the dry, choking flavor of packed earth. It was a basement room, and it was dark, graying near the center, where candles and oil lamps made a futile effort to relieve the gloom. I blinked against the smoke sting and glanced at the unmoving shapes outlined in the dim glow.

"Here?" I asked the Cook.

"Where else?"

"It's your game." Straightening, I looked around, waiting for my eyes to adjust to the darkness. Beside me the Cook shuffled about, apparently seeking a familiar face. If he could see a face. He's told me that though he wasn't born on Endrim, he considers it his home; I suppose that's because so many ex-Sensitives live there. He'd been my guide, more or less. I'd received the impression that parts of the port were as strange to him as they were to me. I hoped this wasn't one of them.

A figure near the far wall moved, unwound into a spider shape vaguely resembling a man. The Cook moved forward and hooked an arm, beckoning the house head to him. They spoke in low tones while I settled myself against a wall latticed with narrow cracks and made a pretense of relaxing. I was tense. I was a new Captain and this was my first independent cruise, and my first crew choice. I was tense.

They came over to me finally, the house head moving in a slow, stooped slide-walk. Spacer. I watched him, and in the darkness I saw the left side of his face, creviced where a set of capillaries had broken. A blown Cork, one who'd snapped so far from reality the pieces were scattered like sand. His eyes found mine, he saw my expression and he smiled, a tug of his lips just slightly askew from the shape of his face.

"Not your man here, Cap'n, no, not me," he said in a broken Sensitive's slow tones. "Quiet boy we got, back new. Fresh one, no scars, you see, huh?" His voice was blurred by the ruined muscles in his neck.

"Let's see him," I said.

"Back. Wait, hold. 'Kay."

He turned and slipped into the shadows. I glared at the Cook, but he didn't seem to see me.

God.

Then the blown Cork was back, and behind him was another man. Correction: a boy. And just like that, with a man coming at me out of the darkness, I snapped. Not on the surface, no: underneath, so deep inside me I didn't sense it then, or even later when it all surged out. It was then, right then, that I snapped. It was then that I made my first mistake and committed my first murder—a homicide of myself, and of this young Cork. Not tangibly. Not real so you could touch it—but real so it would be in my mind forever when I saw it for what it was.

His hands moved nervously at his sides, finally hooking the loops of his overjacket and fidgeting in and out of the leather curls. He didn't look at me, just toward me, and he spoke softly in answer to my questions, almost too low to be heard. I tried to act the well-prepared professional.

"Name?"

He told me.

"You're from Endrim?"

He shook his head and named a place just out from the Center.

"How'd you get out here?"

He'd shipped passage. That startled me. Passage from the Center to the rim was hardly inexpensive, and twice as expensive to return; there were many old spacers caught on the rim who'd been born near earth, who couldn't return to their homeworld to die. Not even a non-Company trader will take on a man after his fourth rejuve, and those spacers caught on Endrim were next to creditless. Sometimes a charter ship will give mercy passage, but not often, and when a psi ship does, the man becomes a sort of galley slave, and generally ends up working harder than he ever had in a life of spacing. For most, though, running to the rim is a one-way ticket, and Endrim is the last stop. It's the final haul, the last jump before death—yet here was a man little more than a boy who'd shipped passage to the soul dump of the galaxy. It was odd. It was more than odd, and I said as much.

He shrugged, and his hands twisted in the loops of his jacket. Endrim was where he wanted to be.

"Experience?" I asked. "Contract?"

He'd been on two local runs, and had been laid off when the shuttle lost its in-system permit, something that was constantly happening with these non-Company mindships. No Contract with a major company, not even a civil service slot. In effect, he was completely without experience. It would have been suicidal for me to take him on.

"Contract him," I said to the Cook, turned to avoid the Cook's wide-eyed stare, and pushed my way out of the commune into the cool night air of Endrim.

When we cut ourselves, we use small knives.

He was a fair Cork. In time, with experience to back his instincts, he could have been a good one. He had a natural sense of calm, a quiet manner that set one at ease, relaxing tightened muscles and soothing anxieties to a throb rather than a pain. He was a Sensitive, and he did his job. Just talking with him eased the soul.

When we were in drive he was everywhere, talking, calming, relaxing, easing: a mind among our minds, a valve for our combined tensions—a release. A Cork.

During those weeks of our first run under my command, I watched him with half attention. He always seemed to be only a few feet away, a constantly stabilizing force because of his familiarity. When I was setting a course or reviewing the flow of the mind-structure powering the ship, he was there, a lamb-soft presence that our previous Corks had never been. Where they'd been huge, powerful, and consuming, he was small, an undercurrent sewer for our frustrations. He channeled the dirt and the insanity out of our minds, keeping us, Sensitives and Physicals alike, on the tightrope between the sane and the mad.

I say us. That includes the Captain, though he is a Physical. Most of all, it includes the Captain.

I've heard Corks described as maternal images, psychic wombs into which the power minds of a ship crawl during stress, there to be cradled and loved. I've heard them likened to sewers as well, draining the filth of our souls; the poisons that power a mindship have to be sucked away, and so the Cork was the valve that cleaned us all. In a way, our young Cork was both. The only sane mind in our crew, our valve, our Cork.

I admit it: to a degree we were all insane. There can't be a truly sane mind aboard a psi ship, Physical or not; it's a contradiction in terms. Sane minds don't provide the energy needed to twist space and send a ship skidding into the Back Region, where all the laws of Einsteinian reality exist slightly warped. Sane minds are passage payers, not crew. Sane minds are useless in space—with one exception, and that's a Cork. If he blows, everything blows.

And that's your *real* one-way ticket.

I didn't see him again after that night in the commune for two weeks out from Endrim. I'd been aware of his presence, but there's a difference between awareness and confrontation. One is nebulous, the other is stark and real. It's an important difference. It was, for me.

I'd fixed the lines and set the degrees for the dive down the gravity well to Centauri: in the Back Region the well acts like a magnet on a mindship, providing the pull for a rim-to-Center run, so all that's required is a vector set and a guard crew to watch for Black Holes. Going *up* from Centauri is another matter, however; you're fighting all the way, riding light currents while dragging against the gravity of the galactic core. In a run Out that's a real struggle . . . and it's during a run Out that your Cork receives his greatest beating. That's why I found him in the lounge sipping at a drink of absinthe and beer; going In he could afford to wander outside his station near the Control Room—going Out he'd have no time for socializing. For now, he could sit there, listening and drinking, watching with a distant, passive look.

I went over.

We made small talk, untroubled talk between a Captain and one of his officers. He seemed reticent about that part of his life before he came to Endrim; in passing, when I asked him about his early days before he left the Centauri area, he became less talkative. He seemed to wind in on himself, a slight hardening of the wires in his neck—nothing definite, just a sudden withdrawal. He circumvented the entire subject with a single soft phrase, bringing the conversation around to me and my own past. Strangely, the shift didn't strike me as abrupt. Perhaps I'd wanted to talk about myself and had only been marking time until the inevitable return inquiries began. It was friendly and shallow talk. It seemed so.

I talked about my life on my homeworld, a dustbin planet in the western end of the Arm. He listened, and his attention seemed to act as a salve, drawing out things from my past that I'd let rest for years, things of which I'd been aware, but which for some reason I'd kept buried:

Being alone during a sandstorm and crouching in a corner of cold steel while wind pelted the outside walls with a rain of dry sand; watching a brother die and being too small to help him, too young to make the proper moves; then being alone again, never wanting to be alone again, leaving the world days later, finally spacing; being where walls were still cold steel, where other winds still pelted the outside with dry sand, but where you *weren't* alone, where there were other minds joining yours with theirs, and their mind with yours. Speaking of a gut need to *stay inside*, safe from the naked outside of vacuum and dust, to hide within a framework of cozy steel, running from space into space. I told him about a box I'd seen once that opened into another box, which flowered to reveal a third box, each layer peeling away in turn, until there was nothing left but a final cube, which couldn't be opened. In languid tones I told him all of this, and at the time I thought it was all idle conversation, talk between a Captain and one of his men.

I see now I wanted him to understand why I had to kill him.

He listened, and his hands danced at the ends of his arms, alien hands with separate lives. Or not so separate.

I didn't ask him about himself again. It seemed distant and relatively unimportant.

We talked, and after a while, I left.

We made the run into Centauri under the line. We'd charted most of the space assigned to us when the *Charter* had left the Demios Base four months earlier under a different Captain and a partially different crew. Now it was time for a trade run, and they told us we'd have to pick up our cargo on Endrim, a shipment of absinthe from the factories there, to the colonies along the eastern end of the Spiral Arm. But first, there were two more runs in the center of the Spiral. The first took us across the galactic plane: five weeks without incident off ship, and only one incident on.

The Cook pointed it out. He was a bulky man, the Cook, short and graying and heavy around the jaw where the webbing of broken capillaries cupped his chin, but even so, he was a perceptive man. Before the accident that made him a Physical, he'd been one of the best Corks under Contract. I'd just left Control when he approached and plucked at my side.

"It's the Cork, Captain. I think he's ready to snap."

"What?"

"He's sitting, not talking to anyone. Something's wrong, I can feel it."

I stared at him, letting it sink in slowly. The Cork. "Where is he?" I asked.

"In the mess. He's just sitting there, Captain. Drinking."

That was bad. I strode down the hall, found myself moving into a trot, came to the lift shaft, and dropped the three levels to the lounge. He was sitting by himself just behind the Cook's coffee console, sipping at a steaming cup of coffee laced with absinthe. He was staring at his hands.

I asked him, "What's wrong?"

Nothing. He shrugged and tried a weak smile. I slid onto the bench opposite him and nervously keyed the remote on the table before me. Muscles jumped in spasms along the outsides of my ankles as I waited for the coffee: it's a nervous thing I get. I watched the Cork. He kept his eyes on his hands, occasionally taking a sip of his coffee.

"Cook says there's something the matter. . . ."

He said no, nothing was wrong.

I felt uneasy sitting there with him; everything about him was calm and gentle—and yet I felt uneasy. I realized that I'd almost deliberately avoided him since that day in the lounge. Being near him made me uncomfortable; I couldn't have explained it.

"Dammit," I said, "*say* something."

He did. Quietly, he started to talk. Nothing in particular, commenting first on the smoothness of the run, the attitude of the crew, who he thought was involved with whom, how much he liked the ship, how happy he was to be Corking under me, how he liked the Engineer, how he was glad the others liked him. He rambled, continuing on without saying anything. His hands drifted across the tabletop as he spoke, brushing it gently as though smoothing a bed sheet. He talked, and finally I stopped listening. I didn't want to listen, not really. I pushed away from the table. He stopped speaking and looked up at me.

Was something wrong?

"No," I answered wearily. "No. Everything's fine. Just OK. I'll see you later."

I went out feeling weak. Something nagged at the back of my mind and I brushed it away, just as I brushed away my last view of the Cork sitting there watching me leave, his eyes blank and, apparently, uncaring.

I saw him about the corridors of the ship. He moved through the halls slowly, his head lowered as he took a wandering path along the rim corridors of the vessel, on those decks where the artificial gravity was activated. Moving like a wraith, he seemed lost in thought, but we knew that the distant look in his eyes was the look of a Sensitive in contact. He left varying impressions on the crew. Some thought him a touch insane, others that he was more sane than any of us, and was lost in our insanity; still others didn't care. Both extremes, madness and insanity, were wrong, by my thinking; his mind was a mixture. He was different, apart from us; dispassionate might have been the word for it, but for the fact that he was hardly cold. I found him once or twice when he thought he was alone, shaking himself back and forth and muttering something low and rhythmic under his breath. In anyone but a Cork I would have said it bordered on madness, but the ways a Cork maintains his sanity sometimes seem stranger than madness. . . .

That was the way it seemed to me at the time. Now I understand that I didn't *want* to recognize his distress; I didn't want to see how he was crumbling inside. He was the Cork. And I wondered why I picked him.

So it went. He wandered and listened, and spoke little of himself—little of substance, little of *him*—and in his station he took up our insanities.

And on our third run, three weeks out from Centauri, up from the Center, he blew.

Mind-drive:

I stand apart from the ship in my analog web, looking down at the ball of light webbed with a network of power and energy, sparked with arrows of mental light, a hundred mental waves turning in on themselves, waves on a muddy shore, churning up soot and soil, foaming in coils of power. Central to that silent storm is the prism of the Cork's mind-field, which seems to draw the darkness in a whirlpool even as we generate it, funneling the black richness of our emotions through the Engineer and out of the ship in a beam that shoves the *Charter* through the Back Region, a helix blue and white behind us.

Behind the ship are the stars. Ahead, the golden glow of hyperspace. We move through . . . and in.

I stand apart from the ship, held in the electric stress of the web structured about me by the shipboard computers. I guide the mindship with carefully directed bursts of power, power applied through the field my crew members create around me. I stand apart with my mind, outside the ship, the noneyes of the Captain's Set overseeing the flow of the mind-drive.

Like a golden bird, we fly.

Below, a hundred sick men pour out the filth of their souls, and that filth is funneled by the Engineer. Below, a hundred sick minds are filtered through a sane one, our safety valve, our Cork.

But here . . . we fly. The stream of energy pulses, eternal, unchanging.

The *Charter* flies.

I can feel the weight of Center dragging at me—a sensation akin to that one feels when climbing a mountain under a heavy pack. It sets me aslant. I compensate and the ship shifts, and we move sluggishly through the stream.

Images in my mind:

Twist—

Squatting in sunlight, sweating from open pores, dying—waiting and no one comes. He's dead. My fault. They're all dead: Desert world.

(Thoughts from the prism: gentle, cool, draining off the memory.)

Twist—

Dark, cold room around and over me, sounds throbbing in my bones, in my skull—alone, panicking—

(His hand comes into my mind and draws away the madness, silken fingers brushing my thoughts—cold.)

Twist—

The Control Room, chaotic: fires, smashed consoles and screens, the labored breathing of the madman in the Captain's Set, blood trickling from his nostrils, a river down his chin. Screaming, I shove him from his chair, watching his body curl over on itself like paper tossed into a fire. Screaming still, I clamber into the Captain's Set, knowing I can't do what I need to, finding the wires, shoving them in—

(And the Cork comes, plumbing the poisons from my mind, and I am purged . . . cleansed. . . .)

And the ship dives on.

In the Control Room I jerked forward as something took the *Charter* and *shook* it.

Walls canted around me. I fell sliding from the Set, catching myself before the wires could tear from my skin. In the distance alarms wailed.

Somehow I was back in the Set, strapping the emergency bands across my chest. Another shock threw the ship forward. I slammed into the restraining bands and bounced back, stunned.

"Engineer . . . status report." Calm. Tendrils of calm played with the panic lacing my consciousness. I gripped the armrest, forcing myself to relax.

Forcing—

I cut off the hurried string of numerals from the Engineering section. "The Cork," I asked, "where is he? I want him up in the Control Room with me. *Now.*"

"Yes, Captain."

Punching a key on the board to my left, I studied an exterior view of the ship. The screen showed a bowl of gray curling to either side, unmarked but for a puncture of black dead center ahead. A Black Hole. I felt a chill start a slow crawl up my spine.

"He's not in his section, sir."

"Then find him."

"Yes, sir."

Not in his section. The implication drove home and fell away. I stared at the screen, no longer registering the scene of disaster rapidly approaching. *Not in his section.*

"Captain?"

"What?"

"We've located him, sir."

"Where?"

"In the . . . ah . . . mess, sir. Drinking coffee."

God in heaven!

"Send him up."

"Yes, sir."

The ship lurched forward again: the tidal forces from the stellar freak ahead, the "Black Hole," final result of a collapsing star, the mass of a million planets compressed into an area four miles across, possessing gravitational properties that could reach even to the Back Region. . . . I sent out signals to reverse thrust. The image on the screen flickered, faded, then grew large again. I'd need more power. *Much* more power, if we were to survive.

Behind me a pneumatic hiss signaled the entrance of the Cork.

"Where in hell were you?"

He started to explain. I cut him off. "Never mind. You'll be stationed here. I want you near me when we push past that hole."

He didn't answer. I was busy once more, making course corrections and feeding new figures into the computer brains that lined the walls of the Control Room, relaying the decisions and revisions they arrived at along the mental circuits binding the ship. Around me the computers hummed, the screens winked and glowed, and I felt the ship gathering power as its many minds drew their strength together, preparing.

During a pause, I glanced up at him.

He was ready to blow.

You get to know the look after a while. The slouched posture, the eyes, the trembling hands fumbling with the buttons and zippers on a jacket. His gaze didn't meet mine. It wasn't a new thing, but now it seemed to have an unvoiced meaning, where before . . .

"Oh god."

He didn't seem to hear me.

I groped in the slot under the left armrest and came up with a syringe kept there for the Captain's use during a hard drive. It was full. A third of it would be enough. I grabbed his arm and plunged the needle in, and it was then I sinned. I gave it all.

He seemed unaffected.

"Just stay," I said, "just keep thinking . . ."

He didn't answer. He didn't seem to hear me.

I turned from him and made the connections that would send me over to mind-drive. I blacked out.

Black:

Shrieking:

Writhing and alive, the hole:

Light.

Mind-drive:

It spins from everywhere and it bends in on us, a great obsidian sore. I throw the ship forward—

—*boxes, each flowering into the next, and* (A ghost form comes and takes the fear from me, swallows it into himself)—

—battering past the gravity well, slamming through seas of tidal pull, while the collapsed sun sinks forever below us, dragging us, the Back Region consumed with heat, wrinkling in the black-pitch energy storm, bending around us, warping around us, falling from us—

Twist—

Seething sun golden madness leaping now larger always larger—

(Hands come, take our madness.) (Frail hands, like tissue.) (Tissue in a maelstrom.) (Breaking.)

A hundred sick minds pour out their insanity and the

sewer swallows the ichor, and it drives us on, funneled behind us.

The Black Hole erupts.

I slide the ship around and away—cut forward and pitch into overdrive.

And we are gone, splicing from the unreal to the real, in and out and—gone. Where we'd been, the Black Hole blossoms, spreads like ink, and drains away.

The ship moved through a fold in space and slid into the graindark midnight of Outside. We drifted through a sudden calm. In objective space, the Black Hole was light years distant, already a dying memory. Around us the stars were brilliant on a velvet sky. There was silence, blessed silence.

Silence. . . .

Everywhere. . . ?

. . . no.

From some dim corner of our collective consciousness there came a moan of pain and agony, not an audible moan, not a physical scream of torment—but a whimpering mental whine.

The Cork.

I returned to the Control Room, tore off my straps, and swung down from the Captain's Set. I found him slumped on the floor inches from my feet, his arms outstretched as though he were groping for something that was now forever out of his reach. . . .

His mind was gone, lost in the madness I'd forced him to drain. He lay in a huddle at the foot of the Set, wound in on himself fetuslike, his pale hair tumbling over eyes that were blank and staring. He'd clamped down on his tongue sometime during the flight and now a stream of thick blood dribbled past his lips and onto the floor, where already it was crusting brown. His clothes were in ragged strips. His arms were bleeding where he'd struck himself agains the sharp edges of the Set. He was whimpering when I came to him, spitting up blood with each sigh. I bent quickly, removing the wires from his forehead. I pulled him into a sitting position. His body was limp and sagging in my hands. I stared at him and after a time I let him down and left him there to whimper alone, in silence.

Some nights I wake shrieking and huddle under the bedclothes warm with my sweat, and ask myself—why did I do that, why did I pick him, why *him?*

As yet I've found no answer, but it doesn't trouble me too greatly anymore. I have release, of a sort.

At night the silken fingers quickly come, and steal the pain away.

Chapter One

Eighth month, third day, anno Domini 3146

He'd been awake for hours, lying in the darkness of the room and watching the dusky glow of his cigarette crawl toward his fingertips. The fingers were stained yellow, callused under each knuckle with a layer of thick white skin. At times, nervously, he would worry at the callus on his forefinger with the nail of his thumb. When he was sitting alone in the galley lounge aboard ship, or at his station during drive, or at times like this, lying awake in the early hours before false dawn, he would worry that lip of skin until the irritation made the flesh under the callus become inflamed, or until his nerves were unable to stand the monotony any longer, and then he would bite the dead skin free. Inevitably a new callus would form within a few days, and the process would begin anew.

The storm was over. Now there was only a gentle rain misting the balcony beyond his window with a faint post-moonlight haze. Kilgarin looked at the woman sleeping beside him. She lay turned away on her stomach, her back bare above the quilt. There was a soft tracing of brown fur across her shoulders and shoulder blades, just thick enough to be noticed in the blue light from outside. The down moved as she breathed. Just then, as he watched, she shivered and tried, in her sleep, to snuggle more fully under the covers. Kilgarin drew them up about her neck. Her stirrings ceased and she made low throat noises as she shifted once more, turned her face toward him, and drifted gently back to sleep.

He stood and drew on his robe, bracing himself against the moist wind off the Endrim sea. His legs felt cold, his arms wet. The breeze tasted of salt, but Kilgarin knew it was only an illusion. The sea fronting the tavern district was fresh water, as were most of the smaller bays and lakes on the young frontier world. He closed his eyes and welcomed the memory of other planets, especially the clear, crystal memory of his only visit to earth. He'd spent his leave near the sea, on an untainted shore in the eastern hemisphere. The water had been warm, salty. There'd been a woman. . . . Kilgarin broke off the thought, opening his eyes and staring at the motion of shadow in the room, and the window showing the town below.

He was a tall man, a little over two meters, with black hair drawn back from his forehead and bound with a leather wrap at the base of his neck. His arms were well muscled, his shoulders broad and thick, but his chest was thin, his waist was narrow, and his hips were a bit wider than normal, all signs of his non-Physical background. His legs were heavy and strong: he'd spent most of his hours off the *Drowner* walking. On the worlds the mindship had visited, Kilgarin had wandered for hours through forests and deserts, over hills and across plains: it gave him time to fix a sense of *place* in his mind, making the planet more real than it would have been seen only from a port window or studied from the base of a ship's fin. His wrists were thick and his hands were callused, and that by itself was odd for a Sensitive, especially odd for a former Cork. Kilgarin enjoyed working with his hands, and had gone out of his way to find craft work, finally settling on wood carving as a hobby. His pieces were primitive—he readily admitted it—but they'd gained some favorable comments, particularly from a friend he'd had aboard the *Drowner*, a former art critic who'd worked as Communications Sensitive until he'd blown, the Centaurian named J'kar, who'd mentioned something about "an assurance to the work that amazed" him. Kilgarin smiled at the memory. He looked at his hands, then tucked them under his arms and glanced out at the balcony and the port city beyond.

The air was cool out there. He relaxed against the brick wall, closing his eyes and trying to visualize the town. It was something he did when he settled on a planet for more than a day; he tried to place the buildings and streets in his mind. It gave him a kind of mental freedom then, to arrange his life around those things—as though he were studying a new game board, learning, in a way, to play the game.

There: the steeple of a church. And there: the row

of prefabricated buildings, which had been erected by the Company before the advent of the new Independence government on Endrim, little white-and-blue dollops on a green strip. And closer: the thick structure of the Company's factory complex, the processing and refining plants, the managerial offices separated from the rest by a rectangular fountain/pool. And also there, fittingly, the first of the city's taverns, on the same block as the plant, just a half mile outside the Sensitive District, a small windowless tavern built into an older building's basement. And here: the newer buildings erected under the Independence government, black iron balconies set close to pseudo-brick facades. Kilgarin opened his eyes. It was all there, including the landmark he'd neglected to remember, accidentally or deliberately: the spaceport. The ships in the port glistened under the arc lights of the maintenance buildings, their snub prows running with rivers of blue light, the cleansing autohoses swooping about them in the glow of the bright spots. Kilgarin half-turned from the sight, and saw instead the Company refining plant. Neither pleased him, but both were the cause of his being there on Endrim, his reason for picking this planet for his retirement. He rubbed his hands over his eyes, sighing.

Behind him the girl moaned. He listened to her rustlings with slight amusement. He'd slept with professional women before, and he knew how foolish it was to have illusions about them—especially since his abortive affair with Marka three years before, and even more so, now that he owned a brothel himself. But still . . . something of the romantic nestled within him, and he turned and watched her movements as she stretched under the blankets, smiling, almost, with affection. It was simpler to make love to a woman like this. She was firm bodied, as were all the women in his brothel; her breasts were heavy, flattening as she shifted to one side, and there was a coarseness to her features no makeup could remove, tight lines at the edges of the mouth, tension in the molding of her face. Life was difficult for a Physical on Endrim. Even though the city was a port, its inhabitants rarely found work in anything but a tourist-service capacity. The refineries employed only Company contractees from off planet, for reasons Kilgarin couldn't comprehend, with the result that hopefuls immigrating to this rim world often found themselves without a job. Many tried for a shipping Contract, but more often the less qualified Physicals sought work in one of the taverns or hotels. How many whores in the city? Kilgarin didn't want to know. In a way he felt responsible for their misfortunes, though he didn't treat his own women unfairly—yet somehow that didn't matter. To Kilgarin, at moments like this one, his very participation in the economy of the world—regardless of the motives he knew worked within him, and which he understood—brought out a normally buried sense of guilt.

There was a sound in the street below. He stepped to the balcony and looked over. A figure drifted by, cape floating from firm shoulders. Two men on the opposite corner called again—it was their first call that had attracted Kilgarin's attention—and the girl in the cape, positioning herself by the doorway of the building, motioned them over. Kilgarin grunted and turned his gaze to the rooftops.

He stared at the white buildings of the port, arranged at angles to the central mile-square landing strip. He felt nothing, and sensed pride because of that emptiness. It'd taken him time to heal the wounds he'd sustained aboard the *Drowner*. The six years he'd spent as a Cork since his eighteenth birthday hadn't been easy for him. He was glad to forget what he could.

He turned and reentered the apartment. It was still strange to think of it as his own. He'd never possessed anything as large as this building, and it made him uneasy—for a moment. Shrugging off the gathering concerns, he smiled to himself and walked softly back to the bed to awaken the sleeping girl.

Kilgarin moved down the short flight of steps into the bar's foyer, where a man in a high-waisted tunic briefly probed his mind, satisfied himself that Kilgarin was a Sensitive, took his tip, and led him into the main lounge. As he walked to the counter Kilgarin felt the doorman's eyes on him, admiring his blue tunic and leather trousers; he smiled, and still smiling, settled himself on a swivel stool before the ancient ex-Cork bartender and ordered a beer cut with absinthe. The old man did things with glasses, slid a mug across the counter, and accepted the credit chit Kilgarin gave him in return.

"Any of the others around, Pul?" The absinthe burned in Kilgarin's throat, dry and bitter, reminding him it had been years since he'd tasted honest Endrim wormwood.

Shrugging bony shoulders the bartender said, "A few, not many tonight. J'kar. Wils. The twins were here, but not now. Bad time tonight, ships out, you know?"

Kilgarin nodded and sipped his drink.

"J'kar told us you were coming," the old man continued, muttering through broken lips. "How long Out, huh?"

"A couple of months. J'kar must have left the *Drowner* on our last pass through Endrim, right?"

Pul passed a hand over his stubbled chin, eyeing Kilgarin's emptied glass. The younger Cork pushed it toward him, asked for one more. The old man complied and Kilgarin asked, "How is he, Pul?"

"J'kar? Now, OK, guess. Bad for a bit. Couldn't move, too much trembling, face all swollen, red. Broken bad. But what hell, happens to us all, y'know?"

Kilgarin said yes, he knew, accepted the glass, and swung down from the bar, glancing around the shadowed room. In a corner by one of the draped windows, two men were talking. One had his back to Kilgarin: red hair over a thick, florid neck, the collar of a blue Sensitive's jump suit lapping a gray vest that barely stretched between broad shoulders. Kilgarin walked over. The man facing him noticed his approach and said something to his companion. J'kar blinked around, his lopsided face splitting into a grin when he recognized Kilgarin. He made room on the bench, half-turning to face his friend and make the introductions.

"This here straight, his name's Kilgarin. Old buddy, back to back, sweat same ship five years, the *Drowner*. Looks like a fed cow, hey? Bet you been slopping off since J'kar left, no one whips you 'round, huh?"

Kilgarin smiled. "Something like that." He gave the older man his hand. J'kar took it and pressed it loosely. There was something wrong with the muscles in his wrist. "How are you, J'kar?" Kilgarin asked.

"Living, OK. This mate here, his name's Whyte."

The two men greeted each other formally. Whyte's eyes were a soft yellow and seemed somehow out of focus; Kilgarin realized, startled, that the man's right eye was sightless. Whyte's features were devoid of emotion, though his lips were tucked back in a noncommitted smile as he shook Kilgarin's hand.

J'kar nudged Kilgarin's hand with his own. "C'mon, drink. We'll get another."

Kilgarin complied and they ordered another round from the console in their booth. When the glasses came, Kilgarin started to lift his, but J'kar stopped him with a toast. "Shipmates," said the broken Sensitive, and both Kilgarin and Whyte drank with their eyes watching each other over the rims of their mugs.

"What now, Killy?" J'kar asked. "Here, good? No more Contracts?"

"Certainly not this year. Perhaps never again, if things work out. I've just about come the route, J'kar; your luck only lasts so long, and mine's been pretty strong, I suppose . . . but, well . . . you know."

"Sure, best, that. I guess. Whyte, Killy was fellow on *Drowner* till last spring, would've been this year five together, but I had this accident, y'know." J'kar flexed the muscles in his arms, smiling with just a hint of regret. "But Kilgarin, still going, him. Right?"

"Until now, anyway," Kilgarin said, uneasily. J'kar's inability to speak coherently was something he hadn't expected, though he knew he should have—it was normal with a Sensitive who'd collapsed. In fact, Kilgarin had almost managed to forget the incident which'd broken the former art critic; it came back now with J'kar's every-slurred word. "I've gotten myself a place."

"Now? Oh, right: you quit." The Centaurian seemed confused for a moment, finally nodding as though he'd settled something in his mind. "You and your brother, getting together now? You mean place for you two?"

"My brother?"

"Sure, him here month ago, this bar. Ask Pul. Asking 'bout you, sure. Hey, didn't find you, huh?"

Kilgarin worked on his drink, thoughtfully. He shook his head. "No, he didn't. The last I knew, he was back home on Wellington, schooling."

"Well, now here. Or was. Ask Whyte."

The other Sensitive broke in, changing the subject. "What sort of place you got, Kilgarin?"

With half-attention, Kilgarin told the two broken Sensitives about the building he'd bought in the Sensitive District. It was a mechanical description; in the two weeks since he'd landed on Endrim, he'd given the report a hundred times to every ex-shipmate he met. He always extended the same offer of work, and always, it was accepted. He knew what information would interest his listeners, he knew how to pace all the elements of the tale, and for a time he'd enjoyed working the reactions of his audience. But only for a time. For Kilgarin, the process of telling a story had become a craft so instinctive it no longer intrigued him, and a part of him regretted this, more deeply than he would have thought possible.

When he'd been Cork aboard the *Drowner*, before the run just past, he'd spent most of his free ship time in the galley lounge, spinning long and involuted stories for his mates, each a creation of the moment and each what they needed to break the tedium of mind-drive. He'd gained a minor sort of fame, and he supposed there'd been a few disappointed newcomers on his last run, when he refused to work up a single tale. As certain as he was that word had gotten around about his story-telling ability, he was equally certain that word about his accident *hadn't* been circulated. Such subjects were taboo, both out of compassion for the Cork (who was *always* aware of what was being said and thought about him) and out of a superstitious notion that if it wasn't mentioned, it hadn't really happened.

Thinking about that very effective method of dealing with tragedy, Kilgarin wondered briefly if any of the men who'd been with him when Baeder died could even *remember* how close Kilgarin had come to breaking. So complete were those emotional erasures, Kilgarin reflected as he sipped at his beer and told J'kar and Whyte about his brothel, that it often seemed as though the bad events were merely dream memories, fading away.

He then remembered his brother, Marc, and realized he'd been practicing his own emotional erasure. By centering on his own problems, he'd managed to avoid thinking about his brother's. The boy must have broken loose, Kilgarin thought. It was something he'd expected since he himself had left the family. Marc Kilgarin was an unstable boy: it had been apparent in the way he moved, and especially in his hands, which were incapable of rest. Kilgarin remembered how, when the four members of the family used to gather for dinner, young Marc would sit with his fingers knotting and unknotting in his lap until his father allowed the family to begin eating. They were like pink birds, those hands. Kilgarin smiled at the image; it was one Marc would have liked. If the boy were here on Endrim—

Kilgarin shook himself, looked from his own hands to the faces before him and finished the description of his new project. "Want to come aboard, J'kar? I could use a friend with a dose of common sense."

J'kar tapped both hands on the tabletop, nervously drumming a quick rhythm, blinking at Kilgarin, then at Whyte, then at his hands. Kilgarin glanced at the Centaurian's fingers, the memory of his brother's hands still strong in his mind. J'kar's knuckles were red and bloated, and both little fingers were obviously paralyzed, apparently by the same nervous disruption that had ruined his forearms.

"I'm asking you to come in with me," Kilgarin said again, this time with more emphasis, hoping his tone would tell J'kar what he needed to know.

The older man stopped tapping, sat one hand in the palm of the other, and rubbed the two hands together. He was still silent, but the storm of emotions Kilgarin felt boiling in the air between them was almost overpowering—so strong Kilgarin couldn't determine which emotion was the dominant one: frustration, anger, love, gratitude, shame, or that other emotion, the one for which Kilgarin had no name. He knew nothing like it in his own experience, yet it seemed to touch something closed tightly within him. A sense of . . . owing? Kilgarin almost caught it completely, but then the emotion passed as J'kar regained control. Kilgarin sighed, pushing the remainder of the feelings aside: he knew he couldn't afford to open up fully again, not in the way he'd opened aboard the *Drowner*. He wasn't strong enough yet, not yet. He pressed his hands together and noticed that his palms were wet. The leather strappings around his wrists were also moist with sweat, glistening in the dim light.

J'kar looked at him again, and the Centaurian's face was stiff and immobile. He nodded, saying nothing, and glanced at Whyte, who also nodded, and then J'kar shoved against the table, sliding it back and easing out past Kilgarin. The Cork watched as J'kar walked to the bar and took a drink from Pul. Whyte followed Kilgarin's gaze and smiled gently when the Cork turned back to him. Amber eyes smiling: one solid, one faint.

"He's had the full route," Whyte said.

"I know," Kilgarin answered. Then: "You too?"

The man furrowed his brow, then grinned again, less sure of himself for reasons Kilgarin didn't care to read. "That's why we're together, him and me. Who else, either of us?"

"You want in?"

"Contract pensions go only so far. Of course I want in."

"What about J'kar's pension?"

"The way he broke, he gets nothing. You know that. You were there, you saw it happen."

"You've been supporting him?" Kilgarin asked; Whyte nodded. "Tell him I meant the offer. Make him understand. And both of you, be there tonight. There's going to be a party. A small celebration."

"We're not good at socials, Kilgarin."

"Stop protecting him, Whyte. Be there." Without glancing at J'kar, Kilgarin walked briskly out, pausing at the door to pay his tab and straighten his vest and tunic, very distinctly aware that on his body, at least, there were no scars.

Behind the bar a narrow alley dropped down a series of wide steps to a small plaza. Kilgarin stopped beside the fountain, shifted himself onto the stone rim, and stared into the waters below. Bits of metal were scattered over the bottom of the pool, some engineer's effort to give the fountain an aura of history: green and blue and gold, the credit chits glittered in the moonlight—unaffected by the motion of the fountain waters, the chits were only for viewing. Kilgarin ran his hand through the water, cooling the heat that throbbed under the skin. No outward scars, oh, no. But there *were* reminders.

Suddenly his hand clenched into a fist and slammed hard against the stone rim, splashing water over his thighs. He sat trembling, watching his image split and reform in the spreading ripples. After a moment another reflection moved in beside his own. Marka. She tried a smile.

"Still remembering, Killy?" Her voice was soft behind him.

"No memory, Marka. Just a nerve spasm, only that." He cradled his bruised knuckles and glanced around at her. "You came up rather quietly just now."

"I saw you leaving the tavern. Are you sure you have no memories? This was our place, once. . . ." She laughed at him, tilting her head as she moved closer. "I waited for you to come back, that night. I wanted to explain. I even went to the port, but I couldn't find you. I guess you didn't want me to."

"If you believe that, what am I supposed to say?"

He edged off the fountain and stood facing her. She'd lost weight since the last time he'd been on Endrim, three years before. Her shoulders were narrower, two sharp strokes under the tan material of her blouse. Her hips were flat, nudging out only slightly below her waist, sinking straight into her thighs. She wore a jumper, something knit from black synthetic wool: it was frayed beneath her breasts and at her waist. She went barefoot, apparently no longer attempting to conceal the ruin of her left foot with boots—perhaps she was proud of the limp she affected,

Kilgarin thought, proud of the accident that kept her from being a mindship Physical.

She felt him studying her and drew her arms more tightly together under her bosom. When he continued to stare, she laughed. The laughter was a return cut. They each knew the other's weakness.

"I know I tried to hurt you, Killy. I was just trying to get back at you . . . for being so cold. He didn't mean anything to me. He was just a customer."

"Have you found passage Out yet, Marka?"

"Who'd take me on, Killy? Who needs a Physical who can't do work? Oh, I've survived, but it hasn't been good here these past few months . . . no jobs, and none of the Company plants are contracting . . . everything's taken. Newcomers everywhere for work in the taverns, so who'd be desperate enough to take *me?* You?"

"Maybe," Kilgarin said. "In a way."

Her smile faded a moment, then returned, a wry upturned line. "I can't live on might-be's and maybes, Killy. I'm almost through my pension. . . ." Shivering suddenly, she uncrossed her arms and rubbed her palms along the sides of her face, as though trying to wake herself from a half-sleep. She tossed her mane of crimson hair, eyed him casually. "How long are you down this time around? Still with the *Drowner*?"

"Not anymore. I'm finished."

He caught the surge of hope, not so clear as a Sensitive's broadcast, but there: dull and blunt, searching. He cut it out of his mind. He didn't want to know the reason for the rush of hope inside her. Practical or emotional, why she cared didn't matter to him. That she *did* care was almost enough to touch him—but he pulled away, not wanting more delusions. He pulled out of the momentary Sensitivity.

"For good?" she asked. "You're done shipping Out?"

"I almost pushed it one run too many, Marka. My Contract is up, so I cashed it in, and now I'm setting up on my own. That's what I meant by taking you on."

He explained it all, careful not to look at her again. The plaza was paved with cobblestones, new stones, washed clean by the previous evening's rain. "You can come in with me," he finished. "I'll need someone experienced to handle the girls."

"That would be nice." Her voice was so low he almost missed her answer. Almost, it was the same girlish voice she'd used when they'd sat on the balcony of his hotel room that distant summer, holding hands and pretending to an age they'd left behind centuries before. Kilgarin brushed off the feeling of déjà vu.

"Come to my place tonight," he said. "There's a party. Ask J'kar; he'll know where." He turned and started to move out of the plaza, walking quickly. Suddenly he stopped and called back over his shoulder, "Come tonight, Marka. We'll need you. We'll all need you. Tonight."

If she answered, he didn't hear.

As he came down the main street, Kilgarin saw a woman with a cat sitting in the doorway of a prefab apartment building. The cat was on her lap and the woman was trying to force its mouth open and feed it a tab of concentrates. The cat was resisting, frantically pawing at the woman's wrist with a declawed pad and hissing through the corners of its lips, a sound rumbling in its chest that bristled the small hairs at the nape of Kilgarin's neck. The cat had been Reformed. Its eyes were hooded by thick looming brows, its chest bulging with tufts of black hair and raised ribs, its back straightened to a humanoid line. To accomplish this the spinal column had been fused and the legs broken and reset in an upright position. However, whoever had done the Reforming had neglected to reshape the cat's ankles; they were now at the wrong angle for the legs, effectively crippling the animal. The woman had dressed the cat in a bright yellow waistcoat and short red knickers; a red hat sat on the cat's lumpy brow, tied under the chin with a yellow braid. Kilgarin paused under a streetlamp and watched the woman and her pet. She persisted in force-feeding the cat until finally the animal howled and squirmed free. It sprang to the street and stumbled forward a few steps on its unbalanced hind legs, and then dropped to its forepaws, scrambled a foot or two more, finally collapsing on its back in the gutter, mechanically stroking the air with its useless, twisted limbs. The woman said something Kilgarin couldn't hear, scooped up the cat, and slapped it twice. The cat whimpered. It was a sound Kilgarin had thought only dogs could make, and hearing it come from the cat did something to the pit of his stomach. He walked briskly away, trying to wipe out the image of the girl with the cat dangling limply from her hand, and the implications that echoed in his mind.

The pneumatic tissues of the tavern tent fluttered like batwings in the evening air. Kilgarin ducked through the doorway and strolled down an alley littered with food and liquor stalls on either side. Overhead the roof rose and fell silently, settling as he paused at one gaily curtained stall, filled a plate with steaming meat and a mug with cold beer, paid a little man with loose, rubbery jowls, and found himself a seat at the end of a table running lengthwise down the center of the cluttered, cavernous room. There was little wind inside the tent, and the tavern was hot and thick with humidity. The lanterns placed at six-meter intervals did little to relieve the darkness, so at each table several candles had been set to burn on worn plastic plates. Kilgarin pushed his candle aside and worked on his meat and brew.

He could feel the stares of the Physicals sitting a few meters down the table. They obviously recognized the blue dress colors of a mindship Cork, and Kilgarin knew they were all wondering what a Sensitive was doing in an all-Physical tavern. He wondered himself. Perhaps, he thought, he just needed to be away for a while; the silent pressures of the Sensitive District were beginning to unnerve him just a bit, and here, in the main port area, where emotions were less sharply developed, he could relax the psychic barriers all Sensitives were forced to erect in their own company. Perhaps. As he thought it, the released tension ebbed out of him, like the physical draining he experienced before falling asleep. He leaned forward and closed his eyes, suddenly conscious of the hardness of the wood under his elbows, the heat on his neck, the pressure of one leg crossed over the other. Every physical sensation crystallized into focus: the nearby sound of spoons against bowls, the clatter of plates on wood, the undercurrent of voices—all of it seemed to jump at him, as though he'd removed cotton from his ears and could suddenly hear unimpeded. He sighed, pushed away from the table, and walked back to the stalls for another beer.

The attendant at the stall watched Kilgarin fill his mug, wait for the foam to subside, then fill it a bit more. Kilgarin nodded at him politely as the man took his chit. The card slid back out of the stall's electric eye and was still warm as Kilgarin returned it to his pocket under the attendant's intent gaze. "Something wrong?" Kilgrin asked finally, taking a sip of his beer.

The attendant looked startled. "Oh. No, nothing. . . . You're a Sensitive, aren't you, friend?"

"They pay you for questions?"

"No, just for my eyes. The questions are my idea. They keep things from getting dull. You *are* a Sensitive, aren't you?"

Kilgarin shrugged. "What if I am?"

The man shifted his weight on the stool and inched forward. "Have to keep it all moving," he said as the Cork relaxed against the stall wall. "You don't find many friends on a port world."

"No," said Kilgarin, "I suppose you don't."

"Take that fellow, for instance," the young man said, indicating a short crewman passing them. "I spent half an hour with him yesterday, talking, even stood him a drink. Half an hour. I was interested, that's all, just trying to make conversation. I thought he was from Centauri, or maybe even from earth, and I wanted to find out what they were like. Just interested. He took me for a half hour and a drink. Then when somebody else comes up to the stall—it was getting into the dinner hour—he just walks away. Like that. What do you do? The drink I don't mind. But the time . . . you spend it, just trying to keep things moving . . ." He broke off and resumed his smile. Kilgarin met it with one of his own. "I mean, what can you do?" the attendant said, helplessly.

"I don't know," Kilgarin said. He held up his stein and raised his eyebrows in inquiry. "Drink?"

The young man grinned and shook his head. "I'll get my own." He did, and settled back, downing half his beer with a long pull. "I'm not supposed to," he said, "I'm on duty. But what the hell, you know?"

Kilgarin laughed. "You just try to keep things moving."

The attendant blinked at him and nodded slowly. "Yeah. I guess you do."

A short way into the District the streets became cobbled again. Kilgarin and the attendant from the tavern tent (who'd introduced himself as Raymond Velacorte after he'd shared Kilgarin's third stein) walked together in the gutter, taking alternate swigs from the bottle of Endrim Pernod and water that Raymond had supplied. It wasn't the best absinthe Kilgarin had ever tried, but it served the purpose—which was to provide them with something to drink while they talked. The latter was provided by Raymond, who was eager to gain Kilgarin's friendship—a not uncommon desire expressed by many Physicals toward Sensitives; in a way, it made a weak Physical feel more important to associate with a Sensitive—and though Kilgarin didn't think of Raymond as weak, he recognized the motivation and accepted it. The young man had a seemingly endless capacity for monologue. Kilgarin didn't mind. When the time came for him to talk, he would talk. Until then, he listened.

Raymond was a big man, a heavy man, but his heaviness wasn't the product of strength: his flesh rounded his waist and crowded his armpits, and his walk was slow and awkward. From time to time he would nudge into Kilgarin when his balance faltered, which was every second step. At one point Kilgarin had to grab him to keep the Physical from stumbling over the curb. Each time the young man laughed, nervously. He'd become accustomed to his clumsiness, he said; it no longer bothered him. Kilgarin soon realized that there were other things that did.

"Sorry," Raymond said. He braced himself and stepped away from Kilgarin's helping hand. "I've been like this for years. Can't understand it. Almost kept me off the ships, but once I had that Contract—well, I suppose it *did* keep me off, in the end. No renewals for Raymond. No, no. Endrim's not so bad though, don't you think? How long are you Down this time, you know yet?"

"For good," Kilgarin said. "I've had it, all that bouncing around."

"What bouncing around? It's not so bad. You get to see things, wench it up a bit. You know how it is." He accepted the bottle, gulped at it, and belched. "Nobody makes you do anything, not really. Machines do all that. Hell, most of the time you're asleep. All the time in drive, sometimes, you sleep. What's so bad about that?"

"*You* sleep, Raymond. That's what Physicals are for. You just dream and love and hate, and clean up the halls and work in the hydroponics, and lead your lives like any normal man or woman. I don't suppose it's such a bad life, but it wasn't *my* life. Do you know how close I came to going insane this last trip out, Raymond? That close. I still don't know how I survived. Two of the people I was involved with, didn't. A third, a Communications man who was only my friend, not even a part of the disaster—he cracked up, snapped because he was close to me. Don't make the mistake of thinking everyone has it like a Physical. Some of us fight for our lives."

The young Physical was silent, letting the bottle swing

at his side as he walked. Then: "Kilgarin, I'm sorry. I really am. I must be a terrible ass, clumsy mouthed too, I guess. I forgot about what you were. I never met a Cork before, you know that. I'm sorry."

"No trauma," Kilgarin said. "Forget it."

"No, I'm really sorry."

"So am I." Kilgarin took the bottle, uncorked it. "When did you first hit Endrim, Raymond?"

"A year ago. Maybe two."

"Always at that tavern?"

"Just this past month." He stumbled against a lamppost, caught himself. "Stupid. Things like that keep me out, job after job. You don't Contract for crawler jobs, you know. Things are really tight down here, specially for Physicals. There's no room at the plants, all the jobs are taken by off-worlders—you've got me *why*. A girl I had a few nights back was telling me she worked three shifts at once, figuring she'd manage to hold one job at least if the others fell through—that and sleeping every john who had the credit. Not a very optimistic girl, but practical. She had herself a nice place in the District and she kept it clean. You can't really ask for more, if you're a Physical. No crawler ever gets a pension or walking time, or anything else—" He stopped speaking. Kilgarin glanced around at the sound of a muffled cry.

Raymond had halted and was hugging the belly of a streetlamp, the light running over his shoulders and pants in rivulets of electric blue. Kilgarin saw that the young man was shuddering, his chest heaving. Not knowing precisely what was wrong, and not wanting to touch the other man's mind to find out, Kilgarin could only touch Raymond's shoulder and supply a moment of pressure to transmit his concern.

"Sorry," Raymond said, in a soft voice that for an instant reminded Kilgarin of Marka. Abruptly Raymond shook his head, "No, I'm not sorry, really. There's nothing to be sorry about. It was just the thought that you could go back to the ships and wouldn't, and that I . . . well, it was a silly thought, and I guess I *am* sorry, after all."

He straightened and palmed his cheeks as Kilgarin backed away. The Cork didn't want to meet the young man's eyes; he'd just received an emotional blast stronger than anything he'd felt since leaving the *Drowner*. There was anguish there, and self-pity, and fear and hate and confusion—all of it momentary, returning to the subconscious where Kilgarin hoped it would remain. He disliked having his mind invaded.

Raymond drew himself together and stepped into the light of the streetlamp. "Kilgarin—are you all right? You look odd."

"I feel odd," Kilgarin said. He started to drink from the bottle and realized it was empty. They crossed the street to a small store where an old man in a stained and wrinkled undershirt sold them another decanter. Back on the street, they continued in the direction of Kilgarin's town house.

"I had a family once," Raymond said. "Brothers and sisters. On earth I would have been an only child, because I was the oldest. We were lucky in a way, but my father didn't think so. The colonies aren't the best worlds to raise children on, but you weren't allowed more than one child on the civilized planets, and mother wanted quite a few. My father told me that after she died. She was the one who wanted us, he told me, and he was the one stuck with us. I think he loved us, though. My brothers said no. Neither of them could understand him, but I could. So could my sister. It's funny, but I think I was the only one he could never really care for. Too clumsy, you know? More than I am now. He couldn't accept that."

"What did he do?"

"He was a laborer on one of the community farms. What else could you do on a colony world? He told me once that in the ancient days on earth you had only two ways to escape from the peasant, laborer life: you could become a priest or a thief. There was something else, about squires for knights, but I never understood any of that."

"Let's sit down," Kilgarin said. They climbed the steps of a two-story building with a stone porch, stretched their legs out, and looked east toward the rainbow lights of the tavern bazaar. The stars over the tents and lighted alleys were opaqued by the city glow. Most of the eastern horizon was in pitch blackness, the night sky obliterated by the lights of the city and the port. The western sky over the plant area and the nearer Districts, was brilliant and undulled, cloudless and stark with the richness of the galactic Arm. Endrim's atmosphere acted like a lens on clear nights like this, Kilgarin thought, bringing it all into focus and shattering the night into vividness. From the porthole of a ship the stars would seem one dimensional and flat; the exhilaration of a night sky was something experienced only by planetbound creatures. Those who'd been there knew the truth.

"It's lovely, isn't it?"

"Yes," Kilgarin said, "It is."

"Do you have any family, Kilgarin? People you've left behind?"

"Left behind? Sure. A family? Not really. Six years can do odd things to certain bonds."

"You think so? You're probably right. You have any sisters?"

"A brother. My mother and father died three, maybe four years back. He was a Sensitive too, my father, but he never used it. I think it burned him out from inside."

Raymond unwound his arms, grunting as the kink slipped in his shoulders and neck. "Burned out? How do you mean?"

"You can't let your Sensitivity sit. It'll rot you. Like wine, or anything that ferments if you bottle it up. When you finally tap it, there's an explosion. Anything that was once there is expelled"— he unfisted his hands—"and lost."

"You make it sound pretty frightening."

"It is."

"What about your brother? Is he a Sensitive too?"

Kilgarin set the bottle down carefully on the steps beside him. "I don't know. I haven't thought about it." He shrugged. "It's not a dominant gene. Fifty-fifty; maybe I used it up for the family. We hadn't noticed anything by the time I left. Marc was still too young for anyone to tell. It's connected with puberty, except in freak cases. Something about hormone distribution. The planet you come from counts too; whether it has a high electromagnetic field. The stronger the field, the weaker your Sensitivity. Wellington's field was pretty weak. I suppose Marc could have it." He took a sip of the wine and returned the bottle to the stoop. "I guess I'll find out soon enough."

"What do you mean?"

"From what I hear, he's on Endrim, looking for me. Tomorrow I suppose I'll go search for him in the communes, send him packing back to Wellington. I don't have anything to offer him here. What good would a boy be in a brothel?" Kilgarin laughed. "It *will* be good to see him, though. I don't really know him anymore; I've been sending him credits since our parents died, but that's the only contact I've had with him in years. . . ." His voice trailed off. He looked down at the bottle.

"How'd you get in, Kilgarin? I mean, get a Contract?"

"Easily enough. You can sign on at eighteen. I took a year's training, and from there"—he spread his hands—"I moved up, rung by rung. It's not hard, if you tend toward the suicidal."

"Training, hey? They don't train Physicals, so what—?"

Kilgarin smiled. Raymond's attempt to change the subject was painfully transparent—as transparent as Kilgarin's dislike for talk about his family must have been.

"You think a Sensitive can just bounce into a ship's crew?" he asked. "You have to work, my friend. It's not like being a Physical. You have to train, because if you don't you can't last a week. You're a dead man. There're a lot of broken Corks around as proof, men who never learned to break away, to stand outside. Have you ever been in the District before?"

"A couple of times. I can't remember. I was probably drunk."

"Must've been fun for the crowd around you. Drunk normals blast like a damned foghorn."

"Blast?" Raymond blinked at him, eyes glistening from the light on the building above them.

"Don't worry about the semantics. Call it broadcasting your emotions. Have you ever really *looked* at the Sensitives in the District, Raymond?"

"How do you mean, look?"

"Their faces."

"Oh, sure. You know, I never mean to stare or anything, but—"

"But you could see it, couldn't you? There's something shattered inside them, and it's echoed in their voices, in the way they speak, and it's sculptured on their faces and their hands. You have to watch the hands of a Sensitive, Raymond. His hands will tell you things his thoughts and words never can."

As Kilgarin spoke Raymond took his bottle from his lips and stared at it, as though the absinthe had become suddenly sour. He placed it on the stoop beside his feet and closed his eyes, leaning his head back and twisting it from side to side. "I've got a muscle wrong in my neck," he muttered. He glanced at Kilgarin. His eyes were in shadow, and his voice was soft—like Marka's—as he said, "What's wrong with you, Kilgarin? You've been a Cork a long time. Why aren't you like the others, the broken ones?"

The Cork smiled bitterly, a self-mocking tug at his lips.

"I got out before it worked on me," he said. "Bonus Contracts or no, I wasn't going to spend another term on that ship. I've no desire to break myself, if I can help it." He rapped his hands together, rubbed them on his knees. "And I can, Ray. Believe me, I can."

"How do you now when you've had enough, Kilgarin?" Raymond asked. Both men were speaking quietly; realizing this, Kilgarin laughed.

"You can tell. Sometimes something happens which almost pushes you over the brink, and you know you've had enough. The stupid and greedy ones stay on for that extra high-risk Contract. The smart Sensitives get out at once. When Lucille died, and Baeder and J'kar broke, and I found myself looking for a length of strong rope . . . well, I knew it was time I cashed in and pulled out."

He upended the bottle of absinthe, drank, set it down, and wiped a hand over his moustache and beard; he needed a shave again.

"It was a mixed ship, you see, men and women. We cared for each other, something most psi-ship crews never do. Maybe that was what made us all so susceptibile when things began to go sour. I know all the theories—sometimes a bisexual mindship can be as bad as a single sex charter, if not worse. But it'd worked for the *Drowner* for the twelve years before I shipped out on her, and it'd worked for most of the six I spent aboard. Until I came back from a leave on Endrim and mated with a girl names Lucille.

"There's one thing a Cork should never do, Raymond, and that's look into the mind of a woman he's loving. You see things you never expected you'd see, and sometimes . . . things you don't *want* to see. I wanted a simple physical mating . . . she wanted more. She felt more. It wasn't what I wanted, so I broke off with her. That's when she started with Baeder, a Communications man I'd counted among my friends. They shouldn't have done it, Raymond; not then. Not right after she'd broken up with me.

"You see, I'm a Cork, and a Cork has to touch everyone's mind. Everyone, even ex-lovers. Lucille was a Technician, she should have realized she wouldn't be able to make a clean emotional break . . . but she tried to; she tried to transfer her desire to Baeder, who wasn't really strong enough to take that kind of strain. Both of them were constantly aware of me, and I was constantly aware of them. We couldn't get away from each other to heal. We never had that chance. The tension kept building and building, and one day when we were heading back toward Endrim . . . it broke.

"Everything broke: Baeder, Lucille, a friend of mine named J'kar. And almost, I broke too . . ."

Kilgarin's voice trailed off. In reflex his foot straightened out, knocking the absinthe bottle over, sending it tumbling down the stone steps to smash on the pavement below.

"Lucille died before we reached port," he finished. "Baeder and J'kar were left here in a hospital; Baeder died, J'kar's slowly pulling back together. I kept on with the *Drowner* for six more months and then I quit. I had to. Otherwise I'd go insane."

"I see," said Raymond.

Kilgarin spat into the street and looked up at the man sitting next to him. "You know something, Raymond?" he said. "I think you do."

The party had been in progress for over an hour. There were thirty or forty people clustered together in the three rooms of Kilgarin's private suite, and almost half of them would have been invited by the Cork if he'd seen them. In some cases he had; as it stood, though, most of those present had heard about the gathering through the District grapevine, and knowing Kilgarin from other parties, had felt free to invite themselves. The other half were either strangers or friends of friends . . . and some of these were undesirables, people who for one reason or another were avoided by the majority of the District population. As he sat perched on the kitchen sink, seeking a moment's solitude, Kilgarin decided that perhaps the two were the same—strangers and undesirables. Apparently those who didn't know Kilgarin personally felt no compunction to be polite or careful. In the morning, Kilgarin knew, the apartment would be in shambles. It didn't matter. Enough friends would remain to help set things aright. That too was the way of their crowd.

Kilgarin had drawn his feet up and hooked his arms around his knees and now he peered over them, watching the movements of the three brothers dancing in the next room. The music was loud, yet at times the voices around him seemed louder. The moments were few when the melody would reach him clearly, but at those moments Kilgarin would close his eyes and feel himself sway in sympathy with the rushing beat. He was doing this when a hand touched his wrist. He looked up, smiling, to see J'kar.

Whyte hovered in the background, his hands tucked self-consciously into his overjacket pockets. J'kar's expression was stiff and formal, and his voice was without emotion as he said, "Whyte say you told to come. So we come. And I take your job, huh?"

"I'm glad you're here, J'kar. I really am."

"Sure. Just the man to liven things up, right? Good thinking, you." The ex-Communications man sniffed, relaxing visibly. He half-turned and settled his hip on the edge of the sink. "So what's happening, you in sink, them dancing out there? How many people and who, huh?"

"Couple'a dozen or so. Some old mates and their friends. You know them," he said. "But what's wrong with you joining them, J'kar? You can't play social outcast forever."

J'kar shook his head slowly. "Something, you. Really something. What you think, I'm glad the way I am? Think I want everyone know, give me claps on back, offer money, smiles? Sure, friendly me. Maybe not let them too near, huh?"

"Sorry, J'kar. You know that's not how I meant it."

"Sure, well. Guess everyone's close enough edge, huh. Sure."

He shoved from the sink and left the room, limping past a couple entwined in the doorway. Whyte caught Kilgarin's eye and lumbered over. "You shouldn't be too rough on him. He hasn't healed over."

"And your protecting him will help?"

"Maybe a little."

Kilgarin swung off the sink. He brushed arms with two men talking near the food dispenser console. "You're just helping him stay inside himself, Whyte. Sure, he's hurt—he's lost a lot these past twelve years, from what he told me when we were on the *Drowner*, together with what happened to him six months ago. Strong people who lose their strength don't really have much to fall back on, except the sympathy of other people." He frowned at Whyte, then turned and moved toward the doorway. "Think about that the next time you excuse him."

He located Raymond near the speaker system. The Physical was crouched under the two triangular apertures, clutching his glass in both hands and eyeing the Sensitives moving past him. Kilgarin slid in next to him and took the young man's glass. "Thanks," he said, and downed it. "Want another?"

Raymond shrugged. "I haven't figured out where to look."

Kilgarin led him across the room to a small table beside the balcony windows. Pul was there, squatting on a stool and gazing across the rooftops, his featherlight hair blown back from his forehead by the evening wind. "Hey, old man," said Kilgarin, "fix my friend a drink." The old Cork swiveled around and fixed Raymond with a suspicious stare.

"A normal, Killy?"

"I said fix my friend a drink."

Pul hurried to his feet and worked with glasses and bottles, and something with ice in it appeared in his hand, topped with a shadow of yellowish green. The old man gave it to Raymond, who tasted it and nodded.

"Thanks, Pul," Kilgarin said. He brought Raymond onto the balcony and found a place by the rail a safe distance from a threesome crouched in the shadow of the farther wall.

"Why did he look at me like that?" Raymond asked.

"Pul's an old man. He's not too quick."

"Not *that* old, Kilgarin. Am I crashing something private?"

The Cork laughed. In spite of himself he found Raymond's whipped-dog attitude amusing. "No, nothing private, really. You're just not a Sensitive, Ray. That bothers some people."

"Does it bother you?"

"If it did, you wouldn't be here."

"Who was that old man, anyway? A friend of yours?"

"He's a bartender in the Llyia's, one of the private pubs. I guess bartending's in his blood; if there's any such thing as a servile instinct, Pul's got it. If automatic bars ever come to Endrim, old Pul will just shrivel up and die."

"He's a Cork?"

"*Was* a Cork. He broke about fifteen years ago; some people never come out of it."

Raymond was silent, and after a while Kilgarin went back inside.

The brothers had stopped dancing, and now a young girl had assumed their place on the spot of bare flooring. The lights were dim and improperly directed, so Kilgarin was unable to make out her face. She was one of his, though; there were ten of them at the party at least. He studied her from the edge of his bed. Only part of her body was visible in the shifting light, swathes of skin and strands of hair, all of it moving and swinging. He looked away. Standing apart from the knot of unfamiliar people near his bed, in the shadow of the arch that led into the hall, was Marka.

She'd changed her clothes. In the semidarkness, and perhaps because of the drinking he'd done, it seemed to Kilgarin that she'd recaptured something of the woman she'd been three years before. She'd done things with her hair, and she wore a dress of some lightweight material, a single piece that covered one breast, uplifted the other, rounded her hip and swirled about again to flow to the floor. She saw him as he approached and she raised her glass in a mock salute.

"To the rebellion," she said.

"Which one?"

"In the Outworlds, of course."

He smiled and took a drink from a passing cart. "I'm not with it in spirit, but I'll drink to your toast."

When she'd finished her wine, she said, "It's a fine party, Kilgarin."

"I'd like to say the gallant thing about it being because you're here, Marka, but I don't think you'd take it quite properly."

"You're right," she said. "I wouldn't."

They smiled at each other, and then someone said something behind him that made him turn around.

"*I'm* James Kilgarin," he said to the portly man who'd asked for him. The man swung around from the group he'd been querying, sized up Kilgarin with a flicker of his eyes, and nodded, as though silently agreeing.

"I'm Oliver, Fellow Kilgarin," the man said. "I represent the Charter Company here on Endrim." The company name was meaningless; all of the small offices belonged to one major licensing organization, chartered by the earth Federation Colonial Office, and that organization was the Company. Oliver was a Company man.

"You were invited, Mr. Oliver?" Kilgarin asked him.

"No, uh, I'm afraid I'm not here socially, Fellow Kilgarin."

"I gave up the Fellow when my Contract expired, Mr. Oliver." Kilgarin separated from Marka and moved closer to the squat, red-faced Company agent. "And if this isn't a social visit, then what do you want?"

They were attracting a crowd. Oliver realized this and apparently found it disturbing, for he inhaled heavily and removed a packet from his waistcoat. "Your brother's name is Marc Kilgarin?"

Kilgarin felt a chill of premonition. He resisted the temptation to probe the man's mind and learn what the interruption was all about. He answered Oliver's question carefully, added, "Why?"

The fat man zipped open the packet and shook out a square wafer and a plastic chit.

"These are your brother's effects, Kilgarin. The chit is the money he had on his person at the time of the accident. The wafer is his Contract."

Kilgarin accepted the items. Something warm was rising under his ears. The wafer was weightless, the chit cool and sharp, biting into his flesh as his fist closed over. "Accident, Mr. Oliver? What accident?"

"Your brother was killed aboard the Company ship *Charter* two days ago. It occurred while he was acting in his capacity as Cork for that vessel. The details are all recorded on that wafer. The Company expects to hear from you within the next forty-eight hours concerning your decision on the fulfillment of the terms of your brother's Contract."

Oliver frowned, then added briskly, "I'm sorry, Fellow Kilgarin. The Company offers its condolences." He left the room, passing between two of Kilgarin's former shipmates from the *Drowner*. The taller of the two men glanced from Oliver to Kilgarin, his hands moving at his sides. Kilgarin caught the look the Sensitive threw him and shook his head; hurting Oliver would do none of them any good. He looked down at his fist clenched about the wafer and the chit, and then he brushed past Marka and hurried down the hallway, hearing the first hesitant whispers beginning behind him.

He knew what they'd be saying; not the precise words perhaps, but the feelings behind the words—and he hated the pity his friends were going to feel for him. It was just too much, added to his own.

He sat on the ledge of the chimney, staring over the roofs of the buildings that cupped the spaceport peninsula. The spotlights of the port were swinging in narrow arcs across the cloudless sky, beams of topaz and sapphire straining against the night. There were the sounds of the tractors in the distance, or perhaps the cranes rumbling in their concrete beds, sounds too familiar to an ex-spacer: a ship being readied for a morning launch. He hated that sound.

For a while he examined his hands. They lay in his lap, one resting loosely on the other, relaxed in a way Marc would never have allowed. The plastic chit and wafer glittered in the moonlight as he looked at them. He closed his eyes. His mind was empty. He couldn't think.

When he looked up again, he could see Marka standing in the arch that led onto the roof from below. She was silhouetted in the glow from the plates in the stairwell ceiling. She'd spoken his name and he'd turned to her, but he couldn't recall either the word or the movement. Against the yellow light she seemed ethereal, hair sparkling in the golden wash. There were too many shadows for him to make out her face, but her voice, when she spoke again, was the young voice he'd known years before.

He didn't understand what she said. Once again the words were lost. Something seemed to have dropped away inside him; his mind was no longer able to connect words with their abstract meanings. Finally she left the stairwell and came over beside him. Her fingers were cool on his arm. He showed her the things in his hand, and she took them from him and slipped them into her shift.

He tried to say her name. No sound came out. She pressed her head against his chest and glanced up at him, her features outlined by the stairwell light. It was Marka. Her features were soft, not the harsh features he'd seen earlier in the evening. He didn't understand her expression, but a part of him responded to it and he dropped from the ledge and stood facing her. Her hands were holding his, and as he slipped down she drew him closer. He enfolded her tightly, impulsively. His mind felt sucked clean. He couldn't think and didn't *want* to think. Marka pressed against him, whispering, but even though he tried, he couldn't make sense out of her words.

He woke in the morning, aware of the sunlight filtering through the window beside him. He was in his bed and the sheets covering him were moist with his own sweat. He tried to recall his dream—a feeling of darkness and pressure—but was unable to summon the details. He rolled over wearily, feeling a feminine arm pressing into his side. Remembering Marka, he smiled and shifted to face the woman sleeping next to him. He ran a hand along her back and she shivered, and settled again, and when he slid his fingers into the warmth of hair at the nape of her neck, she turned over completely and dropped her hand against his hip, smiling at him, groggy with sleep. He took her hand away and sat up. The girl asked him what was wrong, but he didn't answer; he found his robe on a chair and pulled it on as he walked into the kitchen. He needed coffee, he thought, and maybe something stronger. He wondered if Marka had left during the night, and then wondered if she'd ever been with him at all.

The coffee was hot and bitter, and he sat on the windowsill drinking it for a long time, waiting for the stranger in the next room to leave.

An hour later, dressed and warmed by a hot breakfast, Kilgarin started toward the distant spaceport, and the duties that awaited him there.

Chapter Two

Eighth month, fourth day, anno Domini 3146

He was met at the entrance to the *Charter*'s private field by a short man dressed in Physical grays. There was a moment's wait as the man examined the Contract wafer and Kilgarin spent the time studying the lines of the ship above him. The *Charter* had been built more recently than the mindship Kilgarin had crewed, but still, despite the lack of bow lights and the addition of another cargo hatch under the main airlock, the *Charter* was fairly standard. Six main thrusters to lift the ship off a planetary surface, several smaller engines for guiding it within a primary gravity well—the external equipment was familiar to Kilgarin, painfully so. In many ways the ship was a duplicate of the *Drowner*.

Finished running the Contract through a portable scanner strapped to his waist, the small man returned the wafer to Kilgarin, noticing the expression on the ex-Cork's face. The man nodded, his features twisting in a parody of a smile. Kilgarin realized that the other man was a blown Sensitive, partially healed.

"You sense it too, don't you?" the man said. "The ship? It's a hate ship, Fellow Kilgarin. It destroyed your brother; that's why you're here, isn't it?"

"You knew my brother?"

"I was there when the Captain signed him on. He was too young, your brother. He didn't understand what sort of a ship this was."

"You were there?" Kilgarin studied the Physical. "Are you the Mate?"

"No. I'm the Cook. We don't have a Mate aboard the *Charter*. Just me."

"The Company allows that?"

"There was no choice. The cargo comes first, yes? That's why the Captain took your brother. He had to." The Cook sighed. "Maybe."

Kilgarin frowned as the short man took his sleeve and drew him up the ramp into the air lock. The fingers holding Kilgarin's arm were loose, twitching; the Cook was agitated beyond his ability to control the finer movements of his limbs. Once inside the ship Kilgarin was led down a passage lit on four sides by translucent light panels. They came to the mess and turned in. "I want to talk with you before you see the Captain," the Cook said. "It's important you understand."

Kilgarin wandered across the wide, low-ceilinged lounge, becoming aware of the forces present in the room. This was the nexus of the ship, the focal point for the psychic energies of its crew. The room was roughly circular, sloping toward a central point, a counter and console arrangement that Kilgarin recognized as the main food dispensing area. Overhead glowplates cast a soft light too delicate to create a shadow. Kilgarin walked a few steps into the lounge, peering down the rows of tables and booths, aware of the tensions that lived in the room. He felt himself opening up to the emotions in the lounge in the same way he'd opened to the emotions aboard the *Drowner*. It was different here, however. The emotions he received were twisted and misshapen, ugly, inhuman. Waves of hate beat against him, within him, and he turned away, cutting off his reception and closing in on himself while he regained his breath. He felt unclean, as though he'd been physically invaded.

When he finally straightened, Kilgarin saw that the Cook had been watching him, eyes bright and gleaming. "You see?" the small man asked. "This ship is insane. I've been with her three years, and it's always been this way. The first time I stepped aboard I nearly dropped. It's strong."

"How do you stand living with it?" Kilgarin asked.

"You learn. It's not easy, but it's not hard, either. Think about it. There's nothing here that's not inside each of us."

"But there's so much . . ."

"Quite a few crew members have a little of it in them. Even the Captain."

"The Captain. I wanted to talk to him." Kilgarin

glanced at his hands, forcing them to be steady. "About my brother. He shouldn't have been contracted, not for something like a Cork's position. You know that, if you knew him."

"I knew it, but not the Captain. The whole business was new to him. He'd been a Mate until our previous Captain was killed. He's never had to meet a crisis like this before, picking a Cork . . ." The Cook's voice faded. He smiled, wrinkling the left side of his face. "Try to understand him, Kilgarin. Living in a ship like this can damage a man's sensibilities . . . he didn't mean to hurt your brother. The boy seemed strong. He made a good Cork, until we had that accident."

"A good Cork, on a ship like this. . . ?"

"Listen: we hit a Black Hole, our Cork was breaking, the Captain had to hold him together, any way he could. He tried too hard. You've played the wafer, haven't you? It's all there."

"The how, yes," Kilgarin said. "But not the *why*. I have to know why the Captain contracted him. I don't care what happened; that's done, my brother's buried already . . . but I need to know *why* it was done. Showing me that this ship is insane doesn't tell me any more than I already knew. I don't believe a Physical Captain can be affected that much living here. There has to be something more. I've got to find out what it is. You're a Sensitive; you can understand that, can't you?"

The Cook looked at Kilgarin, his mouth working as he tried to phrase an answer. "The Captain's changed," he said finally. "He hides inside himself, but he's a good man. A good Captain, now."

"Maybe he is," Kilgarin said. "I'll find out for myself, won't I?"

"I guess you will," the Cook said with resignation. "I guess you will."

On Kilgarin's second knock the door slid silently open. He stepped through into the Captain's quarters and moved down a narrow hallway that curved with the main corridor of the ship. There were sounds from the refresher cubicle set apart from the main cabin, the hum of the cleaner fading as Kilgarin entered the main room. He waited, standing with his arms folded and letting his eyes adjust to the bright lighting—harsh compared to the rest of the ship—as he looked around at the one-and-one-half room suite.

The walls were bare, the sparse furniture completely functional, the only item betraying any real wear being the viewing console tucked off near the inflatable bed. The console was still turned on when Kilgarin entered, though unfocused and untuned; images moved across the screen in random patterns, the sound too low to be audible. Kilgarin glanced at it only briefly as he scanned the room, looking for some hint of the Captain's personality in his choice of objects and design. The room looked frankly uninhabited. Kilgarin shivered, then laughed at himself nervously. Intimidated by an empty room.

"Yes? Can I help you?"

Kilgarin turned at the sound of the voice and faced a man roughly his height and weight though obviously older. Kilgarin estimated the Captain to be approaching thirty. The man stood at the door to the 'fresher, drawing on his jump suit and zipping up the suit's front as he stared at Kilgarin. Kilgarin smiled. The Captain started, his eyes widening, a frown flashing for an instant, then fading away.

"I'm sorry," the Captain said, "but for a moment you looked like someone I knew. It's nothing. Are you signing aboard? Did the Cook send you up?"

"Not exactly, Captain. As a matter of fact, he tried to convince me not to come."

The Captain scowled—firmly, this time—and moved across the room to the viewing console. He flicked the screen off and returned his attention to Kilgarin. "He did? Can you tell me why?"

"I'm Marc Kilgarin's brother."

"I see."

"I wanted to talk with you about the way he died."

"Weren't you told?"

"Things like that . . . information gets garbled. I prefer to hear it from you. You were there when it happened."

The Captain's face relaxed and he sighed, settling onto the stool molded into the desk before the console. His shoulders moved restlessly as he spoke. "I was there. We'd made it all the way to Centauri with our cargo, we'd shuttled to some of the colonies in the western Arm, and we were heading back to the rim. Three weeks out from Centauri, he blew. Like that. I tried to save him, but it was impossible—between keeping the ship together and saving your brother, it was all I could do to maintain my own sanity. There was nothing, nothing I could do for him." His hands moved over his knees, pulling at the material, straightening it. "I'm very sorry it happened the way it did."

Kilgarin leaned against the wall that ran into the narrow hall, feeling the muscles in his arms knot as he forced his hands to his sides and into the loops of his suit. He felt dizzy from the emotions surging through him. Up to that moment he hadn't truly encountered his brother's death on a personal level—he'd been shocked, grieved, pained—but until the Captain had told in simple words how it had happened, the death had had no gut meaning for Kilgarin. Now it did. For a brief moment he closed his eyes and trembled. When he opened them once more, he searched the eyes of the Captain.

He wanted to know the reason for what had happened. No more and certainly no less. It was part of being a Sensitive: he was all too aware of the random nature of events, and how the most well-intentioned plans may have disastrous effects. What mattered was not the effect but the intention. He needed to know the Captain's intention in hiring his brother, and in driving Marc Kilgarin to his death. At that moment it was the consuming force in James Kilgarin's life.

He searched the Captain's eyes, but the other man's feelings were buried too deeply. Nothing was visible, only a cool barrier. Kilgarin paused, hesitating. He was not sure he had the stomach for a direct probe of another man's mind, so soon after leaving the *Drowner*. Was there an alternative?

No.

Gathering himself, he concentrated on the field of the Captain's mind—*and he pushed.*

His mind dove forward, into the Captain's soul.

There was a moment of darkness for Kilgarin, during which he floundered, searching for some common ground of orientation between himself and the Captain. At last he found it: the mindship world, the crew/officer relationship. Steadied, Kilgarin plunged deeper, into the other man's subconscious—and found himself stopped by the mental counterpart of the barrier he'd seen in the Captain's eyes. Here, however, it was more than an unemotional attitude. It was a block rising between the conscious and unconscious. Kilgarin pressed, but the mindblock was unyielding. He searched for an opening, but there was none. He tried to filter through, but couldn't. There was no way past the block, none at all; he was totally and completely halted.

He stepped back mentally. It was a mindblock, and not one erected by a machine—those were clumsy, ill-fitting affairs, useful to hide select information, but not whole areas of experience. No, it was psychologically organic, which was, of course, a flat impossibility. The Captain wasn't a Sensitive, could *not* be, if he were part of Crew Administration. There were strict Company regulations about Sensitives being in charge of a ship, enforced with careful screening of all applicants to an Administrative position. The Captain could not be a Sensitive, therefore he could not have planted the block himself; it was too complete.

Then who? And more importantly for Kilgarin's purposes: why? What was the Captain trying to conceal, so well that he kept the secret even from himself? The reason for Marc Kilgarin's death? If so, who would help him hide it?

Stunned and confused, Kilgarin withdrew. Less than a second had passed; the Captain hadn't noticed the changing expression on the ex-Cork's face. The man was still straightening the material of his trousers and only now looked up at Kilgarin.

"I've already explained it to the Company representative here on Endrim," the Captain said. "There was some discussion concerning my behavior, but that's all finished with. They decided I'd acted rashly, but considering the circumstances surrounding the matter they thought my actions perfectly excusable. You should know that they docked me two months' pay for endangering the ship. They think that settled the matter, and though naturally I'm—saddened by what happened, I agree with them. There was nothing I could do. Nothing. You understand that, don't you?"

His voice grew lower as he ended his speech, and Kilgarin had to strain to make out the last few words. He was still trembling from his experience inside the Captain's mind, and was already beginning to feel ashamed for attempting the invasion in the first place. It was against all codes of conduct to do what he had done. Kilgarin felt his face and hands growing warm as he listened to the Captain's hurried apology. When it was over, he nodded, quickly.

"I do understand, Captain. I just wanted to speak with you about it. You *were* the last person to see him alive."

"He was a fine Cork, Fellow Kilgarin. One of the finest."

"Thank you."

"Have you decided what you're going to do with the remainder of his Contract?"

"I could buy it out," Kilgarin said. "I've a little money saved, though I'd planned to use it on other things."

"Are you a Sensitive yourself?" The Captain eased himself off the stool and stood cracking his knuckles; he seemed distracted.

"It runs in the family."

"So I understand. You could finish his Contract term yourself, then, couldn't you?" The Captain's eyes rose and looked fully at Kilgarin for the first time. The Sensitive shrugged and found himself looking away. "Let me know when you decide," the Captain said. His eyes began moving again. "Just about now, I could use a good Cork."

"Is he always that way?" Kilgarin asked. "He made me feel like a child, an absolute fool."

Beside him the Cook shrugged. They were walking down the broad avenue leading from the port area into the tavern district. "It's hard to say. Sometimes he's worse. He turns on and off; sometimes he sees you, sometimes not. He was like that with the Cork, your brother, going Out."

"Do you know him very well?"

"Well enough, I suppose. We came aboard the same time, when the *Charter* was commissioned. He was First Mate, and I was Cook. We talked sometimes, not much."

"When was that? When the *Charter* received her commission?"

"Forty-three. Forty-four? No, it was forty-three."

"She's only been commissioned three years?" Kilgarin shook his head. He pointed down the street they were crossing. "Pul's place is down that way. Free drinks."

"Go," said the Cook, and crossed the street ahead of him.

Though it was still early in the day, the Llyia's was partly filled with crew from the five or six ships staying over at the Endrim port. Even so, Pul filled Kilgarin's order promptly and found time to join them in a toast, raising his own glass to his lips with a trembling hand. "Gets this way a bit, sometimes," he said when the hand trembled too much and spilled absinthe on the bar. "In the mornings, not so good. Old, 'y'know?" He eyed the Cook, who was watching him rub the liquor into the counter top with a rag. "Who friend, Killy?"

"Calls himself Cook," Kilgarin said. "He's with the *Charter.*"

"Heard about that ship, bad. People speak, round port. Here, at party last night . . ." Pul frowned. The muscles in his cheek jumped and tugged at his lower eyelid. "Wasn't. . . ?"

"That's the one," Kilgarin said quietly.

"Drink?" Pul asked, in apology.

"Let me finish this one," Kilgarin answered. He turned to the Cook a moment later. "Isn't the *Charter* a cargo ship? That's why she's on Endrim now, right?:

"Absinthe. You have it. After Endrim, we head into the Outworlds, along the eastern Spiral."

"Bad that," Pul said, leaning forward. "Company not strong, not there. Heard? Like Centauri in '28."

The Cook nodded. "But if the Company says go, we go. The cargo pays for the charting . . . or so they say."

"Let's not talk about that," Kilgarin said. "I want to think about this a moment. Pul? Another beer?"

The bartender gave it to him and Kilgarin sipped at the sweet liquid, staring past the edge of the bar at the pipes winding in the console behind the counter. He let his gaze travel along the pipes, his mind drifting back to memories of his years on Wellington. Not much of that time was left within him. Most of the memories were dulled, but some were still bright and alive. Wellington. His homeworld.

It was a cold planet, not semitropical like Endrim, half again as far from it's G-type star as the earth was from Sol—one-and-one-half astronomical units, in the old measure. During the winters his father would spend most of the day collecting wood and bargaining for the native mineral they called coal. When summer came—mild summers that were over before they'd really begun—Kilgarin's father would bring him out to the fields, where they'd labor from dawn until sunset to bring in a crop of Roots, the all-purpose vegetable that had been designed for the Wellington climate by the Company botanical engineers—and for which they extracted a harvest percentage. He remembered the feel of sweat crawling down his spine, and he remembered the bitter chill that would lodge below his ears, and remembering, he shivered and sipped at his glass of beer.

There were other memories; pleasant memories. His brother was six years younger than he, and Kilgarin could recall the day and hour of Marc's birth very clearly. It'd been during the early days of spring, in 3128. They'd received word about the trouble on Centauri just a week before, which was why the time of year remained so clearly in Kilgarin's mind. His father had been worried, wondering if the attempted rebellion would affect the Company's attitude toward its other colonies—and how this would in turn affect the upbringing of Charleton Kilgarin's second child. As it turned out his fears were unfounded. There had never been any reprisals, at least, none that were apparent to the young James Kilgarin. His brother was born a week later, small and pink, a wizened old man's face squinting out of white bedclothes, small hands—even then—moving and exploring. Mouth squealing. Kilgarin's initial feelings were mixed. For some time he had a vague feeling of discomfort, and once, when he was alone with the infant, he found himself wondering how to dispose of the child. When he realized what he'd been thinking, he'd become upset and then ill, and was unable to go into the fields with his father for several days. After that he treated Marc with distant respect, which later hardened into cool reserve.

Remembering this, Kilgarin found himself shaking, and he groped for his glass of absinthe and beer and downed it in one long swallow. The Cook was watching him with an odd expression. Kilgarin ignored him and ordered another beer, and only after he'd finished half of it did he turn to the diminutive ex-Sensitive.

"Something bothering you, friend?"

"You," the Cook said.

"Don't concern yourself with me, friend. I'm capable of handling myself."

"Sure. But it's still bothering me, and you asked. Maybe there's something you should know, Kilgarin. After your brother died, somebody had to Cork the *Charter*. Only one man could. Me. Yes, I used to be a Cork, nine, ten years back. I broke pretty bad, and it took me four years to get back even this much"—he gestured with a hand that moved awkwardly, nervously—"control. Four years, and then I became a Cook. But after your brother collapsed, the *Charter* was falling, and it needed someone to save it—the same man who saved it before. Me. You know what that does to a blown Cork? To go back?"

"I can imagine," Kilgarin said softly. The Cook's voice was cracking with emotion as he went on.

"Sure, imagine. So listen, maybe you know, maybe you

don't. But you know this much—I can still feel things, and right now I can feel you. You're burning up inside. It's not good, what you feel. It's a waste, a hurt. I don't want to feel it with you, but I can't stop it now, inside me. You can imagine, sure. But you can't know." He cut off Kilgarin before the Cork could speak.

"Just be careful, Kilgarin. You understand pain . . . but maybe not enough. Too much pain inside you, and you can break. Like I did, or like him." He swept a hand over to indicate Pul. Ill coordinated, it caught the rim of his glass and sent the mug spinning off the counter and into the console. Glass shattered loudly, the spell was broken, the room became noisy once more.

"Sorry," the Cook said quietly.

Pul shuffled over to clean up the glass. "Forget it. Breaks all the time."

Kilgarin looked into his own glass and smiled. "If you can read me, Cook, then you already know what I've decided to do."

"It's a mistake."

"Can *you* tell me where the Captain could get a mind-block?"

"No."

"Then I have to find out for myself," Kilgarin said. He swung off the bar stool and stood up; his smile was empty and mechanical this time, as he added, "I want to know why he killed my brother, and *that's* why I'm signing aboard."

The Cook said nothing. He shook his head once, and then, limping, he followed Kilgarin out the tavern door.

Raymond was on the third floor of the brothel, in a room opening off the main hallway, sprawled over one of the suite's large beds, arm draped across the bosom of a thick-waisted girl whose gray hair had been tinted a delicate blue. Kilgarin left the Cook outside and entered the room, catching the eye of the waking girl and gesturing for her to leave. She did so, hurriedly. He took her place on the bed beside Raymond and poked the sleeping Physical in the ribs. The young man stirred, opened his eyes, closed them, opened them again. Kilgarin said hello. Raymond jerked to a sitting position, wide awake. "Where is she?"

"I sent her downstairs," Kilgarin told him.

"Oh." Raymond relaxed, closing his eyes again. "Did you need to do that?"

"Send her away? I'm afraid so. I wanted to speak to you privately."

"I hate waking up alone," Raymond said. He kept his eyes closed. "That always happens. I hate it." One eye opened. "What did you want to talk about? Did I do anything wrong? Hey, if you want me to pay for the girl—"

"No, don't worry about that," Kilgarin answered. He got up and bent over the bedside console. "Breakfast?" Raymond nodded and Kilgarin selected items, punching out their coordinates on the keyboard. "I just wanted to tell you I'm signing up again. Taking another Contract."

Raymond swung his legs off the bed and reached for the container of hot coffee that had appeared in the food slot. "You're not serious. You said it'd be suicide for you. Didn't you?"

"Things have changed since last night." Kilgarin sat down beside the Physical and picked up the tray of food he'd ordered.

"Your brother?"

Kilgarin nodded.

"But if it's so dangerous for you—"

"Maybe I overestimated the danger," Kilgarin said. "I'm not a weak man. I've always been proud of that."

"Still. You're lucky you're alive, after being a Cork as long as you have. That *is* what you said, isn't it?" Raymond peered at him over the piece of toast he was nibbling.

"That's what I said. I hope I'm wrong. But that's really not what matters. I wanted you to know, because I want you to take care of this place for me while I'm gone."

The Physical shook his head. "No. Sorry. I can't do it."

"If that's the way you feel," Kilgarin said, standing, stopping in mid-turn when Raymond's hand caught his arm.

"You don't understand," the young man said. "It's not because I don't want to. It's because I'm coming with you."

"I just want her to know," Kilgarin said. "That's all."

"You don't have to explain. I understand. I'll wait here; you go upstairs."

Kilgarin left the Cook at the doorway to the tenement and walked up the two flights of slick plastisteel stairs. The building was not in disrepair, not physically. It was a good building, and would remain a good building for decades: when the Company built these tract apartments they'd built them to last. Yet the building was in decay: a spiritual decay, Kilgarin thought. The building and its occupants had been abandoned by the colony in favor of a new look, one preferred by the port's new Independence government. The older buildings of the Company's construction, though useful, were treated with contempt. They were now the slums, and the people within them, the derelicts. Though the people survived, they didn't live. People like Raymond, fortunate to have a job. People like Marka. Who didn't.

She opened the door and blinked at him, her face puffy with sleep. She gazed at him a moment and then stepped back, holding onto the door as he entered the cluttered room.

"I expected you earlier," she said.

"I had business at the port."

"Of course." She walked across the room, skirting the ragged bedding in one corner. The bones of her rib cage were visible under her olive skin, her breasts rising and falling as she limped. "I'd offer you something if I had anything to offer," she said. She stepped into the fresher by the kitchen. "I'll be with you in a minute."

When she came out again, the paleness in her cheeks was gone, her eyes were less bloodshot, and she looked almost young. "Well?"

"I'm taking up Marc's Contract," he said.

Something moved behind her eyes. "Why?"

"I have to know why he died."

"He died because you weren't here to stop him," she said. "Isn't that obvious?"

"I'm not here for lectures, Marka."

"I know that."

"I won't ask you to come along. I can't."

"I know that too."

Kilgarin nodded. "That's all, then. Maybe we'll get together before I leave."

"When does the ship lift?" she asked him.

"Three days. We'll be taking a cargo run along the western Arm, to most of the Outworlds. Charting."

"That's where the rebels are," she said. Then, about the ship: "Can you handle it?"

"I don't know," he said.

At the door there was a brief moment when her breast touched his arm; he wondered if he should ask her about the night before, but decided against it. He didn't want to know. She stepped back and thumbed the lock for him.

The door slid open. He left. A moment later the door slid shut behind him.

Kilgarin wasn't prepared for the *Charter*'s mess to be crowded that evening. It was usual for a mindship's crew to take leave as soon as the vessel cleared port, but for some reason the Cook couldn't or wouldn't explain, the *Charter*'s crew was different. When Kilgarin arrived at the ship in company with the Cook, he found the halls busy with crew members, intense-looking men and women hurrying from cabin to cabin, pulling on jump suits as they walked, tabbing jackets and brushing back hair. The Cook left Kilgarin in the recreation room and went off to prepare the evening's menu, and after the small gray man had left, the Cork collared a passing Physical and asked him what was happening.

The boy gave him a brusque once-over, apparently decided that Kilgarin belonged on the ship, and answered. "The Captain just released the route, Fellow. From Barron to Rylon, first off. Then down the Outworld Belt." Kilgarin released him with a deeply felt thank you, and the Physical rushed off.

Rylon. No wonder the crew had gathered for mess. There'd be an hour or more of excited speculation, Kilgarin knew. Rylon was one of the three major Company ports, Endrim being one of the lesser stopovers. Kilgarin had never been there himself, though he'd heard rumors about the planet, stories from Sensitives who'd experienced some of the exotic thrills the port had to offer. If Endrim was an industrial port, with all the economic and social gestalts such a designation implied, then Rylon was a pleasure center. According to the more elaborate tales, the Company had bribed the Federation Colonial Office to write it an unlimited charter for the planet, in much the same way they'd managed to receive full exploitation rights for Endrim's native wormwood industry.

It was going to be an interesting voyage, Kilgarin decided. In more ways than one.

The Cook reappeared twenty minutes after Kilgarin had settled in the rec room. Returning with the Cook to the cafeteria lounge, Kilgarin received a tray and took his place on line. Most of the crew had been served already and were scattered about the room in groups of five and ten, talking loudly between mouthfuls of soup and bread. Against one wall the ship's Sensitives were gathered, twelve men and women on one long bench, supporting their trays on their laps and speaking softly, their hands moving in both broad and subtle gestures. Kilgarin filled his plate and mug, processed his credit chit—though he'd signed aboard that afternoon, he wouldn't officially be a member of the crew until 0100 the next day—and crossed the room to join his fellow Sensitives.

There was room at the end of the bench. One of the women slid over to make room for him. A moment later the Cook arrived and proceeded to make introductions. Kilgarin nodded to each of the Sensitives in turn. He was particularly struck by the Engineer, Wells, and the chief Technician, a Centaurian named Ty'ger. The Communications agent, Ryork, was the most cordial, pausing to shift her pet—a small anthropoid with large silver eyes—to her shoulder before shaking Kilgarin's hand.

"You're from Wellington, aren't you?"

"I am," Kilgarin said.

"So is Wells. You too should have much to talk about."

After this she was quiet, her attention returned to her pet, which she fed with scraps from her plate as Kilgarin watched her, absorbed.

"Have you heard?" the Cook asked him, breaking the spell.

"About Rylon? I have, yes. Your first time there?"

"Once," the Cook said. "But not about that. I'm talking about the Outworlds."

"You're not going to let what Pul said worry you, are you? Don't. He's just a broken old man trying for a little attention."

"Still," the Cook said. His muscles remained fixed along his jaw, taut with worry.

"Still," Kilgarin said. "It's nothing to be concerned about."

"What about you, Fellow? Have you ever been to Rylon?"

The voice belonged to Wells, the Engineer. Kilgarin turned to him. "No. The last ship I crewed mostly did charting work. We ran the western Arm."

"What ship was that, Fellow?"

"The *Drowner*, out of Centauri."

"The *Drowner*?" This time it was the wiry Centaurian, Ty'ger. His bleak eyes rose to meet Kilgarin's. "You said the *Drowner*?"

"That's right," Kilgarin answered. He lifted his beer. "You know her?"

"Someone who crewed her once. Perhaps he still does."

"What's his name? I know most of the crew."

"Orion," Ty'ger said slowly. "J'kar Orion."

Kilgarin felt something tighten between him and the other Sensitive. Like a physical presence something had come into the lounge and gathered around them, dark and cold. Against his will Kilgarin felt the alien emotion invading him, thrusting through the defenses he'd erected months before and which he'd only recently begun to relax. He clamped down tightly, shutting off his Sensitivity. There was a flicker in the dark eyes of the Centaurian. It faded and was replaced by emptiness.

"I know him," Kilgarin said. "He's had some trouble lately."

"That's too bad. I would have liked to see him. We could have talked." Ty'ger smiled vacantly. He seemed to have lost interest. "It's been a long time," he added.

Kilgarin said nothing. The other man made him nervous; he seemed to be drawn to a wire tightness. His movements were strained as he turned back to his meal; Kilgarin was disturbed by that appearance of tension, and watched the other man for several minutes before looking away.

Wells brought up the subject of their mutual homeworld and the two men spent the remainder of the mess hour talking about Wellington. Wells (whose name was the last remaining indication, he said, of a distant connection to the planet's founder) came from the southern hemisphere, where the temperature was more earth normal, but as the traditions of the colony were planetwide, he and Kilgarin had much to talk about. They traded stories about the colonial schools, discovered that they'd both spent a month at the same correctional facility for adolescents, and learned that aside from this accident of birthplace, neither had much in common with the other. Kilgarin found the conversation diverting, however, which was more or less what he needed. The pain of his brother's death was receeding, though slowly. As he had many times since the incident aboard the *Drowner*, Kilgarin wished for the intercession of a Cork—something he could never experience. At best, he could distract himself, but only for a short while and only superficially, as he was doing with his dialogue with Wells.

The pain would always remain. There were no Cork hands for him—no other soul to take the guilt away.

Chapter Three

Eighth month, fifth day, anno Domini 3146

It was a cool midnight. Kilgarin took the boardwalk path along the Endrim shore, listening to the clap and pad of his footsteps and watching the line of lights pointing out into the harbor channel in the distance, and smelling the fresh early-morning air. (Salt, dammit. There was *salt* in that air!)

His middle felt warm and full. There was something about ship food—though usually tasteless, there was always enough of it, served in a style that made it, if not spectacular, at least appetizing. He paused for a moment and leaned on the boardwalk railing. The waves rolled in toward the shore, driven by the milky, strangely smooth moon overhead, in lazy parody of the waves he'd seen on earth. There was no sound to this ocean. Kilgarin listened, but he could hear nothing more than a faint whisper that rose and fell with his breathing.

He thought about his brother. How much did he really *know* about Marc Kilgarin? Enough to justify his commitment to this "quest"? Not really. Then why was he determined to join the *Charter?* To find the reason for his brother's death, or—?

He sighed and turned from the water. He didn't know, and he didn't truly care.

A shape moved at him out of the darkness. Kilgarin had time to push from the railing, take a step out onto the boardwalk, and then the shape was upon him.

They fell to the boardwalk, Kilgarin landing on bottom, feeling the weight of a man on his chest, feeling arms tightening into a lock around his neck, feeling knees digging into his hip and abdomen. He tried to jerk free, but the man holding him began to apply pressure to his grip. Blood pounded in Kilgarin's ears. With a grunt he twisted onto his back and slammed his elbow and knee into his assailant's chest and groin.

The man gasped and relaxed his leg grip. Kilgarin gained leverage, shoved, pulled free, and lunged away. Hands caught at him, tripped him. He skidded along the planking, sensing the motion of the man behind him as his attacker dived. The man hit him squarely in the small of the back and carried him over the edge of the boardwalk, under the railing, and onto the sand below.

Turning, Kilgarin snapped the heels of his hands hard against the jaw of the man struggling to get on top of him. The man spun back and sprayed to a stop in a gray dune. Kilgarin got to his feet, staggered, and sat down. His heart was racing. With an effort he forced his breathing into a regular pattern. He closed his eyes and opened them again, and glanced at the man lying next to him, stunned.

It was Ty'ger.

"Well?" Kilgarin asked.

Ty'ger glared at him. Two flushed patches marked his jaw where the Cork's palms had caught him, promising nasty bruises by morning. Edging himself up on one elbow, the Centaurian worked a hand along the back of his neck. "You know how to fight," he said.

"It's something you pick up when you like to visit unknown ports," Kilgarin told him. He waited.

"They told me you're a friend of J'kar."

"That's right. You're not, I gather?"

"I wanted to make you take me to him," Ty'ger said. His voice was husky, and he paused to clear his throat. "I have things I want to talk to him about."

"Like you talked to me?"

"You wouldn't take me if I didn't force you. Not when you found out what I want."

"How do you know?" Kilgarin asked.

"I know." The Centaurian got to his feet with difficulty. Kilgarin followed him to the stairs leading up to the boardwalk.

"Try me," he said. "I'm willing to listen. It's my job; I've had enough practice."

"Don't you think I know that? I can tell. I know what it's like. I know what you're thinking and how you feel. You think there's something wrong with me, and you want to know what it is so you can warn your friend. I can hear you. You think I can't, but I can, Kilgarin, I can." The other man's voice went low and the Cork strained to make out the last few words.

"You don't want to believe me," Ty'ger whispered, "but you know you have to. You know what I am. It's something you can't help thinking about; you keep worrying it's happening to you. It's why you quit Corking. I can tell, Kilgarin.

"I can hear you."

He walked away, his footsteps a soft clap and pad on the boardwalk planking. Watching him, Kilgarin felt a brief chill. He didn't need a Sensitive's training to understand what was wrong with the Centaurian—but only a Sensitive could sympathize.

Ty'ger was one of the growing number of Sensitives who were constantly "on," whose minds were in perpetual reception of the thoughts and emotions of people around them. It was obvious now that Kilgarin knew what to look for. The man was abnormally thin, and there was a haunted look in his eyes. And the way he moved: the strained quality Kilgarin had noticed earlier, like someone moving in a room filled with glass figurines . . . all too aware of the boundaries of privacy around him. A part of Kilgarin's mind had recognized it earlier, he realized, without his conscious mind understanding. Kilgarin realized something more. Ty'ger was right. It *was* something he feared at times was happening to him. It was something he feared more than breaking.

And perhaps because it frightened him, it fascinated him too.

Sighing, he started off after the Centaurian's receding form. His footsteps echoed on the planking—clap, pad, clap, pad—and then faded as he turned down the street which led into the city.

"Why do you want J'kar?" Kilgarin asked. The two Sensitives were following the alleys on a wandering path from the central port area. They were on the fringe of the Sensitive District; ahead of them were the shops and taverns frequented by Endrim's large Physical population. The odors of cooking food drifted to them, sweet on the moist sea air.

Ty'ger took his time answering. "I've known J'kar almost all my life, Kilgarin. You've known him for six years. Which of us knows him better, do you think?"

"I don't know. How much does a man change in six years?"

" 'It depends on the man.' That's what you're thinking. You've changed, I've changed. It follows that J'kar must also have changed. Perhaps. I don't think it matters. A man is what he is made to be, no more, though perhaps a good deal less. Tell me, Kilgarin: what do you know of J'kar? Of his life before you met him on the *Drowner*?"

"Damned little," Kilgarin admitted. "He used to be a critic of some sort on earth. He formed a school of art . . ."

"J'kar is a brilliant man. Talented like his father. We went to school together on Centauri; I know him like a brother. Let me tell you, Kilgarin: he conceived an entirely new approach to aesthetics. I couldn't begin to explain it. It had something to do with Sensitivity and its affect on the appreciation of art—perhaps even the creation of art. I can't understand it, though I've had it explained to me a thousand times. It's the difference between us, him and me; some people are born to art, others . . . are not. J'kar told me that once when we were children. It was something his father taught him. His father taught him a great deal."

Kilgarin walked silently beside the thin Centaurian, listening, his hands thrust through the loops of his jump suit. The odor of cooking became stronger and sweeter.

"You know about the Centauri Police Action, don't you? You're about twelve years younger than me, but you should have been aware of what was happening."

"My father mentioned it."

"Good for him. These rebels in the Outworlds should have learned from our mistake, but no, they're making the same errors we made. Yes, Kilgarin, 'we.' I was eighteen at the time, but my brothers and sisters, and my father had been active in the anti-Company movement for several years before I was able to join them. We believed in what we were fighting for, Kilgarin. We were fools. It doesn't matter who owns a planet, the Company or the people—you still have to trade at Company prices and make the Company's deals. Look at Endrim. It declared Independence seven or eight years ago. The Company let it go, because it acted peacefully and because it had no chance of becoming self-supporting. Seven years. Look around you, Kilgarin. Has anything changed?"

"I suppose not," Kilgarin said. "The new buildings—"

"—mean nothing. You may have noticed that only

Company personnel work at Company plants, yet there are hundreds of people available native to the planet, who go without work. Hundreds of people on the dole, supported by the Endrim government. Ever wonder why the Independence people let the Company get away with it?"

"Of course I've wondered."

"Because they have no choice. The Company is the only game in town, Kilgarin, and it makes this planet pay. In another few years the Independence government will go bankrupt—and when that happens, the Company moves in. Business as usual. Revolution is rot."

"Why haven't the Outworlders figured this out?"

"They're as stupid as we were, that's why. The Company's seen to it that no single planet has the ability to support itself without trade. Those who get close"—his voice rose, and he lifted his hands from his sides, waving them expansively—"get crushed. They crushed us. They'll crush the Outworlds. And they'll do it through people like J'kar Orion."

"What do you mean?" Kilgarin asked.

"Do you know what he did?" Ty'ger turned his eyes on the Cork. The pupils were dilated, the eyes moist. "His father, his brilliant father, a Company man, bought by the Company, controlled by the Company—his father told him to spy on us. And he did. He was my closest friend, Kilgarin. I loved him and trusted him more than I did my own family. And he betrayed me. It cost my mother and father their lives. It cost my brothers and sisters their minds. It cost me my soul."

Kilgarin looked away. Ty'ger continued, his tone like the rasping edge of a saw.

"They killed my mother and father outright; both of them were too old for retraining. My brothers and sisters were much younger—Eiline was only twenty—and with a little work, their minds could be emptied of revolt. And of everything else. I saw Eiline after they'd fixed her. She didn't recognize me. She smiled when I spoke to her, and she nodded at my questions. Something must have been left inside her, I think, for when I started to cry—she cried too. She never said a word. She just sat there crying.

"Since I was the youngest of the lot, my mind was the most easily reclaimed. That's when I learned about my Sensitivity. It was an accident. They were probing, excising little bits of brain here and there, and they hit the Treacher Lobe and burned out their instruments. They burned out some of my mind as well. That's why I'm a Receiver. Day and night. Even in my dreams.

"They let me go after that. They knew I'd never have the control to work against them. They've been right so far.

"All I want is J'kar, Kilgarin. Sometimes it doesn't matter that much to me, and I stop thinking about him for a while. Then the memories come back, slowly at first, and with the memories—hate. You know about hate, Kilgarin; I can feel it inside you. There's a woman, but you don't really hate her, do you? But you understand how I feel. I know you do. You know why I want him."

Ty'ger paused by the gutter and toed the neck of a small decanter lying tilted toward a sewer grating. "Was I right in saying I'd have to force you to take me to him? Don't bother answering. You know I am."

"What do you want me to say, Ty'ger? I'm sorry."

The Centaurian looked at Kilgarin. Light from the nearest streetlamp crossed his face, somehow missing his eyes, which remained in shadow. "I know you are," he said, nodding hesitantly. "I know. But can you see . . . that doesn't really matter?"

This time it was Kilgarin's turn to nod—with hesitation.

They found the tavern in a side street that curved to a plaza similiar to the plaza near the Llyia's. A narrow flight of steps bordered by an iron rail led to the heavy wooden door of the tavern, which opened to a wide atrium. Kilgarin went through a side door into a sitting room where they would be served by a waiter. He and Ty'ger took a booth by the window, Kilgarin sitting on the side facing the room.

"I've never been to a Physical pub on Endrim before," Ty'ger said. "The way they're watching us. . . . Their thoughts are confused, Kilgarin. I can't make them out."

"Don't let it worry you," Kilgarin replied. "There isn't that much trouble in the city. Out in the fields . . . that's another matter. Sensitives aren't greatly appreciated by the laborers."

Ty'ger shrugged. Kilgarin glanced around and caught the attention of the waiter, who took their orders and moved off to the wall console. When they had their glasses, Kilgarin raised his, smiling. "Good charting."

"Hm." The Centaurian sipped at his wine. His eyes shifted, gazing over the rim of his glass. "You're definitely aboard, then?"

"I signed the papers this afternoon, before mess."

"And I can tell you still don't know why."

"I'm pretty sure. I want the Captain's motives. Besides, is there ever enough of a clear reason for an action?"

Ty'ger snorted. "There should be. But I see what you mean."

Kilgarin relaxed; the other man was winding down, the pressure on the fringe of the Cork's dormant Sensitivity easing as Ty'ger calmed.

"Those Physicals, Kilgarin . . . I don't like what I'm receiving."

"What do you mean?"

"They're tense," Ty'ger said. "They've been drinking." He turned slightly and indicated a table in the corner where several men were sitting hunched over mugs of beer. One of the men leaned forward and spoke urgently to the others. His voice carried, but his words were slurred and incomprehensible at that distance. "They're looking for trouble," the Centaurian said.

"They won't find it with us," Kilgarin assured him. He slipped out of the booth, dropped a credit chit next to his drink, preferring the unquestionable—and therefore less time-consuming—standard coin at the moment to the credit tab, which would require processing. Ty'ger did the same. Together they crossed the room, passing in front of the whispering Physicals, and stepped out into the atrium. "You still want a drink?" Kilgarin asked. The other man shook his head. "Then let's go," the Cork said. They went outside.

A few minutes later Ty'ger leaned close to Kilgarin and said, "I'm still receiving them, Killy. They're about a block behind us."

"I noticed."

"What do you want to do? Wait for them?"

"It's their game, Ty'ger. Let's just keep walking. The District isn't far from here."

"They know that, Killy."

"Then it's up to them, isn't it?"

They turned a corner and started down the sweeping street that eventually led to Kilgarin's bordello. Here the storefronts were dark; this was primarily a business area and most of the shops were closed after sundown. Ty'ger glanced over his shoulder. "They're coming, Kilgarin."

"Any particular spot you'd like to meet them?"

"Not really."

Kilgarin pursed his lips in thought. "There's an open

building a block ahead. I suggest we stop there, if they give us time."

He crossed the street, Ty'ger beside him. The Physicals followed. Entering the shadow of the large glassine-walled office building, the two Sensitives ducked behind a column that rose to the building overhang, present more for decorative purposes than functional. Voices echoed on the street, footsteps sounded on the plastcrete surrounding the building. Kilgarin tensed. Ty'ger said something softly. The two of them lifted their hands from their bodies and waited.

The footsteps came closer, stopped. Voices conferred. Three of the Physicals stepped into view and turned. The chunky man in black pointed at Kilgarin and shouted, but the Cork was already in motion. He struck the black-suited man in the middle, a full tackle that knocked the Physical back, both of them thudding into a bony teenager who was grappling for a hand weapon, all three of them going down in a tangle of limbs. Ty'ger launched himself after Kilgarin, over the fallen Physicals and into the second group, his head tucked low and his arms spread wide and grasping.

Behind you, Kilgarin. Knife.

Kilgarin started at the sudden invasion of his mind, but quelled his amazement and moved, curling into a ball and rolling aside. The third Physical of the first group—a broad-shouldered redhead with a sparse, ill-kept beard—tottered past the Cork, the glint of metal in his fist bright in the comparative darkness. Kilgarin continued his roll into the redhead's legs. The man tripped and came down, his knife clattering onto the plastcrete. Kilgarin kicked it away, followed through with the kick and toed the redhead hard in the groin. The bearded man doubled in agony.

Good. Now help me.

Ty'ger?

Don't think, Kilgarin. Move.

The Cork came to his feet and dove over the bodies of the three downed Physicals. Ty'ger had been caught by the second group, and while two young men in dark jump suits held his arms, a burly half-bald Physical was slamming calculated blows into the Centaurian's abdomen. Kilgarin landed on the bald man's back, his weight bearing him over.

He felt the sharp *crack* as the falling Physical's chin shattered on the plastcrete, and then he was up again, his fist moving along a narrow curve that ended on the side of another attacker's head. Kilgarin cursed. Another mind than his own had guided the blow, putting too much force into it. His hand stung as though his knuckles had been broken.

Ty'ger, don't try that again. You'll get me killed.

Then get your heart into this, Kilgarin. These men want to kill us—or hadn't you noticed?

There was a prodding in the back of his mind. Kilgarin whirled and ducked. One of the first group of Physicals went over his shoulder—the redhead. He palmed the forehead of another—the black-suited man—spinning him back. Ty'ger, freed from the men holding him, danced over the form of the man Kilgarin had slammed into the ground. The Centaurian's foot came up, met the kneecap of the redhead, who was trying to maneuver behind Kilgarin; the Physical screamed, tipped over backward, and went down, clutching his leg.

A matter of moments—not quite twenty seconds more—and it was over.

Kilgarin stared at the sprawled bodies. Some of the men were unconscious. Two of them were bent over in obvious pain. The sixth man looked dead.

Don't touch him, Killy.

Kilgarin paused with his hand hovering over the collar of the bald man whose chin he'd shattered on the plastcrete.

"We're not fighting anymore, Ty'ger," he said aloud. "You can leave my mind alone."

He's dead, Kilgarin. There's nothing you can do.

Kilgarin's hand tightened into a fist and drew back from the bald man. He straightened and tugged at the folds of his jump suit.

What do we do now? Ty'ger thoughts were like a whisper in a corner of the Cork's mind. He shrugged to cover the trembling in his hands.

"I don't know," he answered. "We'd better get out of here. I'd rather not have my Contract in contest over a liability suit."

What about the others?

"Leave them," Kilgarin said firmly. "They won't report us. Right now the dead man's *their* responsibility. Not ours."

You're sure?

"I'm sure," Kilgarin said.

Mindlock.

Kilgarin had experienced it twice before, with Marka and aboard the *Drowner*, with Lucille. With both women it had happened in the midst of their lovemaking, and it had seemed somehow expected and proper—until he discovered what she'd wanted from him. Most of a year had passed since then, and he'd managed to forget what a mind-lock could feel like: now it came flooding back, invading his mind and reaching into his soul.

His first reaction demanded release. Ty'ger presence, while helpful during the battle, was now vaguely threatening. Yet as they made their way along the side roads of the port city, hoping to lose anyone who might be following, Kilgarin discovered that he enjoyed the exploratory touch of another mind. True, Ty'ger's thoughts were structured in absolutes—right and wrong, black and white—and Kilgarin's instincts reacted against such shallow identification, but another part of him welcomed the elemental simplicity. Gradually he accepted the Centaurian's continued probe, and Ty'ger came in, fully.

You fought well back there, Kilgarin.

You lead a hard life, you learn hard tricks.

I noticed. We're a great deal alike, you know that, don't you? Both of us from frontier worlds, both of us trained to admire the strong and despise the weak. That's why we worked together—like brothers.

Kilgarin drew back slightly. The Centaurian noticed it and laughed within the Cork's mind.

You don't trust me, do you, Kilgarin?

Not completely. Why should I?

I saved your life back there.

And I saved yours.

But you're still afraid of me.

I still don't know you.

You will, Kilgarin, the voice inside him said, laughing, *you will.*

Images came, thoughts and memories from another man's mind. Kilgarin examined them, amused to see that he himself was prominent among them. From Ty'ger's viewpoint—effectively an alien viewpoint—Kilgarin was relatively small. His chest, narrow for a tall man, seemed concave to Ty'ger's eyes. His hands, which Kilgarin had always thought were the most impressive part of his body, looked gnarled and ugly, the calluses on his thumbs and palms—to Kilgarin the mark of a craftsman—were to Ty'ger the scars of a laborer. Kilgarin drew back from the image Ty'ger had of him. He knew that what he'd seen was tainted by the Centaurian's peculiar ethics, but even so he wondered if there'd been validity in the man's picture of him.

I ask a great deal of a man, Kilgarin.

So I see. How do you live with yourself, Ty'ger? How do you get by, day after day?

I wait. My moment will come, Kilgarin. I've accepted that.

And if it doesn't?

How do you *survive, Kilgarin?*

I dream. He thought of his brothel, only several blocks away, but already light-years distant in his thoughts. *Someday I'll get out.*

I dream too, Fellow Kilgarin. Someday I'll get in.

Another image supplied by Ty'ger rose in Kilgarin's mind. It was J'kar, but a J'kar Kilgarin never knew. Younger, a blocky redhead of about twenty, whose eyes seemed darker than was objectively possible. Kilgarin remembered those eyes and how they had followed him and his brothers and sisters at the final meeting of the cell, studying and absorbing details, always shifting whenever Kilgarin glanced their way. Those were the eyes of a murderer.

And the voice. In Kilgarin's (no, Ty'ger's) memory the tones were gone, and all that was left were the words, mouthed without emotion, spoken with mechanical precision. Kilgarin felt his stomach turning. It was the voice he knew, and yet it wasn't. Had J'kar changed that much? Was it even the same man?

Or was Kilgarin's view distorted—had he been tricked by the burly Centaurian, a man he'd accepted as his friend for six years?

You know it's true.

No, Ty'ger. He's changed. He isn't the man you knew.

Why should you believe that? You've seen what he was—what he is.

Because I know him. I have to believe I know him.

Other memories arrived as the mindlock extended through the levels of their minds, peeling away the barriers of thought and emotion. Dazedly, Kilgarin wondered what Ty'ger was seeing of *his* past.

The Cork remembered his father, a Centaurian of average height who'd managed to dominate a room by his presence and bearing. He recalled his father's manner, the bunching of muscles in his upper arms as he lifted his son and sat him on a chair, and the laughter in his voice when he spoke to the young Ty'ger.

He remembered his mother, a stern woman who always ended a conversation, demanding the final word. He remembered also her moments of softness, when she'd sing to him in the morning hours when the others were out working in the mines. He remembered the last he saw of her alive, a gray-haired fighter who'd taken two men with her before the Company agents had torn her face away.

His brothers. Big men, taller than he, wider and broader in their humor than he would ever be. He remembered the way they walked beside him when he was a child, careful to keep him in view and always dragging him back when he wandered away. His sisters. Like his mother, stern; each of them as strong as his brothers—except Eiline, who was the changeling of the family, golden and gentle, the one he loved most.

He remembered what they did to her, and his mind shut off the scene of her tears.

Kilgarin remembered the past of another man, and as he did that past became his own.

You loved your brother, Kilgarin?

I hardly knew him.

But you loved him.

I suppose.

Then you understand how I feel.

Yes, thought Kilgarin. Then, a moment later: *No.*

Ty'ger shifted himself to look at Kilgarin more closely. They were seated on the stoop of a moderately well-kept building within the fringe of the District. A near street-lamp lit the scene, yellow light washing over the gray stones of the stoop, touching the blue material of Kilgarin's jump suit and the darker blue of Ty'ger's. The two men sat at opposite ends of the steps. Kilgarin had his knees up, arms around his legs, his back braced against the stone railing where it joined the building.

The Centaurian frowned. *What do you mean—you don't undertand?*

Your view is too simple. It doesn't leave room for judgment.

And your view does?

At least I want to find out the reason why something happened, Ty'ger. I don't want blind revenge. I want to know a man's motivation.

Is that what you think it is? Is that how you see yourself?

The Centaurian slipped to his feet and stood with his arms hanging straight from his sides. His face was contorted and his eyes were bright.

Let me tell you about yourself, Kilgarin. You haven't faced the truth once in all your life. You're afraid to let someone get close to you—you're afraid you'll become dependent on them—see—see? Ty'ger laughed triumphantly. *You're closing me out! You don't want to listen to that, do you? All right. Then listen to this, Kilgarin—perhaps it won't hurt quite so much.*

The only truth is what happens, in plain and simple reality. I've seen the inside of too many minds to think any *man's intentions can be good. We're evil inside ourselves, Kilgarin. We're sick and foul and filthy. The only ones who come close to being pure are those too stupid to be anything else. You won't admit it, Kilgarin, but it's true. Look at yourself: you hate. I've seen it inside you. You can't face what this woman Marka's done to you, you can't admit your pain. But is that your so-called motivation? No, because your conscious mind thinks it's something else. So what is truth, Kilgarin? What truth do you hope to find in the Captain—what truth do you expect me to find in J'kar? They're guilty, both of them. The only difference between you and me is you don't have the guts to—*

The thought snapped off in mid-pulse.

"Maybe we'd better go," Kilgarin said quietly. "I've got things to attend to at the brothel."

When he returned to his town house, taking the long route to work out the kinks in his body and to allow himself time for thought, Kilgarin found Whyte and J'kar waiting for him in the bordello's brightly lit anteroom. The two broken Sensitives rose as Kilgarin entered. Whyte held a folder in his hands, and bent it back and forth as he faced Kilgarin, greeting him. "Your man said we could wait. J'kar wanted to talk with you, asked me along."

"Friend of yours, Raymond," J'kar said. "Told me this afternoon. About ship, you. Felt you needed help." He paused, a ridge forming between his brows as he wrinkled his forehead in thought. "Checked ship. They need Physicals."

"You've signed aboard," Kilgarin said flatly. J'kar

ducked his head in a nod, smiling. Whyte held the folder out to Kilgarin.

"He hasn't had the Contracts filed yet, Kilgarin, but they're all legal and holding. He wants you to keep them for him, have them made into a disk."

Kilgarin took the file and glanced within. He felt a cold weight lodged in his middle, but could do nothing to get rid of it.

"Why aren't you coming along, Whyte?"

The ex-Sensitive indicated his bad eye, smiling wryly. "Two reasons. That, and the fact J'kar wants to do this himself. He felt you needed help."

J'kar was frowning, and the frown deepened as he studied Kilgarin's unmoving expression. "You want me along, Killy? Right? Like you wanted me here?"

Kilgarin's grin was forced. "Of course I do, J'kar."

"Wanted to thank you for that, asking me here." The Centaurian grinned back and jerked his arms in an expansive wave. "I knew you'd want me on *Charter*. Whyte said no, but I knew. You, me, mates, right, Killy? Like before, Killy?"

"That's right, J'kar," Kilgarin said, glancing at Whyte and then turning away. "Just like before."

Two days later, after taking on its cargo of absinthe for trade to the Outworld planets, the Company ship *Charter* lifted from the Endrim port. Kilgarin stayed at the air lock until the last moment, watching the field gates and the window of the massive observation tower.

Marka never came.

It wasn't until the next day that he found out why.

Chapter Four

Eighth month, eighth day, anno Domini 3146

She was in the recreation room with Raymond when Kilgarin entered. She glanced at him from behind her disarrayed hair and smiled wryly as he sat down. "You don't seem very pleased to see me, Killy," she said. Raymond twisted around to face both of them, shifting awkwardly on Kilgarin's side of the narrow game table. Kilgarin motioned him back.

"The Cook told me you were here," he told her. "I didn't believe it."

"We tried to catch you before the ship took off, Kilgarin," Raymond said, "but you were already in Sensitive, and the Cook said we weren't supposed to disturb you until the *Charter* was on course and you came out of it."

"Why didn't you tell me you were coming along, Marka?"

"I didn't know until the ship was ready to leave."

"She caught me at your place and asked me to take her down to the port," Raymond said. He looked nervously from Marka to Kilgarin. "She said you'd want me to."

"I appreciate it, Raymond. I'm just a little stunned."

"That's obvious," Marka replied. She lifted her cigarette to her lips, drew on it. "When you feel like talking, please let us know." She returned her gaze to the game board.

Kilgarin pursed his lips, frowning. He stared at Marka, his hand tapping lightly on his left leg where it crossed his right. Raymond pushed the pieces on the board about aimlessly, starting when Kilgarin abruptly got to his feet. "I'll speak with you later," Kilgarin said to him. Raymond watched as the Cork walked out of the room.

"Why is he like that? I thought he'd be happy the Cook signed you on board."

"Then you don't know him very well, my friend." Her hand dipped as she ground out the ash of her cigarette on the small tray set into the tabletop. "Shall we play?"

The Cook shrugged his shoulders. "The boy said you wanted her. He said it was OK to take her on. Her foot wasn't as bad as some. Another ship might have said no, but here"—he spread his hands—"it doesn't matter. Why? What's wrong? Isn't she your woman?"

"It's not that," Kilgarin said. "I just didn't expect her. I don't know how to handle it. It doesn't seem right, her coming here without telling me."

"Did you ask her to come?"

"In a way. I thought she'd said no. When she didn't come to see the ship off, I decided to forget her . . . but now . . ."

"Now you can't?"

"How can I?" Kilgarin asked.

The Cook scratched a thick hand over the gray shadow on his chin. "Do you want to?" the Cook asked.

"I don't know. This is the second time around. I just don't know."

"Then see her," The Cook said, "and find out."

Kilgarin followed the corridor around the inside shell of the ship to one of the main cross-paths. He bent, ducking under the low hatch, and came up in the area of the ship set off for the Physical crew. Elsewhere on board the *Charter* the walls were colored a neutral tan. Here, the colors varied from section to section, first a bright red, then a pastel blue, followed by a gold, and so on. Each bay had its own color. There were psychological reasons for this, Kilgarin had been told, reasons that dealt with creating a strong sense of identity in the Physical members of a mindship crew. One of the hazards of the psiship class structure was the gradual dissolution of individual identity, something that affected the Physicals far less than it did Sensitives, but still affected them enough to destroy their efficiency as psi fuel. The Company's concern was not with the problems of the individual but with the effectiveness of the ship; thus, the colored walls were less noble than they appeared to be at first. Perhaps this was why so many of them had been repainted with a layer of concealing white.

The rest of the ship was tomblike in its quiet. Here, however, the halls were filled with sound, from the distant clatter of footsteps to the light music of static harps—the latest product of the earth artisan guild—and other less distinct instruments. Kilgarin traced the music to a pod bay, which grew out of the vessel's "eastern" wing. He'd been told he could find "the cripple woman" there.

As he moved he became aware, once again, of the aura of violence permeating the ship. It chilled him, and it took a moment for him to shrug the sensation off before he could proceed through the hatch and into the pod bay.

The bay was dark, the blackness irregularly broken by the glow of cigarettes and the winking lights of several ship's indicators. Kilgarin recognized the pod's lines. It was a lifeboat, minimally connected to the ship, designed for quick ejection in the event of the mindship's destruction. According to Company regulations the pods were to be kept in proper working order and inviolate until shipwide emergency. Kilgarin wasn't surprised to find the lifeboat serving as a recreation room, however; it was done on every ship. It was tradition.

Marka was seated in a corner under a softly throbbing light screen display. She glanced at him as he settled beside her. "Are you ready to talk now, Kilgarin?" she asked him.

Kilgarin drew his legs up and wrapped his arms around his knees. He found the callus on his thumb and worked at it nervously. "I didn't expect to find you here," he said.

"We've been through that already," she answered. "I'm here. Let's go from there, Kilgarin. I think I'm making my feelings fairly plain. Isn't it up to you to do something about it?'

"Marka, why are you here? Really?"

Her eye caught a flicker of light from the display screen over her. "I'm not the sort of person who thinks in terms of 'whys,' Killy. That's for you to do. I do what I think is right and important. I do as much as I can, and no more. That's the way I've always been, even before you left on your last run. You act, I react; you hurt me, I hurt you. You love me . . . I love you. You're the one who's suspicious, not me. I know what I want, Kilgarin. For now, at any rate."

"I know what you're trying to say," Kilgarin said.

"Then do something, Killy. I can't go back to Endrim now. *Do* something."

He reached forward and touched the skin of her arm,

ran his hand along the tight muscle to her shoulder, and felt the crisp material of her ship tunic lift as his fingers and palm cupped the jut of muscle and bone. "I'll try," he said. "For now."

The *Charter*'s schedule demanded a maximum of speed for the run to Rylon, and because of it the ship's psychic field was strained to its limits by the demands of the Engineering sector. Kilgarin found himself Corking during most of his waking hours, including the small amount of time Company regulation allowed for the rest of the Sensitives. There were hours "on" and hours "off" ordinarily, and the latter hours were intended for rest and a form of gentle "coasting" through the Back Region. However, with the agreement of the crew—many of whom were eager to reach the Rylon pleasure port—the Captain shortened the breaks to three-fourths of their normal length. Kilgarin found the strain almost unbearable at first, but gradually, as he grew to understand the structure of the psychic field peculiar to the *Charter*, Kilgarin gained control over the situation. Occasional outbreaks of anger and violence were usual for a ship of the *Charter*'s reputation, and aside from these minor upsets, the early days went well. Kilgarin soon found himself enjoying his work once more; apparently, it relieved an unrecognized pressure within him. He tried to explain this to Raymond on an evening three days after they left Endrim.

"You aren't aware of being a Sensitive until you reach puberty," Kilgarin told the young Physical. They were sitting in the lounge, drinking from mugs of coffee laced with absinthe. "And even then, you don't recognize it for what it is. There are too many other feelings, sensations, emotions—and each of them is strange and new, each struggling for domination. The Sensitivity is obscured. Gradually your conscious mind shoves it into a corner of your unconscious. If it isn't discovered by a mind-probe, or by accident, it can go unused and slowly deteriorates the more subtle instincts—such as intelligence. You go mad. That's what happened to my father. A Sensitive who suppresses his talent decays mentally. It may takes years, but it happens . . . eventually.

"There's something else. If a Sensitive learns about his ability and trains it, he becomes bound to it. Like a man who builds his muscles; he must keep working them all his life or the muscles will go to fat and kill him. It's the same with Sensitivity."

Raymond nodded, the corners of his mouth drawn in a tight, intent frown.

"I tried to ignore my Sensitivity, Raymond," Kilgarin told him. "Worse, I tried to suppress it. That was a mistake. I could never have kept it up. I need this"—he gestured with his mug—"even this ship, even the men here. I need it."

"I hope you're right," the Physical said. The creases in his forehead vanished as he smiled. "Will you be at dinner tonight, not to change the subject?"

"I should be," Kilgarin said. "We'll be in mind-drive for only another hour or two."

"*Another* hour or two? You're in drive now?"

Kilgarin laughed. "Talking doesn't take much concentration," he said. "I had a certain reputation for storytelling once, and I'm afraid all that talking got to be an unconscious habit. But why dinner?" he asked, rising. "Is the Cook planning something?"

"No. But Marka is."

"Oh?"

"The four of us from Endrim. We'll be sitting together, at the same mess." At the Cork's expression of concern, Raymond said anxiously, "Just for tonight. She and J'kar and I were tired of eating with the other Physicals. You don't mind, do you? You don't have to sit with the Sensitives, do you?"

"I don't think it's wise," Kilgarin said, "but there's no reason why I have to—"

"Then it's all right," Raymond said happily. "Marka seemed to think it was important."

"She would," Kilgarin said.

Mind-drive:

Kilgarin strolled down the corridors of the ship. His gaze traveled over the squares of flooring that stretched ahead of him, touched the seams where the floor joined the walls and rose to the ceiling that glowed overhead. His head tilted as though he were listening to a distant sound. His eyes went out of focus, and he paused. For several seconds he remained motionless. At last he shook himself, glanced around the corridor, brow furrowing. He whispered something to himself, shook himself again, and continued down the corridor, strolling.

Mind-drive:

His room was small as far as quarters for Sensitives go.

There was barely enough room for him to stand upright. He keyed the heat-sensitive tab on the wall next to his door and the desk and chair folded out of their wall shelf with a nearly silent hum. Kilgarin sat down, zipping open the sleeves of his jump suit and rolling them back, detaching them from the shoulders and placing them on the desk. Bare armed, he flicked a switch on the wall and accepted the tidy transparent pouch that dropped into the open slot below the controls.

Wood and metal fell from the pouch onto the desk as Kilgarin peeled it open. He picked up the knife and the half-worked block of wood, and began carving.

As he worked, he hummed softly to himself. Twice the knife nicked the underside of a finger. He never noticed.

Kilgarin passed the Captain on his way into the cafeteria lounge. The older man saw him, paused to grip the Cork's shoulder, and smile vacantly. "Glad you're with us, Kilgarin," the Captain told him. "If you ever have any problems, anything you want to discuss, be sure to let me know." The grip tightened a moment and then dropped away. Kilgarin thanked the older man and went inside the lounge.

Marka was already seated behind a table that was tucked in a corner by the hatches to the lifeboat bay. Her arms were folded on the tabletop, but she stretched as Kilgarin came up, ending the stretch with her fingers knit together behind her neck. "Raymond is getting us food," she said. "He tried very hard, doesn't he, Kilgarin?"

"He means well."

"I'm not complaining," she said. "I think it's pleasant. He's nice. But he'd probably blush to death if he ever heard me say it." She laughed. To Kilgarin, it was the same laugh he'd heard three years before. Something about it made him uncomfortable. "Do you mind all this? Do you think it's terribly sentimental?"

"I don't really see the purpose, no," he said.

"Must I remind you that you dragged the three of us along with you? Not by force, naturally. But we're here because you want us to be. That makes you a bit responsible for our well-being . . . don't you think?"

"I suppose," Kilgarin said. He didn't like the direction the conversation was taking, and was about to change it when J'kar arrived, tugging at the bulky folds of his ship tunic. The Centaurian slid in next to Kilgarin, grinning.

"Work down in the gardens, cleaning trays, washing

tubes. Still stink. Tried fresher, but can't get smell off," He pulled at the ragged locks of his hair. "How, all the time? Others, I mean. Physicals, others—how?"

"How do we do it?" Marka took a cigarette from a sleeve pocket. "It's a job, J'kar. We've been doing work like it all our lives. You've never been inside a hydroponics plant before; for you, it's something different. Something ugly." She shrugged, lit the cigarette. "To the rest of us, it's just life. You have any complaints . . . tell them to the Company."

They sat in silence, waiting for Raymond. Finally Marka said, in annoyance, "Where is that boy? He's been gone almost a half hour."

"This isn't your usual mess hour," Kilgarin said. "Maybe he's having trouble finding the right line."

"I don't doubt it," she replied.

J'kar rose awkwardly to his feet. "Wait," he said thickly, "Stay. I'll go." Kilgarin started to get up, but Marka reached across the table and pressed him back. They watched him lumber off between the tables toward the mess lines at the far end of the room.

"He can take care of himself, Killy."

"I wish I was as sure as you are," Kilgarin said. "Damn him."

A shout from the center of the lounge brought Kilgarin's head around. He stared, cursed, and pushed to his feet. Marka followed beside him. "What is it?" she asked. "What's wrong, Kilgarin?"

"It's J'kar," he said. He jerked out of her grasp and ran down an aisle between two partly empty tables. Ahead a crowd was gathering, obscuring his view. He pushed into the crowd, slipped between an overweight Physical and a goggling Technician, elbowed past and out into a clearing. In the center of the clearing was J'kar.

Or rather, J'kar and Ty'ger.

The aura of the crowd was tense with emotion as the diners watched the two men grappling on the floor. Ty'ger had J'kar in a hammerlock and was trying to maneuver his knee into the base of the big man's spine. Both of them were grunting, Ty'ger snarling something unintelligible, his words consumed in the roar of the crowd. J'kar managed to work his elbow against the other man's chest, heaved and threw Ty'ger backward over the polished plasteel. Kilgarin chose that moment to step forward. Someone caught him and drew him back, shouting in his ear,

"It's their fight, let them at it, Fellow." Kilgarin tried to pull away, but the grip on his arms tightened, another pair of hands joining the first.

In the middle of the improvised arena, J'kar was trying to get to his feet. His bad arm was moving without coordination. When he saw Kilgarin, he widened his eyes, cried out, "Killy—" and was hit from behind by Ty'ger, borne down.

Kilgarin strained against the hands holding him. The grip was unbreakable. He closed his eyes, then—and *pushed.*

A surge of hatred swept into his mind. Kilgarin sagged mentally under the onslaught of Ty'ger's emotions. With an effort he forced himself to face them, absorb them. There was no sense to the emotions swelling into Kilgarin's mind—there was only the Centaurian's hatred, a pressure that grew as Ty'ger snapped a choke on J'kar.

Ty'ger, no!

The Centaurian twisted back, his eyes rolling, hands falling from J'kar's throat.

Kilgarin? Is that you? What are you doing to me?

I want you to stop, Ty'ger. Now.

Ty'ger fell from J'kar's limp form, striking the floor, his back arching into a bow, his hands clutching his face as he strained against an invisible force.

You're hurting me, Killy—

Will you stop?

Yes. Yes, dammit!

Kilgarin relaxed. On the floor, Ty'ger ceased to writhe. His body slowly flattened to the plastisteel. Breath trailed out of his lips in a long sigh. Around the arena, the crowd began to mumble in disappointment.

Don't ever do that again, Kilgarin.

The Cork ignored the thought, pushing Ty'ger presence out of his mind while he slipped out of the loosened hold of the men behind him. He crossed to J'kar. The Centaurian looked up at him. "Are you all right?" Kilgarin asked.

"Now, sure," the other man said. He swallowed, frowned. "Who. . . ?"

"He calls himself Ty'ger," Kilgarin said. "He thinks you should know him."

Comprehension darkened the large man's heavy features. He tried to speak, but the words choked in his throat. Kilgarin laid a hand on the Centaurian's shoulder, wondering, at the same time, how he could remove himself from the problem. "Take it easy, J'kar," Kilgarin said. "You'll be OK. Don't get excited."

He looked around for Ty'ger, but the other Centaurian was already gone. The crowd was thinning, people breaking away to return to their tables and their interrupted meals. One Physical pushed through the crowd, his round face contorted with fear. It was Raymond. He was holding a large tray set with several plates and mugs.

"Where were you with the damned food?" Kilgarin asked.

"I—they wouldn't let me through on the first line—"

"Forget it," Kilgarin said. "Take J'kar back to the table. I've got something else I have to do."

"Sit down, Kilgarin," the Captain said. "You'll have to give me a moment. I'm still tied in to the Set; I've been in touch with Barron, working out the details for our cargo transfer. That Communications agent, Ryork; she's done a fine job of keeping me patched in. We've been having trouble with a Singularity—excuse me—"

The Captain returned his attention to his Set, pushing buttons and keys on the console swung over his knees. Kilgarin watched without interest as the Captain spoke into the throat mike that connected him to the Set, which in turn brought him in contact with the psi field powering the ship. After a moment the Captain finished and unplugged from the console.

"Tailor, the man on Barron, tells me we'll be hitting some trouble in the Outworlds. I asked him for details, but he didn't have any." Detaching the throat mike, the Captain rubbed his neck, thoughtfully. "Probably rumor. Quite a bit of it at most of the ports these days." Finished with the microphone, he turned to Kilgarin and said briskly, "You mentioned one of the Physicals, didn't you? Any problems?"

Kilgarin told him about the run-in between Ty'ger and J'kar. Toward the end of his explanation he realized that the Captain had stopped listening. The other man was on his feet, standing before the wide screen at the rear of the control room, his hands in the back pockets of his jump suit. Kilgarin stopped speaking. The Captain said nothing.

"Captain? Are you going to help J'kar?"

"There's something you should know, Kilgarin. I've been with Ty'ger for three years. He's a violent man; I know that, Kilgarin. He hates. More than any man I've ever encountered. But I also know what kind of ship this is—it needs emotion, *any* kind of emotion, to power its drives. Love, hate: it doesn't matter, so long as the emotion is *strong*. It needs a man whose emotions are deeper than normal or natural. It needs Ty'ger."

"You're saying you'll do nothing?"

"That's right, Kilgarin. You're a Cork. You should understand the priorities here."

"I understand them, Captain."

"Good. We should reach Barron in another six or seven hours. You'll be on duty around 0800. Don't you think you should be getting some sleep?"

Smiling, Kilgarin unfolded from the bench that ran along the wall opposite the Set. Smiling, he bowed and said, "Yes, Captain." Still smiling, he left.

The *Charter* touched Barron and remained a day's rotation on the bleak gray world, unloading part of its cargo and taking on the supply of exotic fruits harvested by Barron's small colonist population. Kilgarin spoke briefly with the Company agent at the main port. The agent, a muscular man sliding into middle age, offered to take Kilgarin out to see his fields nearby, but the Cork refused. He'd seen colony farms before. They were one of the main reasons behind his choosing a bordello on Endrim for his retirement.

Kilgarin asked the man what he knew about the *Charter*'s Captain, asking first if he'd ever been on Barron before.

"You'd know more about him that I do," Tailor replied. "He's your Captain. The last time I saw him"—he sniffed at his glass of absinthe, blinking—"was almost two years ago, and he was only a Mate then. You want some Roots?" he added. "Good chewing. Affects motor control, they tell me." He offered Kilgarin a handful of gray leaves. The Cork refused.

"A Mate? How did he seem to you? Ambitious?"

"Never noticed it. Kept it hidden, if he was. The Captain before this one, he was a hard man. Not the sort you could get friendly with. Haven't gotten friendly with *this* one either, mind you, but at least with him I feel I could." He sipped at his glass. "This right from Endrim? Some other kind's floating around these days, you know, from the Outworlds. Going to be some trouble when the Company finds out."

"Have you told them?" Kilgarin asked, buckling his canteen back onto its shoulder strap.

"Tell them? *Why?* Other stuff's cheaper." He drank, finished off his cup. "Not so good, of course—but definitely cheaper."

Kilgarin returned to the ship. Twenty minutes later the *Charter* lifted for Rylon.

Marka approached him the evening before they entered the Rylon system. He was in Sensitive, standing near one of the wall-length screens that showed a view of the Back Region beyond the ship; he didn't notice her until she put a hand on his arm, and then he felt her only dimly, like a voice speaking through the fog of a dream. "Are you going to stay with me when we reach Rylon?" she asked him.,

"I want to," Kilgarin said. He continued to watch the maze of color winding on the screen. Marka stood with him a moment, her fingers clinging to the cuff of his jump suit. She wore a brightly colored dress-shift that curved diagonally around her body, concealing her left breast, her right hip, and all of her left leg. She'd dyed her hair a pale shade of gold and added makeup to her chin and underjaw, in the current fashion. For several minutes she waited, her eyes holding on him. Finally she broke away.

"I'll see you when we berth," she said.

He nodded and said nothing.

It was late afternoon of the following day before the *Charter*'s crew had been processed by the Rylon port authorities. Kilgarin and Marka left the ship after most of the others, waiting to file their Contracts and have their blood ID'd, according to the regulations of the colony. Kilgarin saw J'kar and Raymond pass near them, but he gave no sign of noticing the two Physicals. J'kar seemed distracted; Raymond was speaking to him in a low voice and the Centaurian was nodding absently. Kilgarin watched them until they disappeared into the fourth of the gray and blue stalls provided for port clearance.

When they left the last of the stalls behind, Kilgarin took Marka by the hand and led her down corridors lit with glowing signs. He found a sign that told him what he wanted to know, and headed in the direction the sign indicated. Marka, reading the message over his shoulder, cried out in surprise. "A flier, Killy? On Rylon?"

"I like to get the feel of a world I'm going to spend some time on, Marka. I want to see a bit of it, get to know it."

She stared at him a moment, then shrugged and allowed herself to be led.

The flier rental shop was on the roof of the port building, a vast structure that dominated the city. Several levels of the building were devoted to a business, the rest to pleasure: signs announced some of the various diversions available, broadcasting their messages in several languages, as well as on the Sensitive frequency. Kilgarin found it necessary to shut out the advertisements on several levels. Each sign was more intense than the last.

Taking a lift shaft they arrived on the roof and picked their way through a forest of antennae to a squat building tucked between two triangular neon signs. There were no people here; the crowds were all on the levels below. No one found it necessary to view the moons of Rylon in person—except, Marka reminded him peevishly, Kilgarin. He ignored the comment and rapped on the window of the squat building, knocking until a face appeared, followed by a man. "You from the Company?" the man asked.

Kilgarin said no. "I want to rent a flier for the evening."

He and the proprietor of the flier agency dickered through the window about the size of the flier necessary and the fee Kilgarin was willing to pay. The other man seemed confused at first, as though he couldn't believe someone wanted to leave the city. Eventually, however, the arrangements were completed and Kilgarin took possession of a waist-high skimmer, powered by an antimatter engine. The flier was large enough for both he and Marka to stretch out on, their shoulders and necks comfortably socketed by the skimmer's form-fitting backrest. The proprietor watched them lift off the rooftop and shoot into the darkening sky. Their last view of him showed his round face upturned, his expression blurred by the distance. Then he was gone, swallowed by the glare of neon far below.

"Where are we going?" Marka asked.

"I don't know," Kilgarin said. "We're looking. That's enough by itself, isn't it?"

"I suppose."

Below them the city of Rylon covered the land like a puddle of gold, portions of it glistening red for an instant, or blue, as though catching the dying light from the setting sun. Kilgarin guided the skimmer through the clouds moving in over the city from the north, and the air around them went from dry to moist, warm to cold, and then clear again as they left the clouds behind. The dome's bubble came up around them, shielding them from the rarity of the upper altitudes. They went into a curve that brought them out over a rolling pasture that extended west as far as they could see in the fading sunlight. Rylon was behind them, already sinking beyond the low horizon.

They flew west, dipping low now and then to skim hedges, rising to leap the crests of low hills, pushing forward through the night.

Kilgarin resisted the urge to probe Marka's thoughts and discover what she felt about the world around them. He was afraid of what he might find. He wanted her to be the same—and yet not the same—as the woman he'd known three years before. It was a precarious balance, and one which he didn't want to upset.

Silently they went west, through the alien dusk.

"I think I understand why you wanted to come here," Marka said. She held herself against the chill. "It's nice. It's different, not like the city at all."

They sat together on a rise before a shallow brook. The water bubbled and hissed at their feet, moving more slowly than seemed natural, over rocks that were *just* the wrong shade of red.

"Places like this remind me of Wellington," Kilgarin said. "We had a farm there, trees, our own river. Not a natural river, we'd dug it ourselves, but it served. Nights like this we'd go down to the stream and sit under one of my father's trees, and listen to the water: Marc and I. He was quiet, like my father. Neither of them talked much. My mother—I could listen to her for hours. Sometimes I did. But Marc was quiet, which was good sometimes."

"It must have been very nice," she said. "Do you miss it?"

"Yes and no. I like the cities."

"That's because they're new to you. You haven't lived in them all your life." She lifted her head and tossed her hair back from her face. Kilgarin watched her profile as she gazed up past the trees, at the smoky night sky and the two melon-sized moons. "I was born on earth, Kilgarin. I've told you that. Have you ever been there?"

"Two years ago, after I left you."

"You probably went to Peking. Everyone does. Not many come to Europe anymore, and I don't blame them. Most of the smaller cities have been abandoned, and the larger ones aren't fit to live in. Even Old Rome—that's in Italy, part of the South European Confederacy—even Old Rome is nothing but ruins and tourist traps. That's where I was born. In Old Rome." Her voice was quiet as she finished speaking.

"What was it like?" Kilgarin asked. He glanced over his shoulder, the movement of a small animal near the skimmer bringing his head around. The creature blinked at him with luminous emerald eyes.

"It wasn't very good," Marka said. "I can tell you that much. My mother was on the dole, and when I came along, she didn't have the credit to feed me. I was illegal, you see. An accident; my mother's sterility shots didn't take. She sent me north to Milan, to an aunt who was doing well off her dead husband's pension—she'd never reported his death, she just continued to forge his name on the Company chits. My aunt and I disliked each other from the first. She sold me as soon as she found a buyer. My mother should have done it—eliminate the middleman, you see? The buyer wasn't so bad. I was three when he got me. I was ten when I left. It's truly amazing what you can learn from a man in seven years, Kilgarin."

She looked at him through the twilight. He didn't meet her gaze. After a moment he cleared his throat and said, "Do you want to leave?"

"Don't you want to tell me about *your* family some more? No? Then I think it's time we go." She got to her feet. "Don't you?"

It was just midnight when they returned the flier to the agency. Kilgarin found out the directions to the central entertainment area of the Rylon port, thanked the man, gave him a standard chit tip, and went with Marka to the lift tubes, catching the next aircar to the lower levels.

There was only one other man in the aircar with them, a Rylon native. Thin, wearing body paint on his chest, arms, and legs, he crouched on the bench that ran around the wall of the car, his legs drawn up and his fingers clasping his ankles. His eyes were white, his pupils dilated to near invisibility; his mouth was open and his breath hissed through lips that were cracked and raw. Kilgarin stood half-facing the Rylan; he caught almost nothing from the man's mind, no emotion or whisper of intelligence. As Kilgarin watched, a line of mucus crept out of the man's nostril and slipped down into the corner of his mouth. Kilgarin turned away. He and Marka left at the next stop. The Rylan didn't.

Rylon deserved its reputation, Kilgarin decided an hour later. It was indeed the most complete pleasure port he'd ever encountered, offering diversions he'd never imagined possible, as well as standard distractions for the tourist whose interests lay in more prosaic areas. There were brain devices of varying complexities, neural stimulators and depressants, exotic parlors, foods and liquors, women, men, animals, children—a literal explosion of the perverse. Kilgarin became rapidly ill. The third time he encountered a man like the one they'd seen in the aircar, he realized it wasn't an unusual state for a native Rylan. To one extent or another, everyone who lived and worked on Rylon was addicted to some form of narcotic. No doubt, Kilgarin thought, it was supplied by the Company.

The Central Area was circular, several concentric corridors enclosing an immense amphitheater where spectacles were staged on an hourly basis. The nearer one came to the amphitheater—the visitor was forced to proceed from ring to ring in order to reach the center—the more bizarre became the entertainments offered. Marka and Kilgarin worked their way through the nine rings in a little over two hours, neither speaking to the other; since the riverbank earlier in the evening, both had remained cool and introspective. Kilgarin felt no anger, himself, but knew that Marka was irritated with him, for reasons he didn't care to comprehend. He respected the silence she offered him, however, and kept to it as they wandered from stall to stall, sometimes pausing to examine an article whose purpose was at first obscure. Several times Kilgarin wanted to bypass a stall that Marka insisted on investigating. The Cork knew she was doing it to punish him, for whatever wrong she thought he'd done her. He accepted it, but gradually it began to annoy him. When they reached the final ring, he wanted to take the aircar back to the port area, but she insisted that they visit the amphitheater. For the first time in several hours, she spoke to him directly.

"How can I ever tell anyone I'd been to Rylon and hadn't seen the theater?"

He sighed. "If that's what you want, we'll go."

They avoided a man who was moving blindly through the crowded corridor, his skull enclosed in a helmet that cut off his vision and hearing, and when he was past they continued down the hall, toward the light that marked the theater entrance.

Ty'ger was standing outside the entrance to the theater, talking with a young woman in Physical grays whom Kilgarin recognized as one of the *Charter*'s crew, and as the Physical half of Ty'ger's Sensitive/Physical exploration team. Kilgarin wondered what she was doing here on Rylon with the Centaurian; normally a Sensitive/Physical team acted together only on unknown planets, mindlocked to make a more effective agent than either would be alone. Vaguely, the Cork remembered an image of the woman from his own mindlock with the Centaurian: her name was Luanne, he recalled, and Ty'ger's relationship with her extended beyond the surface of alien worlds. It was unusual, but not unheard-of. Kilgarin debated approaching the two of them, had about decided against it when the decision was taken out of his hands.

"Kilgarin—Marka—just the people we were looking for." Ty'ger was striding toward them, grinning, leading Luanne with a hand tight around her wrist. "We were about to go inside, but Luanne said she didn't want it to be just the two of us. We were discussing it when you two showed up and solved everything. You will join us, won't you?"

Marka flicked a nervous look at Kilgarin, then smiled back at Ty'ger. "If you want us to," she said.

"You're still concerned about the other night, aren't you? Yes, I know you are. Don't be. That was then," the Centaurian said," and tonight is another matter entirely. It's like I told you, Kilgarin. Some days I just don't care about that friend of yours. Some days I just want to forget."

"Ty'ger, you're hurting my hand," Luanne said behind him. He glanced around, looked from her face to his hand around her wrist. He let go and she stepped away, rubbing her fingers along the band of pink skin where his fingers had squeezed her too tightly.

"I'm sorry," the Centaurian said.

"Actually, we were thinking about not going—" Kilgarin began, but broke off when Marka glared at him. He felt himself growing angry.

"Nonsense," Ty'ger said loudly. "You have to see the theater, Kilgarin. Get your credit chit out, that's it; now come along—it seems we're in time for a new show."

He led the three of them into the theater, keeping up a stream of conversation that Kilgarin mostly ignored. The

Cork was concentrating on placing a probe through Ty'ger's mind, and was finding it impossible; there was no way to learn what the Centaurian was actually thinking, because Ty'ger had thoroughly blocked his mind.

Inside the amphitheater they located four seats near the balcony rail. There were headsets connected to the armrest of each seat; Marka and Luanne put theirs on, but neither Ty'ger nor Kilgarin needed to—their natural talents would enable them to read the emotions of the players quite well. The theater was not usually frequented by Sensitives, it seemed, for around the four of them the majority of the audience wore the helmets. Kilgarin viewed the expressions on the Physicals in the amphitheater with distaste. There was a mixture of greed and fear visible in their twisted mouths and staring eyes. Kilgarin felt uneasy, though he hadn't yet let down his barrier against the audience's reactions, something he knew he would have to do during the course of the show.

"Wait until you find out what they're thinking," Ty'ger said, noticing the look in the Cork's eyes.

"I'm not sure I want to," Kilgarin replied.

The spotlights came on in the theater below. Marka leaned forward, bracing her arms on the railing that protected her from the fifty-foot drop to the circular stage. Seven or eight men stood in the glare of the lights, positioned in such a way that each stood at the vertex of a huge star. They were dressed in silver and gold. Each man's hands were encased in heavy plastisteel gauntlets, and the gauntlets were studded with silver spikes. Kilgarin frowned as he received the first thought-pulse from the "actors." Their thoughts were muted and confused, and not one of them projected an aura of consciousness. He probed deeper—and jerked out with a start. The men were nearly mindless: part of their frontal lobes had been removed.

"My god," Kilgarin said.

"Wait," Ty'ger whispered. "Watch."

The spotlights shifted. Seven more figures stepped out of the shadows, moving gracefully into the center of the stage. They were women, modestly clad from the waist down, their legs concealed by tight bands of cloth wound from ankles to hips. All seven moved with a silky ease that astounded Kilgarin: they seemed almost animalistic. Touching their minds, he learned why. They too had been altered, but whereas the men were almost mindless and without emotion, the women still had their emotions intact—only their intelligence was gone.

He watched, stunned, as the preconditioned "actresses" moved into position around the men, forming another star that enclosed the first. The audience became hushed. Kilgarin caught a glimpse of Ty'ger's face, and beside him, Marka's. Luanne wasn't visible, hidden behind the Centaurian's shoulder. Kilgarin returned his attention to the stage. Light glinted on the plastisteel gauntlets.

Slowly at first, then with increasing frenzy, the actors and actresses began to dance.

Kilgarin watched for several minutes. Then he asked Marka if she wanted to stay. When she didn't answer, he got up and left the theater, and found a public lavatory and was sick.

"Another cup?"

"Please," Kilgarin said. He accepted the coffee gratefully.

"You're too pale. You sure you don't want anything to eat?"

"Nothing, Cook."

"You want to talk about it, Kilgarin?"

"No. Leave me alone, Cook. Just let me sit here. Just leave me alone."

After a while he left the cafeteria and went to his cabin. Apart from the Cook, the ship was empty; there were no other minds to intrude upon his. All the other crew members were down at the port. Even the Captain. Kilgarin reached his cabin and shut himself inside. Taking out the transparent pouch with its blocks of wood, he sat staring at them for several minutes, toying with a knife that he'd sharpened to a glittering edge.

Very deliberately, he took the smaller of the two wooden blocks, a partially finished carving of a tiny animal, and he jabbed at it with the knife until the block was cut and scratched, chips of wood lying on the desk around it, and he continued to jab at the figure until the knife blade snapped and he cut himself on the jagged edge.

He sucked at the wound, eyes closed. He didn't hear the door to his cabin slide open, but he heard it when it shut.

She looked at him with eyes that were red and swollen, but not, he thought, from crying.

"What do you want?" he asked. She flinched at the sound of his voice. It was harsh, clipped.

"Cook told me you were in here. He told me you'd been sick."

"Why should you care?" Kilgarin asked. "I'm surprised you noticed I was gone."

"That's not fair, Killy. You know how—hypnotic that sort of thing can be."

"No, I don't, Marka. On my world people would have been killed for doing something like that. People would have been beaten for watching it. And you just sat there . . . enjoying it."

"I didn't enjoy it," she said quietly.

"You enjoyed everything about that place," the Cork said. He glanced at the figurine lying in a clutter of wood chips on his desk. He poked at it with his knife.

"Killy, I was trying to—to hurt you. Because you hurt me. I never thought it'd go so deeply with you—"

"Hurt you?" Kilgarin looked up. "When?"

"On the riverbank, when you were telling me about your family. Flaunting it. I never had a family, Kilgarin, and you knew that. The way you spoke about your parents—your brother—*how was I supposed to feel?*" Her voice had a pleading quality in it. Kilgarin was suddenly less certain about her eyes.

"I didn't realize it would bother you," he told her. Seeing her like this made him uncomfortable. "I wouldn't have said it if I'd known."

She didn't answer. The muscles in her face worked. Turning her head to avoid his eyes, she glanced at the shelf over the bed console. A dozen wooden statues stared back at her. None was higher than six inches. "I never saw your cabin before," she said. "Or those."

Kilgarin waited. Finally she turned back to him. "I'm sorry too, Killy. I didn't think your frontier planet morality was so strong. I'm sorry if I hurt you."

"I'll talk to you tomorrow, Marka," Kilgarin said. She pursed her lips, as though she were about to speak, then shook her head, said something too softly for him to understand the words, and left the room. He listened to her footsteps recede, and pressed the heat-sensitive tab beside the door, and the door slid shut. He went back to his desk.

He didn't like the way he felt. It was too much like the feeling he'd had three years before, when he'd found himself becoming dependent on Marka. It was an uncomfortable sensation. He didn't know what to do.

Lifting the scratched carving, he placed it carefully in the pouch, sealed the bag, and set it back in its niche in the desk unit. The niche whirred shut around it.

Chapter Five

Eighth month, twentieth day, anno Domini 3146

Mind-drive:

The colors come slowly, washing one over another, pulsing from infrared to ultraviolet. Kilgarin feels the colors moving through him, warm to cold, and he sifts his mental hands through that arterial river, letting the strong emotions through and halting the ego-destructive "silt."

Here, a man contemplates suicide—*and Kilgarin's hand reaches, touches, soothes.*

There, a man trembles on the verge of madness—*and Kilgarin caresses, removes.*

Ahead of the *Charter*, bands of color appear from a central point, widening to their maximum width as they run beside the mindship and shrinking once more as they vanish to the rear. Elongated spots of white dot the rainbow streamers, indicating stars and, sometimes, galaxies. All seem alike, here in the Back Region: giants, white dwarfs, neutron stars, the remains of nebulas or portions of a galactic cloud. Each is a speck of white in the river of color. Size varies little, as does intensity. In the Back Region, all lights are the same—only the mindship glows brilliant.

Kilgarin senses other minds riding outside the mindship sphere. The mental field of Wells, the Engineer, is quite apparent, as are the fields of the Communications agent, Ryork, the Technicians, the Navigators, and the other Sensitives who help maintain the psychic sphere. The most prominent of the fields, however, is not an organic one—it is the artificial mind-web of the Captain, the electronic field established by his Set, which allows him to supervise the ship's progress and course. Like a king on horseback, he rides at the forefront, dominating the scene. His presence invades Kilgarin's thoughts. His control is absolute.

He is everywhere.

And so is Kilgarin.

Here, the beginnings of a fight in the recreation room—*and Kilgarin soothes, calms, removes the pain and anger.*

There, a stark burst of hate, a woman's anguish—*and the Cork guides, gentle fingers releasing and revealing.*

On through the darkness, deep into the Back Region, the *Charter* glides. And everywhere there is Kilgarin, their valve—*soothing and alive.*

Mind-drive:

He sat with Wells in the Engineer's quarters in the southern hemisphere of the ship. They sipped brandy and talked, from time to time moving the pieces on the board they'd set on the bed between them. Kilgarin found the game relaxing, though ultimately boring. Wells, on the other hand, was a true enthusiast. Both men had learned the game on their homeworld, but Wells had gone on into collecting and studying the various versions that had popped up during history. He had several antique sets and would display them at the slightest provocation. Kilgarin had learned not to show too much interest, or else he would be forced to suffer a long and involved lecture on the origin of each piece, its history, and its classic use in the strategy of the game of chess.

"How long have you known him?" Kilgarin asked, continuing their discussion.

"The Captain? Lord, six years now at the least. I met him just before he became Mate on the *Charter*. We shipped on the *Lady* together, back—oh—back around '40. He was in Administration then, and I was a Technician. He'd been working his way up on the *Lady* for almost seven years, and I'd been a Tech for about that time myself. Quiet fellow; we had a drink or two in a crowd when we'd hit port, nothing special. Then this *Charter* thing came along and they asked me to join up—it was a new ship, just commissioned—and I recommended him for First Mate. That was in '43. I was friends with the Company hiring officer at the time, you see."

"Hm," said Kilgarin.

"We got along, the Captain and I. A bright lad, even

then. Bit quiet, like I say, but he can handle himself in a tough spot, that's for certain."

"Oh?"

Wells moved a piece, grinning. "Find your way out of that, Fellow." He scratched at his neck, still grinning, and continued, "Sure, he was a quick one. One time when he was Mate we were hit by some sort of epidemic on one of these colonial worlds on the Arm. The entire damned area was down with this bug, and it was killing our crew one after another. Our old Captain sent the lad off to one of the other cities, where they had some sort of serum. Classic. He took along two other Physicals, and both of them got sick, but somehow the Mate managed to get back the serum by himself. He did. You should have seen his face when he came back to the ship, carrying those damned big packs—like a haunted man's. Serum didn't work, though. Bug died out on its own."

"Sounds like an apocryphal story," Kilgarin said.

"Maybe," Wells said, "but it's true."

Kilgarin moved a piece on the board, and Wells gave a laugh. He placed a pawn on the same square with Kilgarin's knight. "Mate," he said, "that's check."

Morning greeted the *Charter* when the mindship made its third landfall of the trip. Kilgarin was one of the first on the surface of the virgin world, in time to catch the earliest rays of the rising sun. The other members of the ship's exploratory team bustled about him, but Kilgarin hardly noticed them; he was totally immersed in the dawn, in the beginning of a new day on a world no man had ever seen before. He wondered if this would be the planet where they'd finally discover intelligent life. The odds were as much for it as against it. He drew a breath of the bitterly cold air, knowing he was foolish to feel the way he did—but unable to help himself, any more than he ever could help himself the first few minutes on a completely alien shore. The air tasted clean in his nostrils. (And wasn't there the slightest hint of salt in that taste? Perhaps.)

He turned back to help the other members of the team unpack the survey craft they'd need to explore this section of the planet. It was part of the Company's charter with the Federation Colonial Office that occasional explorations of new planets be made by the psi traders—this was one of those occasions. Kilgarin welcomed the break from the ship routine.

Marka finished opening a plastisteel crating box and limped over to stand near him. "Are you sure you don't mind if I come with you?" she asked him. "Cook said it could be dangerous for the two of us, if you don't—"

"Cook likes to worry," Kilgarin said. "It makes him feel involved."

"But . . . will it be dangerous, Killy?"

"Teaming up is standard practice, Marka. All of the other Sensitives coming along will have a Physical with them. Ryork's bringing that hydroponics' man, Kerwin, on top of her own pet. Ty'ger's with Luanne. You're with me. It's best, that way. And don't be afraid I won't be able to keep you in contact—what happened on Rylon is over."

"But Cook says if there's any doubt, we—"

"There isn't any doubt, Marka."

She broke off what she'd begun to say and looked at him, oddly. Kilgarin glanced away. After a moment she went back to unpacking the crate.

Kilgarin wondered if the Cook was right, if he wasn't using this teaming as a test of his trust in Marka, and her trust in him. Something had changed in their relationship since Rylon, despite what reassurances he'd made to her; he was less certain of her, knowing that she was falling into a dependence on him, and perhaps, he thought, this was his way of testing her will. He hoped not, because if the Cook was right, and he didn't commit to the contact—the results would be disastrous.

A new voice brought him back to awareness. It was the Captain. The older man was directing most of the landing party back to the ship under the orders of the Cook. Kilgarin smiled at the thought that the small gray man had become the First Mate of the ship, effectively—contrary to Company regulations, which forbade any Sensitive to act in the administration of a mindship. Kilgarin found it amusing—and puzzling. It reminded him that the Captain's motives were still a mystery to him, more now than before, as he learned about the man. Perhaps on this survey, Kilgarin thought, he'd learn just a little bit more. . . .

"Fellow Kilgarin, are you going to accompany us?"

Kilgarin faced about. "Whenever you're ready, Captain."

"Good. I want you to ride in the first car with Wells and me. Ryork and Ty'ger will follow in the second car, with their respective partners." The Captain raised his eyes to the sun, which was bulging over the mountain range to the east, large and sweltering red in the emerald sky.

"This looks like a fairly unextraordinary world," he said. "We shouldn't have any difficulty carrying out a reasonable survey over the next two days. We'll head north, then cut across the tundra to the western sea."

He held up a clipboard and keyed the miniature screen. Aerial photographs flickered across the face of the board, showing a jagged coastline, the white glare of snow, a dark patch Kilgarin guessed was forest. "The computer indicates a probability of heavy metal isotopes here"—the picture shifted, showed a glacier and a hillside of barren stone—"and here. Our survey will concentrate on the more likely of the two spots, in this forest some two hundred miles to the northwest."

Ryork asked a question about the weather, which the Captain answered in detail. Kilgarin wandered away, found Marka pulling on an overjacket that she'd taken from her pack, open on the ground before her. The other crew members were moving past, back up the ramp and into the mindship.

"You ever go on a survey before?" Kilgarin asked her.

"I had a Contract for five years," she answered.

"That doesn't mean anything."

"I've been down once," she said, angrily, turning to snap at him. "One time, and that's when I shattered this." She gestured at her booted foot. "Does that satisfy you?"

"Let's get ourselves settled in the skimmer," Kilgarin said.

He couldn't read the Captain. The man's mind was as closed to him as ever.

It was as though a wall had been erected between them, so carefully mortared no sound could penetrate, so thick no vibration could move from one side to the other. Kilgarin pried at that wall for several hours during the journey north; the palms of his hands became wet with sweat and he began trembling under the pressures working within him—not so badly that Marka, sitting next to him, would notice, but badly enough that if the trembling had grown worse, she would have.

Other thoughts came to him clearly as he worked at the Captain's mind: he could hear the deep mental echo of Wells's ruminations, the smoldering whisper of Marka's brooding—but from the Captain, nothing. He broke off finally and slumped against the neck and shoulder brace of the rear seat in the four-man skimmer; he almost passed out once the pressure he'd been inflicting on himself was released. He lay there, eyes closed, breathing deeply, and when they came, his dreams were troubled.

"Something's moving down there, Captain." Wells pointed through the windscreen that curved down to meet the floor of the skimmer. "See it?"

The Captain grunted something in reply. The skimmer tilted and arced toward the stretch of white-and-gray hillside Wells had indicated.

"There, Captain," Marka said. Her hand went past Wells's shoulder. "It just ducked behind those boulders."

"I see it," the Captain said. "Wells, contact Ryork. Tell her we're heading down, and tell her where we are. I think we've just spotted our dinner."

Kilgarin leaned forward to peer past the Engineer's bulky shoulder. Below, the snow-covered plain drifted into the foothills of a ridge of glacial mountains, sparkling in the noon sunlight. The skimmer was moving in a slow circle over a grouping of crystalline rocks midway up the hillside, dropping lower with each pass. Kilgarin tried to find the object of everyone's interest, but could see nothing in the glare of the snow. "What is it?"

"An animal," Marka said. "Weren't you watching?"

"I was asleep," Kilgarin said.

"There it is again," Wells shouted. Kilgarin jerked his head around and followed the Engineer's jabbing finger. Against the white, something black darted. It had no definite shape—none that Kilgarin could make out—but it moved like something alive. As he watched, Kilgarin saw it jump behind a crag, appear on the other side, make a short hop to another rock, and vanish once more.

"You think we should try to capture that thing, Captain?"

"Not capture, Kilgarin. We're going to kill it."

"But *why?* We don't know if it's edible—it might turn out to be poison—"

"That's what our survey lab is *for,* Kilgarin."

"Yes, Captain," said Kilgarin. He braced himself as the skimmer tilted into a shallow dive. There was a moment of vertigo, a sense of weightlessness, and then the floor moved up against his buttocks, the brace against his neck, the skimmer skidded, jerked, and stopped. They were down.

"Fellow Oberon," the Captain said to Marka, "will you pass forward the weapons?"

She complied, and the Captain distributed the hand

weapons to Wells and Kilgarin. He gave the light rifle to Marka, first flipping the safety into the off position. "Just aim that weapon in the general direction of what you're shooting, press that stub—there, by your thumb—and the rifle's finder will do the rest. You know how to work your handgun, Kilgarin?"

"Yes, Captain."

"Good. It's a bit cold out, so I suggest we activate our climate suits before leaving the skimmer. Ready? Wells, will you lead?"

The Engineer pushed the windscreen up and back over the roof of the skimmer and dropped through the opening to the ground a meter below. The others followed, the pink crust of snow crunching under their feet as they moved away from the skimmer, toward the cluster of rocks farther upslope. The Captain passed Wells and struck out at an angle to the others, circling around the crystal boulder they'd seen the creature duck behind. He moved lithely, his thin frame graceful even under the heavy material of the climate suit. Kilgarin studied him with a grudging admiration; the Captain seemed completely at ease, totally in control of himself and the situation. It was a trait Kilgarin recognized was sometimes lacking in himself. There was no doubt about it: the Captain was an extremely competent man.

A shadow shifted on the far side of the boulder, above the Captain's cowled head. Kilgarin saw it, brought his handgun up—

Before he could fire, the creature leaped.

Wells spun around at the same instant and the Captain realized the animal was attacking him. The two men moved in uncanny coordination, the Captain dropping flat against the hillside as Wells fired in a swinging arc that swept the beam of his weapon through the space occupied by the attacking creature an instant before. The beam intersected the creature's flight, struck the animal squarely in the center of its pitch-black form.

Nothing happened.

The creature landed, rolled, came back to its feet (feet? Kilgarin realized he'd been thinking in human terms; the creature had no feet—not as such), and sprang.

Wells staggered at the weight of the beast as it slammed into the Captain. Kilgarin recognized the symptoms. "Get out of his mind," he called to the Engineer. "You can't help him like that—*get out of the Captain's mind!*"

His *mind*. Abruptly Kilgarin stopped in his forward motion. Wells had entered the Captain's brain, had managed a symbiosis, a mindlink with—at least—the Captain's consciousness. It was impossible—and yet obviously it had happened. But how? And how deeply had Wells gone? Kilgarin pulled himself out of his sudden reverie. It didn't matter at the moment; if the Captain died, Kilgarin would never know the full answer to that, or any other question. He ran forward again, Marka at his side, moving around the boulder to get into position to use his hand gun.

And he staggered, caught in a mental web.

Beside him, Marka stopped also. The two of them stood paralyzed, staring at the struggling forms in the snowbank above them.

Marka . . .

Marka, I can't . . .

Marka, I can't move—

"What's happening?" she asked, frightened. "What's wrong with me?"

You're holding me back.

Your mind is holding me back, Marka.

Marka, let me free.

"Killy, my arms won't work—Killy, I'm afraid. I can't—"

Above them the Captain braced his legs against the chest of the beast and shoved. Snow sprayed as the creature heaved backward, skidding downslope. Kilgarin saw that the animal was covered entirely with black fur, save for a gray patch on its "underside" that quivered as the creature tried to regain its balance. The Captain straightened and dove for his handgun in a single motion, hitting the hillside with his shoulder, grabbing up the handgun and turning, all in one continuous action. A beam of stark brilliance shot out of the weapon, poked hard into the belly of the creature, into the center of its wiggling gray area. There was a wet hiss, a curl of dark smoke, and a stench of burning flesh.

The animal stopped moving almost at once, though the Captain held the beam on it for half a minute, cooking the tender gray area until it was charred as black as the rest of the beast. The stench worsened.

"Well, Fellows," the Captain said finally, dropping his gun to his side, "I hope you like well-cooked meat."

Wells laughed. Kilgarin, finding himself free of the mind-web that had held him motionless, turned to Marka and said, "Cook was right. It doesn't work for the two of us. I don't think it ever will."

He walked away from them, leaving the Captain and Wells bent over the smoking animal, discussing what to do with its remains. He returned to the skimmer. He was tired and slightly ashamed. But more importantly . . . he wanted very much to think.

A sign on the wall of the prefab shed proclaimed that the colony, Tysos's Bluff, had a population of 24,058 and a Gross Planetary Income of some 34 million Company Credits. Below, in finer print, the sign gave the details of the planetary economy: percentage of unpaid Company loans, and so on. Kilgarin read it all, and when he was finished, he read it all again. The wall clock beside the sign gave the time as 1632; the temperature outside the shed, according to the information screen under the clock, was a mild 12.6 degrees centigrade; and the wind, from the southwest, at 2 kph. Kilgarin glanced around the shed. He returned his attention to the sign. He read it once more. He looked around. He could hear voices coming from behind one of the closed doors. The door opened; Raymond stepped out. Kilgarin walked over to meet him. The wall clock now read 1651.

"Trouble?" Kilgarin asked the Physical. Raymond shook his head.

"They're touchy, but I finally convinced them I'm not a Company spy. Ty'ger's in there now. They're giving him a really hard time. They don't like Sensitives in the Outworlds, do they?"

"Not much," Kilgarin admitted. He studied Raymond thoughtfully. "Do you mind if Ty'ger comes with us?"

"He's your friend, Killy. It's up to you."

"Give him a chance, Ray. He's touchy too, you know. It isn't easy being a Sensitive in the first place, and when you—"

"I know. You told me. That still doesn't excuse what he tried to do to J'kar." He eyed Kilgarin. "*Or* why you're so friendly with him. J'kar's your friend too, you know."

"I know what I'm doing, Raymond. I need both of you."

"Just be sure he doesn't come too near me. I'm not as sophisticated as he is; he can tear me apart with a word. But if he tries to touch me, just once—I'll hurt him. I'll really try to hurt him."

"Take it easy." Kilgarin surveyed the younger man; some of the fat had been worn away in the past weeks, but Raymond was still too heavy. He wasn't as much of a threat as he wanted to be—but he was enough of one. "We only have a few hours while the ship's unloading the material from that world we visited. I want to take care of our business here as quickly as possible—and with as little trouble as we can manage."

"Don't worry. I won't start anything. I owe you that much, at least—for getting me back on a ship, for making me feel like—well. I owe you."

"You don't owe me anything, Raymond," Kilgarin said. He looked past the young man's shoulder, smiled. "Here's Ty'ger now."

During the week it must have served as a general products store, but on the weekend and in the evenings, stools were placed along the outside of the counter and a few tables were set in the middle of the dusty floor. There were perhaps thirty men in the makeshift bar when Kilgarin and the others entered; most of them were drinking a thick black beer popular in the Outworlds because of its availability and price. The few drinkers who favored wine or absinthe were obviously city employees. The rest were farmers, proud in the battered clothes and ill-kept beards.

Kilgarin and Ty'ger were conspicuous in their Sensitive blues, made more obvious by Raymond's sober Physical grays. The three men found a spot at the counter, aware of the eyes of the colonists on them as they ordered beer with absinthe from a sour-faced bartender. As he handed them their beers and accepted their credit chits, the bartender asked in a low, urgent voice, "What are you Fellows doing here? Trying to get yourselves mashed? If you're looking for a run, you've found it, you know."

Kilgarin shook his head. "We just want a beer, friend. That's all."

The bartender shrugged and turned away. "Trouble?" Raymond asked.

"You wouldn't want to know, boy," Ty'ger told him.

"You feel something?" Kilgarin asked the Centaurian; the other man nodded, his jaws taut with tension. Raymond glanced from one to the other, his features registering concern.

"Maybe we'd better get out of here," he said. Kilgarin sipped at his beer, shaking his head.

"I don't think it's directed at us," the Cork said calmly. "I scanned this place before we came in. There's tension, all right, but we aren't part of it. Not directly."

"We could have gotten drunk on board the *Charter*,

Kilgarin, if that's what you brought us here for," Ty'ger said.

Kilgarin sighed. He pushed his empty mug across the counter to the bartender, who refilled it, expressionlessly. "You've known the Captain for quite a while, haven't you, Ty'ger?"

"I know what you're thinking, Kilgarin, and yes, he's had that mindblock for as long as I've known him. It never seemed important to me—not an agressive thing, you know. Something passive."

Kilgarin digested this, turned to Raymond. "What's your opinion of the Captain?"

"He's the Captain. What else should I think about him?"

"He doesn't seem odd to you?"

"I haven't known many ship's officers, Kilgarin. How is he supposed to be odd?"

The Cork shook his head. He drank a bit of his beer. "I can't explain it if you haven't noticed it," he said.

"Is this why you asked us out here, to talk about the Captain?"

"That's right, Raymond. I was afraid he'd hear us if we'd talked aboard the ship."

"You don't mean that, do you, Killy?" Raymond stared at him, a half-smile playing at his lips.

"I'm not joking," Kilgarin said. "I don't pretend he's listening to us in our cabins, nothing like that. But he has spies. Or at least someone in the crew who's close to him, and who's helped him erect that mindblock."

Ty'ger's forehead creased. "You're serious, aren't you? You think Wells is responsible for the Captain's block."

Kilgarin nodded, and Raymond almost choked on his beer. "The Engineer? Buy why? I don't understand, Kilgarin—why would the Engineer do something like that to the Captain?"

"Not to him," Kilgarin said. "For him." He explained what he'd seen during the expedition of some days earlier, finishing with, "There's something the Captain doesn't want anyone to know, and whatever it is, he has to hide it so thoroughly no Sensitive can reach it—not even his Cork. He needs a mindblock, but he's a Physical, he can't make one himself; it has to be done for him. Who's the one man on the ship who's known the Captain longest, who's closest to him, and whom the Captain allows in his mind during a survey? Wells. Our Engineer. He's the only one to have gotten past that block as far as I know. He has to be the man behind it."

"You might have something there, Kilgarin," the Centaurian said, setting his mug down on the counter with a click. "But so what? What does it matter?"

"It matters to me," Kilgarin answered. "It means I'm close to learning why the Captain killed my brother."

"Killed?" Raymond said the word softly. He was sweating, and under his ragged black hair his face was pale, his forehead wrinkled in a deep frown.

"What else would you call it?"

"But *killed*—" Raymond shook his head. "I suppose you know what you're saying, Kilgarin. But why are you saying it to us?"

"I may need a little help," Kilgarin said.

"You're thinking we can find out things for you, about Wells and the Captain, and that Wells won't think of probing our minds. Is that it?" Ty'ger smiled. His eyes glistened in the dim light.

"Essentially," Kilgarin said. "I can block off any probing from Wells or anyone else, but doing that limits me. I don't really think I'll need either of you in a pinch, but it will make things simpler to have you around."

The two other men glanced at each other. Ty'ger's gaze went back to Kilgarin first. "I'll do what I can, Kilgarin. It may not be much."

"Me too," Raymond added. "Like I said before: I owe you."

Kilgarin nodded. "Fine," he said. "Let's get another round of beer."

Approaching them, the colonist seemed smaller than he was; his body moved in a shuffle, one shoulder dipping, rising, the other repeating the motion, both hands stuffed shyly into the large pockets on the front of his dusty suit, tousled hair falling over a grainy face. He stopped a short distance from the three shipmates and looked them over, tilting his head back to free his eyes from his ragged bangs. He let his gaze linger on Raymond. Then he looked at Kilgarin, catching the Sensitive's eye. "You two from the ship? One that just landed?"

"We all are," Kilgarin said. The colonist nodded and frowned down at his hands.

"First ship in six months," he said. "First Company ship."

"There weren't many people to meet us at the port," Kilgarin said. He waited for the colonist to comment, then went on, explaining. "Usually in small ports like this, people come to see the crew down. To hear the news. That sort of thing."

"Bluff isn't 'that sort of' world, mister. We've been a little cold around here, past six months. Past six years, actually."

"But *you're* here," Raymond pointed out. "You're interested."

The colonist ignored him. "Staying long?" he asked Kilgarin.

"Another two or three hours."

"Better leave now."

"Why?" Kilgarin asked. Ty'ger touched the Cork's elbow, but Kilgarin shrugged away. He watched the colonist's eyes, which were still fixed on his hands.

"Because you're Company, mister. And Company isn't welcome around here much, anymore."

Raymond coughed. Kilgarin paid no attention to the Physical's nervous hint; he continued to face the colonist, coldly. "You've got something against the Company, Fellow—?" He paused, waiting for the small man to supply a name. He noticed that the room around them had grown quiet, and that all eyes were aimed in their direction. Feet shifted almost inaudibly. A burly man in brown overalls cleared his throat noisely. The tension in the room deepened.

"My name's none of your concern, mister," the colonist said. "And I'm no Company Fellow, either. Told you Company isn't welcome around here. That was a friendly warning, one human to another. Told myself I'd do that much, I don't have to do much more." The vague looked vanished from the colonist's face. His hand came up and brushed the hair back from his eyes. Lean, hard features; the thin slash of a mouth, the black of squinting eyes.

"We didn't come here for trouble," Kilgarin said.

"Then get out now," the man said, "and take your friend."

Raymond's mouth worked, but before the young Physical could speak, Ty'ger cut in. "What's wrong with our friend that's not wrong with us?"

The colonist's facial muscles jerked into an expression that mixed distaste and pity. "You were born like you are, mister, can't help being the way you're being. But him, he can, and he's sitting with you, drinking with you. He knows what he's doing is wrong."

"What's he doing?" Kilgarin asked. Beside him, Raymond began to speak, but was stopped by Ty'ger. The three of them stared at the colonist, who leaned over to spit between the Physical's legs.

"Being with you," the small man said.

Ty'ger grunted. "Are you going to wait on this one, too?" he asked Kilgarin. The Cork shook his head. Both he and the Centaurian moved forward in a single motion. The colonist went back over the bar, into the far shelf of bottles and glasses, sending them flying in a dozen directions. With a cry, the other colonists lunged forward, and it began.

Within moments Kilgarin found himself at the center of a twisted bundle of arms and legs. He snapped his knee up, heard someone on top of him cry out in agony, and slipped through the path the injured colonist's form provided when it collapsed out of the way. Across from him Ty'ger was dodging the wild swings of a middle-aged farmer in faded overalls; the older man held the arm of a chair in his fist, and was brandishing it at the Centaurian with no attempt at aiming. Several times the end of a swing connected with one of the colonist's colleagues, but the man seemed unaware of the effect his blows were having. The room was in an uproar. Two of the lanterns fell from their niches, and half of the bar was swallowed in darkness. Kilgarin searched for Raymond, but was unable to find the Physical visually. One particular tangle of colonists looked promising, and he plunged toward it, opening his mind to draw in the young man's thoughts.

Panic. Pure, hysterical fear.

Reacting as a Cork, Kilgarin slipped into Raymond's mind, made an attempt to soothe the young man's fears, to help Raymond gain control of himself. Instead, he discovered himself slipping into a mindlock, as he had with Marka several days before. There was something different about this mindlock, however: where the link with Marka had paralyzed him, this one freed him in some way. Where before he'd found himself enveloped by emotions he didn't understand, he now felt balanced on the end of a lever mentally attached to Raymond. It was a true mindlock symbiosis. He was in control. Raymond was in control. The two of them thought with the same mind.

Now, Raymond! Bring your leg up, twist it around his knee. Hard, now . . . now, now, now! Hard!

There was a crack that was audible across the room. The tangle of bodies broke apart suddenly, exposing Raymond, lying half across and half under a man whose leg was twisted at an impossible angle. Raymond's face was white with terror, but there was also a quiet awareness in his eyes. He pushed the broken man off him, thrust himself to his feet, whirled in time to avoid the fist of a gaunt man with bulging eyes, ducked and grabbed the man by the arm, jerked him over his shoulder and slung him into three men who were rushing Ty'ger. All four went down with a simultaneous grunt.

To your left, Kilgarin.

Leaning aside, Kilgarin felt a form diving past him. A crash thundered to his right, chairs splintering as the colonist completed his dive by landing in their midst.

The fight ended quickly. Once Raymond and Kilgarin linked the colonists had no defense against the two of them, or against Ty'ger, who fought like a madman. Less than ten minutes after it started, the brawl was over. Kilgarin and his two shipmates found themselves alone in the pub, surrounded by the remains of wooden chairs and tables. The bartender was gone; most of the lanterns were out: the place was in ruins.

"Want a drink?" Kilgarin asked. He went behind the bar and fetched a bottle for each of them. They drank somberly. After several seconds Ty'ger set his bottle down with a muttered curse.

"They weren't really fighting us. They were fighting the Company. And we had to hurt them. Damn." He looked up at Kilgarin and Raymond, who were still working on their bottles. "What happened to you two back there? One moment we were fighting as a team, the next—" He paused. Then: "Mindlink? You two?"

Kilgarin nodded. Ty'ger raised his eyebrows. "Fine," he said. He took another pull on his absinthe, set it down a minute later. "Are we still together on this Wells thing? Yes?" Kilgarin said they were, and Ty'ger shrugged. He seemed colder than he'd been earlier, more distant. Finishing off the last of his drink, he tossed the bottle over his shoulder. It shattered on the floor, glass scattering in a rough circle around a pool of dark liquid. "Fine," he said again. "I'll see you back at the ship."

Kilgarin and Raymond watched him leave. Then Kilgarin took a credit slip out of his pocket—a standard chit for several hundred Company credits—and placed it on the counter where it would be found. Two more bottles disappeared from under the bar. Skirting the wreckage, the shipmates left through the wide-open door.

On their way back to the ship much later that evening, they met the Cook. He was returning from the market section of town, which Raymond and Kilgarin had bypassed during their wanderings because of its lights and activity, and he was pushing a cart that was filled with brown-and-green vegetables and several kegs of a sweet-smelling liquid he called milk. Kilgarin and Raymond took turns helping him push the cart until they reached the ship.

At midnight the *Charter* lifted for the planet Elysson; all hands were aboard.

Chapter Six

Ninth month, second day, anno Domini 3146

In his quarters during the last few hours before they would reach the planet, the Captain briefed his officers on the situation they would encounter on Elysson. Apparently the colony was in active rebellion, the colonists seizing much of the main port area, a few of the Company holdings in the central city, Krysta, and were in the process of attacking the planet's Company Administrative Office as the *Charter* approached. Ryork, the Communications agent, had received this information earlier in the day, as well as certain instructions, which the Captain now relayed. The *Charter* was to land at the Krysta port, and its officers were to make every effort to rescue the Company agent held there under siege. The agent's name was Gunyon. More than this, the Captain didn't think his officers needed to know. They were dismissed.

In the corridor outside the Captain's quarters, Kilgarin approached Ryork for further information. Her pet eyed him with luminous orbs as Ryork turned and blinked at him; Kilgarin was surprised to discover she was crying. She brushed a hand over her face, blinked again, calming herself. "I left Elysson fifteen years ago, Kilgarin," she told him. "It used to be my home once, but I don't know what it's like now. I always thought we Elyssonians were a quiet tribe, frankly. I don't know what to make of all this."

"Is your family down there?" Kilgarin asked. He gestured a greeting at the Cook, who was passing them, and the other man lifted a hand, went on, leaving Kilgarin walking with Ryork and Wells, who didn't seem to notice them in front of him.

"A sister. I don't think she's still there, though."

"What's the planet itself like, Ryork? I like to know that sort of thing."

"An easy planet, Kilgarin, for those who understand it. Good soil, better than Endrim, better than earth. I've never felt soil like it anywhere. The winters are long, but the years are almost half again as long as Standard; there's time for a big harvest, warm summers. It's a nice world, Kilgarin."

"And the people?"

"Fifteen years; I don't know them anymore. But when I was there, they were a hard lot. It was odd," Ryork said, turning her head to gaze at him through the graying bangs of her hair; her pet stared at him also. "An easy planet, but the hardest people I've ever known. The Company made them that way. We would draw in several tons of Shak—it's a wheat that grows in stalks, close to the ground—and the Company would take most of it in interest payment on the land, the tools, and the transportation to the planet. Second-generation Elyssonians were still paying off their parents' emigration fees. Paying for the privilege of being a Company slave."

Her anger touched Kilgarin's mind. He closed it off. "Sounds as though you haven't changed much in fifteen years."

"I have," she said. "Yes. I used to hate the Company a great deal more. But I learned something every Elyssonian knows in his own way. If you want to survive, you have to play the Company game."

She left him. Kilgarin watched her turn a bend in the corridor and disappear. The last he saw of her was her pet, leaning off her shoulder to peer at Kilgarin until she carried him from view.

"Ready for another game, Kilgarin?" Wells asked him. The Engineer slipped in beside the Cork, matching his long stride to Kilgarin's. When Kilgarin said no, Wells laughed. "Pity," he said. "I enjoyed beating you. Captain's the only other worthwhile player aboard, and he can't leave his Set when the ship's in Drive. Pity you won't play."

They fell silent, continuing to stroll down the main corridor toward the lounge. Kilgarin paced the lumbering Engineer, letting his mind relax until external sensations were dim shadows just lightly touching his brain. Inside, his mind opened, the portion of it which acted as a Cork maintaining its efforts as another portion separated and drifted in a gentle probe toward Wells. Kilgarin felt the fringe of the Engineer's mind, the anxieties naturally present in any ship officer, combined with the less natural disorder derived from Wells's position as Engineer, the irregularities of personality shifting on this inner sea. He probed deeper, past the level he usually touched as Cork—and found resistance to his probe.

Quickly he backed off. Something had touched him when he'd tried to slip past Wells's conscious level. Kilgarin paused, thinking. Another mindblock? It was possible, but—

He tried again, extending a probe around the area of his initial attack. He met the same resistance he'd encountered before. It *was* a mindblock, and an efficient one at that. Most of Wells's subconscious was cut off to Kilgarin's probing, and it was done in such a way that Wells's consciousness was not aware of the barrier within his brain. Which meant the block had been erected by the Engineer's subconscious, or by a conscious order that had been consumed in the mindblock's creation. Complicated, but effective. There was no way for an outside mind to discover what Wells was trying to hide.

Warily, Kilgarin withdrew his probe. He glanced at the Engineer, but the man gave no sign of having noticed either the Cork's probe or its removal. *He can't know what's been happening,* Kilgarin thought. *He can't be responsible for the Captain's block. . . .* Yet there it was, the Engineer's own psychic barrier: why did it exist, if not to conceal Wells's culpability in fixing the Captain's mindblock? It had to be Wells's defense against Kilgarin; when he'd realized what the Cork planned, the Engineer must have sought a way to protect himself—and his own mindblock was the result.

What else could it be? Kilgarin wondered.

"Maybe a game later," he said quietly. Wells brightened, looking up from his feet, which he'd been studying as he'd walked. "Good," he said. "I'd enjoy that."

Leaving Wells outside the recreation room, Kilgarin tucked his hands into the loops of his shipboard jump suit and went on down the corridor toward the Library. He was barely aware of the rumblings of the ship around him; the sounds seemed removed, and he knew it was because he'd sectioned his mind in order to probe Wells. He didn't mind the resulting alienation from the physical world; in a way, it was relaxing. The pressures on board the *Charter* were beginning to get to him, and he was glad for whatever relief he could find. It made his load as a Cork easier to bear.

He stepped through a hatchway and stopped. J'kar stood before him, blocking his path.

Gradually Kilgarin realized that the Centaurian was speaking to him; it took the Cork a moment to tune back to awareness, and he did so regretfully. "Talk, please talk now?" J'kar was saying. He was clearly agitated; his face was pale, his eyes bloodshot and wide, his hands moving toward Kilgarin's jump suit and away, as though he couldn't decide whether to force himself on the Cork or not.

"I can't," Kilgarin told the burly Centaurian. "I've got something I have to do."

"Please, you can tell him, tell him please. Wants to kill me. Raymond says you stop him, please stop him, Killy, don't want hurt, no more, please?" J'kar head bobbed on his reddened neck. He was close to total panic, Kilgarin saw. He laid a hand on the Centaurian's shoulder and squeezed reassuringly.

"Everything will be all right," he told him. "I just can't talk to you now. Later."

"No, no," J'kar said. His voice seemed to jerk out of him. "Don't understand, you. Thinks I told soldiers about him, his brothers, sisters, parents, thinks I told. All years thinks I killed them. But wasn't me, Kilgarin, tell him that. My father, he told the soldiers, I didn't, wouldn't—tell Ty'ger that, Killy, my father, not me—tell him—" The Centaurian's mouth worked and his arm twisted out of Kilgarin's grasp. His eyes squeezed shut in pain, his face turning red. Kilgarin grabbed J'kar's hand quickly and snapped the big man around, spinning him so he struck the far wall. For a moment J'kar didn't move. He leaned against the corridor wall, breathing heavily through his nose, his body calming and coming under his control. Finally his eyes opened and he stared past Kilgarin, slowly focusing and shifting his gaze until it touched the Cork. His breathing became more regular.

"You nearly broke again that time," Kilgarin said. "If I hadn't done that, you would have. You've got to relax, J'kar. For your own good, you've got to force Ty'ger out of your mind. He's changed; he won't hurt you. I wish I could make that clear to you, but I've got some things of my own I have to do. Relax now. I'll speak to you later."

"Kilgarin, *please*—"

The Cork stopped. He was already several meters down-corridor from the Centaurian, but he could still hear J'kar's ragged breathing, still feel the fear running out of the man. He shook his head. "I'm sorry, J'kar. It's something you'll have to handle yourself." He started walking again. "I've got other things to do."

J'kar cried out once more, but the Cork had ceased to hear.

Like most ship libraries the room was small, scarcely large enough for Kilgarin to move about in. The walls were bare except for the console and the stool protruding from the base of the machine. Kilgarin sat down and punched out the identity code of his Contract as a ship officer, which would open the ship's entire memory bank to his scrutiny. As a Sensitive he'd never thought he'd need to resort to the Library records—but so many minds were closed to him he knew he'd have to gain the information he needed by any means possible. The code light came on. The Library was activated. He punched out the call letters for the personnel files, feeling oddly unclean and uneasy. The file codes and names appeared on the display screen and he ran through them until he found the file he wanted.

The Captain's.

DATE OF BIRTH: SEVENTH MONTH, TWELFTH DAY, ANNO DOMINI 3117

PLACE OF BIRTH: OREGON, BARSWELL'S PLANET (PROCYON III)

SPECIAL NOTE: IN 3121 OREGON COLONY DESTROYED BY DISEASE. BACTERIA SINCE IDENTIFIED AS MUTANT BACILLUS MEGATERIUM. SUBJECT AND SIX OTHER SURVIVORS SINCE INOCULATED, NO LONGER CARRIERS.

EDUCATION: EDUCATED COMPANY SCHOOL ON ROSHARCH, UNHANSSEN (PROCYON IV) FROM 3121 TO 3133. GRADUATED ADMINISTRATIVE SCHOOL, MAXIMUM HONORS. ALL SENSITIVE PROBES NEGATIVE: PSYCHIC OUTPUT MINIMAL.

SERVICE RECORD: FROM 3133 TO 3134, SUBJECT ACTIVE ON COMPANY PSI CHARTING VESSEL, "LADY," OUT OF NOVA SCOTIA

PORT, VAN DRAM (SIRIUS II). 3133 TO 3137 SERVED AS ADMINISTRATIVE ASSISTANT. RECEIVED COMMISSION TO SECOND MATE 3138. RECEIVED COMMISSION FIRST MATE 3142. IN 3143 TRANSFERRED TO NEWLY COMMISSIONED VESSEL OUT OF CENTAURI PORT (ALPHA CENTAURI V): "CHARTER." 3146, ASSUMED COMMAND "CHARTER" FOLLOWING DEATH OF PREVIOUS CAPTAIN.

PHYSICAL STATISTICS: SUBJECT HEIGHT: 187.96 CENTIMETERS. SUBJECT WEIGHT: 81.648 KILOGRAMS. SUBJECT DIMEN—

The rest was useless to Kilgarin. Most of it was a record of the Captain's physical health, which was good, and his mental stability, which, as far as Kilgarin could tell from the official records, had never come into question. There was a brief record of the investigation that followed Marc Kilgarin's death. It was pretty much as the Captain had told Kilgarin during their first meeting.

—ACTED IN ACCORDANCE WITH HIS UNDERSTANDING OF COMPANY REGULATIONS. AND IN CONSIDERATION OF THIS [the transcript of the investigation went] THE COMMITTEE WISHES TO DROP ALL CHARGES AGAINST HIM, TO COMMEND HIM FOR HIS INTENTION, AND TO CENSURE HIM FOR A LACK OF SUFFICIENT INQUIRY INTO THE BACKGROUND AND EXPERIENCE OF CONTRACTED CORK MARC KILGARIN—

There was more, but Kilgarin didn't read it.
He turned to the file on Wells.

DATE OF BIRTH: NINTH MONTH, TENTH DAY, ANNO DOMINI 3109

PLACE OF BIRTH: CRISPIN, WELLINGTON (FARRIN IV)

EDUCATION: COLONY SCHOOL, 3114–3124. SENSITIVE PROBES POSITIVE.

SERVICE RECORD: ENTERED COMPANY MILITIA ON WELLINGTON 3125. TRANSFERRED OFF—PLANET 3127, TO COMPANY BARRACKS WORLD IN CENTAURI SYSTEM (ALPHA CENTAURI III). PROMOTED TO CORPS EN-

GINEER EARLY 3128, SECOND MONTH, THIRTEENTH DAY. ACTED IN BEHALF OF COMPANY DURING CENTAURI POLICE ACTION, FOURTH MONTH, TWENTY-SECOND DAY, 3128, TO SEVENTH MONTH, THIRTIETH DAY, 3128. TOOK SERVICE CONTRACT FOR TRADE AND CHARTING VESSELS ON EIGHTH MONTH, FIRST DAY, 3128, TO SEVENTH MONTH, THIRTY-FIRST DAY, 3134. RENEWED TERM CONTRACT TWICE, EIGHTH MONTH, FIRST DAY, 3134, TO SEVENTH MONTH, THIRTY-FIRST DAY, 3135, AND EIGHTH MONTH, FIRST DAY, 3135, TO SIXTH MONTH, TWELFTH DAY, 3136. RENEWED FULL CONTRACT FOURTH MONTH, EIGHTH DAY, 3141. SHIPS SERVED: "BLACK FIRE" (3128 TO 3130), "WALKABOUT" (3130 TO 3134), "YEARLING" (3134 TO 3136), "LADY" (3141 TO 3143), AND "CHARTER" (3143–)

PHYSICAL STATISTICS: SUBJECT HEIGHT: 195.58 CENTIMETERS. SUBJECT WEIGHT: 113.4 KILOGRAMS. SUBJE—

Kilgarin skimmed Wells's file. He looked for some contact with the Captain previous to the *Lady,* found nothing. Wells's file was more detailed than the Captain's, obviously because the man had lived longer. Both the Captain and the Engineer had lived lives almost devoid of major incidents, apart from the Captain's early loss and the Engineer's involvement in the CPA—and even these things were not unusual in a colonial society. Kilgarin's own life had been spiced with moments that pained him. They meant nothing, though, because they'd happened to everyone, and would happen to him again. He studied the screen, thinking. His hand drifted to the console, dropped, and keyed out the code for Marka Oberon.

DATE OF BIRTH: ELEVENTH MONTH, SEVENTEENTH DAY, ANNO DOMINI 3121

PLACE OF BIRTH: OLD ROME, EARTH (SOL III)

EDUCATION: NO FORMAL EDUCATION. ALL SENSITIVE PROBES NEGATIVE.

SERVICE RECORD: PHYSICAL CONTRACT SIGNED EIGHTH MONTH, SIXTEENTH DAY, 3137, IN LONDON, EARTH (SOL III). SHIPPED

ABOARD "WALKABOUT" FROM EIGHTH MONTH, SIXTEENTH DAY, 3137, TO SECOND MONTH, FOURTH DAY, 3142, WHEN CRIPPLED DURING PLANETARY EXPEDITION. PENSIONED ON ENDRIM, ENDRIM (SB3487 IV). CONTRACT RENEWED "CHARTER" EIGHTH MONTH, SEVENTH DAY, 3146.

PHYSICAL STATISTICS: SUBJECT HEIGHT: 177.8. C.M. SUBJECT WEIGHT: 53.52 KILOGRA—

Kilgarin shut off the console and got to his feet. He knew little more than he'd known when he'd entered the Library, and the little he'd learned was next to useless. The files weren't designed to answer questions about motivation; they were simply required to list the crew member's vital Company statistics. He'd have to look elsewhere for his answers, he knew.

The trouble was . . . he couldn't decide where.

"Killy, did you hear what I asked you? I wanted to know if we'd be going down to Elysson together."

"I don't think that'd be a very good idea, Marka. Considering what happened last time."

"That wouldn't happen again . . . would it?"

"I'd rather not find out. We're going to have a hard enough time down there without adding problems. I can't take the chance."

"I told you I'm sorry."

"That doesn't make any difference, Marka. It's not a matter of being sorry."

"You don't want to have to worry about me, is that it?"

"Marka . . ."

"Killy, do you know what you're doing to me?"

"You're not making any sense."

"*I'm* not making sense? I thought you wanted me, I let you take me, I *trusted* you . . . and you're not willing to take a chance. And you don't understand why I—" She turned away from him, sitting up on the edge of his bunk. "You're making me feel the way I felt when I waited for you at the port three years ago. I wanted to explain, but you never gave me a chance. The way you'd treated me, I wanted to get back at you. So I brought a customer in and waited until I knew you'd be coming back to the apartment—I wanted to hurt you, because you—" She broke off again. "I knew it was a mistake to start with you again, from the first, I knew it was a mistake."

"Listen."

"Don't touch me. Not just now. Let me alone, a minute."

"All right."

She fumbled in the pocket of her jump suit, pulled out a rectangular palm-sized box, opened it. She sat cross-legged on the edge of the bed; Kilgarin could see the twisted hump of her ankle and arch where it rested on her thigh. She managed to pull a cigarette free of the box and twisted the end to light it. Smoke hovered near her face a moment, drifted away.

Watching her, Kilgarin waited for her to speak.

She didn't.

The main port of Elysson was on the outskirt of the central city, Krysta. The shuttle settled down with a minimum of fuss, the snow on the pad evaporating into steam as the rockets' heat preceded the vessel onto the field. A moment passed, the steam faded, swirled away on the heels of the wind that swayed the stubby ship, and the hatch cycled open. Leading his men, the Captain swung out and down the ladder, dropping to the surface several meters from the scorched plastisteel directly under the ship.

The field was empty, the buildings that made up the port seemingly deserted. Kilgarin dropped down beside the Captain, followed by Raymond and then Wells. Ty'ger and Luanne brought up the rear.

Together they entered the main port building, a tower that looked as though it'd been cut from a single slab of stone. Windows opened onto the field, each window several meters high, four or five meters wide. The light from outside was the only light available inside the port building, and it leaked across the wide empty floor in pale yellow rectangles. There were shadows everywhere, behind every column and post, and behind each of the six crew members. Kilgarin listened to their footsteps; they were the only sound in the port.

They came to an exit, stepped out into the street.

Alleys and sidewalks; cobbled streets; the facades for a dozen different architectural styles. It was a port like any port, but in one major feature it was different. It was empty.

"Well, Captain?" Kilgarin asked. "What now?"

Casting about, the Captain indicated a direction. His breath came in white vapor as he spoke. "Gunyon's office is that way, according to our information. We'll find him there, if anywhere."

The street curved ahead of them, swinging down toward the center of the city and a plaza that was visible beyond the roofs of the buildings, which were farther away. As he strode beside the Captain, careful to avoid the patches of ice that spotted the street, Kilgarin let his mind roam the buildings on either side of the cobbled road. He could sense the presence of many minds, men and women standing behind the curtains and shades of the windowed buildings, children crouched in corners, all listening to the passage of the *Charter*'s landing team. Kilgarin read a mixture of emotions, most of it ingrown and self-directed. Fear was present, and anger, and a slow, corroding resentment that was vaguely directed at the men striding down the street. Kilgarin pulled away; he didn't like what he'd seen. He glanced at Raymond beside him; the Physical kept stumbling over cobbles and bumping into Kilgarin. The Cork wondered if he'd made an error in bringing Raymond along. He thought not—but he'd have to wait and see.

The Captain halted at an intersection. The others waited as he examined the buildings that met at the crossing. Finally he nodded and gestured at a structure that was set between two older, smaller buildings. The Company office and quarters. Kilgarin recognized its utilitarian form.

"Kilgarin and Velacorte, around the side. Ty'ger, Luanne . . . the rear. You and I will take the front, Wells."

The teams split and went to their posts. Raymond clutched Kilgarin's sleeve to stop himself from falling as the two men took their position outside the alley door. "Sorry," he said, mumbling. "Do you think we'll have any trouble?"

"What do *you* think?" Kilgarin answered. Raymond didn't bother to reply.

A sound came to them from the front of the building. Something splintered and crashed inward. Glass rained musically inside the building, followed by a shout and the dull *whut!* of air pistols. Kilgarin tensed, feeling the wave of emotions sweeping toward him as someone clattered down a flight of stairs, running for the alley door.

They're coming, Kilgarin thought.

Where? I don't see them.

Wait, Kilgarin told the Physical. *Wait.*

Abruptly the door over them bulged and flew open.

Two figures slammed out, stumbling over the shipmates crouched below them. Kilgarin straightened, grabbing one of the two men by the collar of a furred vest, lifting the man and throwing him back through the door into the building. He felt Raymond's disorientation and calmed the Physical, guiding the younger man into a smooth kick that shattered the second man's jaw. Without speaking, Kilgarin and Raymond lunged over the doorsill and into the hallway beyond.

Down there, Kilgarin thought. *I'll go this way.*

They parted, Raymond half-stumbling down the steps into the basement, Kilgarin proceeding onto the main floor.

Brushing back the hair from his eyes, Kilgarin surveyed the scene. On his right and left, Ty'ger and Luanne were struggling with three or four men each; the movements of the two were graceful in their lack of wasted effort, neither making a motion that seemed out of place or forced. They drifted from posture to posture, ducking and dodging, Luanne twisting to throw an attacker off balance, Ty'ger ramming his weight into a man's chest, the two halves of the mindlink moving in a give and take dance. It was a perfect lock.

Directly before Kilgarin, however, was the Captain; Wells was nowhere around. A man dressed in a loose-fitting tunic and baggy shorts had his arms around the Captain's neck, and was tightening his grip as Kilgarin watched, paralyzed. Somehow the Captain got his legs under him, managed to bring his weight to bear, and thrust. The former First Mate snapped forward, dragging his attacker off the ground, swinging him with startling speed until the Elyssonian was thrown from the older man's shoulders like a length of rag. The tunic wearer struck the near wall, fell.

The Captain straightened and saw Kilgarin standing in the doorway. "Come with me, Kilgarin." Without waiting for a reply, the older man sprinted for the archway that opened into an oval chamber dominated by a dusty conference table. Kilgarin ran after him, his heart pounding with a mixture of excitement and fear, a delicious feeling of confidence and vulnerability.

Another arch broke the wall ahead of him. He ducked through, saw the Captain's vanishing form as the man went up a flight of steps three at a time. There were sounds of a scuffle overhead. Kilgarin took the stairs in three bounds.

Darkness greeted him when he reached the landing. To his left a dim light glowed, barely enough to affect the gloom. Kilgarin glanced around. The Captain was gone, the hallway was empty, but one of the doors at the end of the passage was half-open. The Cork started toward it, and as he did he saw something move in the opening, a splash of soft light on metal.

He hit the ground as the energy bolt lashed the wall above him, burning a scar deep into the plastisteel. In a single motion he came to his feet and slammed shoulder first against the partly open door, crashing into a room filled with struggling figures. Kilgarin didn't wait to identify who was fighting whom; he drove into the colonist holding the weapon he'd seen glinting through the door. The man doubled as Kilgarin's fist whipped into his stomach; he fell as Kilgarin cracked the side of his skull with the edge of his hand.

It was a computer room, Kilgarin realized. The tall machines ranged along three of the walls, the consoles hulking in the center of the chamber. Between the consoles men were moving in a rapidly paced ballet. One of the men was the Captain; another was Wells. The others were strangers to Kilgarin.

"Over here, young man—" Against one of the machines a shadow moved. "Over here, please, I'm here—"

Kilgarin went quickly to the agent's side. The Company man was lying in an uncomfortable-looking heap, legs twisted at an odd angle under him, his head moving weakly, gray-bearded face turning to stare at Kilgarin as the Cork squatted. "It's my legs, you see," Company agent Gunyon said apologetically. "They're broken."

Kilgarin saw. After a moment, he nodded. "We'll get you out of here, Fellow Gunyon. Don't worry."

"I'm not worried," the old man said. "Just hurry, young man. Will you do that, please?" The agent's pale cheeks trembled. "I'm afraid there's a great deal of pain. . . ."

Swinging around, Kilgarin picked out a colonist and hurt him.

Badly.

"Is he all right?" Marka asked as she and Kilgarin watched two Physicals maneuver Gunyon into the corridor of the mindship. Both Kilgarin and the Captain, who supervised the operation from a few meters away, were bare chested; their tunics had been sacrificed to the construction of the makeshift stretcher that now bore the Company's former Elyssonian representative. The stretcher was a foot short for the old man, but Gunyon didn't seem to mind, though the arrangement must have been causing him considerable agony. Kilgarin avoided looking at Gunyon below the waist. He'd also avoided looking at the colonists the landing team had left behind in the Company Office on the planet far below.

"He'll live," Kilgarin said. Marka's head came around; her gaze pinned him.

"You don't sound concerned," she said.

"I'm not. Now," he added. "In fact, I'm a little bit ashamed of myself."

"For god's sake, Kilgarin—*why?*"

"I don't think it's something you'd understand," he told her. He ignored the look she gave him, turned and left her with the men preparing to bring Gunyon to the medical room on the inner level. He felt her staring after him, but he didn't really care.

Mind-drive:

Kilgarin entered his cabin and stepped into the fresher cubicle. He stayed under the cleansing radiation for several minutes, wishing for the feel of a needle shower spray; he'd grown used to water as a washing agent in the few short weeks he'd been on Endrim. He didn't feel clean without it.

In the room again, he worked the mechanism that released the drawer on his desk. Opening the flip-down lid, he pulled out the tray within and set it on the sloped writing board. The tray was cluttered with bits of wood in the shape of animals, crudely carved by hand, the souvenirs of hundreds of trips to primitive worlds, the only souvenirs Kilgarin ever collected. Among the carvings were several other personal items: a credit tab, a small printed booklet with a metal clasp, a round, concave mirror, half a dozen hologram cubes—two of which were of obvious commercial origin—a dinner bracelet, and a Contract chit.

He picked up the chit and placed it in the player located in the upper half of the desk console.

"—signer swears fealty and liegeance to the Charter Company, a licensee of the Federation Colonial Office, to its executives and officers, its stockholders and—"

"—all personal and professional efforts in the Company's behalf, such efforts not to exceed seventy-four days or fall below sixty—"

"—of legal age, physical and mental competence—"

"—for the maximum signing period of six years, with options for two terms of one year each at—"

"—do so profess these statements to be true, within my understanding and —"

"—Marc Kilgarin—"

"—Contract reassigned—"

"—Kilgarin."

He played the disk twice more, his eyes close and his hands resting flat on the top of the console. When the disk finished its third run-through he removed it from the player and dropped it in the tray, placed the tray back into its slot, and slid the tray home. He slammed the flip-down lid shut. He sat silently, his hands clenching until his fingers became mottled with pressure and obstructed blood, and then he relaxed, remained motionless for several seconds, finally left.

Mind-drive:

Raymond caught up with him on the outer deck, one level below the skin of the ship. He clutched the Cork's sleeve, tried to pull him around. Kilgarin jerked away and continued walking.

"Killy, it's about J'kar—"

"Not now, Raymond," Kilgarin said.

"He needs your help, Killy. He's really afraid of Ty'ger—and frankly, so am I. You owe him—"

"Goddammit, Raymond—I said not now!"

The young Physical gaped at him, his mouth working as he tried to comprehend Kilgarin's anger. "I'm sorry, Killy—I just—"

Kilgarin didn't listen. He continued walking, leaving Raymond standing near a port window, the glow from the Back Region giving the Physical's face a palid cast. Raymond stayed there, watching the Cork until Kilgarin stepped into a lift tube, dropped, and was gone.

Chapter Seven

Ninth month, tenth day, anno Domini 3146

A week after the incident on Elysson, the *Charter* touched port at Wylder, on Helmswuld, where Gunyon was to be transferred to the main Company medical facilities. While the rest of the mindship's crew went into the city for the weekend, Kilgarin found a room on the outskirts of the industrial district and locked himself in with a cask of absinthe and several large bottles of beer.

Two days later he paid off his landlord—a stubby colonial who eyed the credits in Kilgarin's folder with obvious avarice—and walked the half mile to the Sensitive District. He'd accomplished his purpose in renting the room and going on a binge: his senses—inner and outer—were so dulled he doubted his ability to find his way back to his ship. In fact, he half hoped he wouldn't.

He came across Raymond and the Cook in an ill-lit tavern two blocks from the port buildings. Both men were drinking straight beer, sitting in a narrow booth in the rear of the low-ceilinged room. They saw Kilgarin before he saw them, and the Cook went up to him as the Cork ordered at the bar. "You OK, Kilgarin?" Kilgarin started, glanced around. Finally he nodded and sipped at his drink, guiding a credit chit across the counter to the bartender, who clawed at it and slipped it out of sight. The Cook touched Kilgarin's arm.

"Listen, why don't you sit down over here with Raymond and me, hey, Killy? We've been looking for you. Where were you, hey?"

"Around," Kilgarin said. He allowed the Cook to pull

him to the booth where Raymond was sitting, and sat down at the small gray man's urging.

"How've you been, Kilgarin?" Raymond asked.

Kilgarin said something noncommittal. "The Captain's given us six days off," the Cook told him. "He's picking up some cargo in one of the other cities, some special consignment for the Company. All these special trips . . . not much to like about them, Kilgarin."

"I suppose not," Kilgarin said.

"Wells went with the Captain," Raymond said. He lifted his stein. "I thought you'd like to know. Nothing else has happened."

Kilgarin looked up. In the darkness of the room his face was heavily shadowed, but his two crew mates could see the lines of strain that marked the underlids of his eyes. He frowned, bringing out other lines in his forehead. "I'd almost forgotten," he said.

"Why'd you go off, Killy?" Raymond asked him. "Something that happened on Elysson?"

"I suppose," Kilgarin replied. "Up to that point, I'd been working for the Company as I've always worked for it. It never occurred to me what I was doing. But when we hit those men . . . I realized what side I'd been fighting on."

"I understand," Raymond said. "What do you want to do about the Captain?"

"The Captain?" The Cook spoke up. "Is this about your brother, Kilgarin?"

"Don't worry about it, Cook," Kilgarin said.

"I worry, Killy."

"Well?" Raymond asked again.

The Cork shrugged. "Wait until they get back. Nothing much else to do. I'm not even sure I care. Maybe I don't want to care."

"Sure," the young Physical said. "Another beer?"

Kilgarin shook his head. "No," he said. "I'm fine."

There was a curtain across the doorway. Kilgarin ducked, went through, and held the drapes aside for Raymond and the Cook. Inside the room they found several people sitting against one wall, staring into the glowing coals of a brazier on the hardwood floor. Another group, similarly dressed in brief shorts and long bulky tunics woven from a native flax, sat under the room's single window. Three men and two women, they rested against one another in a circle, head on lap, head on shoulder. The youngest of the women opened her eyes and stared at Kilgarin. The Cork looked back at her: dark green eyes offsetting the red of her hair, which was bright against her pale skin. She was conspicuous in the room, the fairest of the Sensitives present. Meeting Kilgarin's look with smiling arrogance, she said, "You want to see J'kar, don't you?"

"We were told he was here," Kilgarin said.

"I'll take you to him," the girl replied.

They followed her through another curtained arch into a hall, which ran parallel to the room they'd just left. There was a scent of something sweet in the air, which faded as they moved down the corridor and was replaced with another odor: the bitter tang of paint. Kilgarin understood suddenly why J'kar was at that commune, and he knew what they'd see when they found the ex-Sensitive. A moment later the girl slipped through a final, uncurtained arch, and Kilgarin's guess was proven correct.

J'kar was perched on a window shelf, his long legs dangling to the floor, his hands bracing himself as he leaned forward to greet his shipmates. He seemed transformed. His eyes were empty of fear, and his voice when he greeted them, was firm and steady. Kilgarin's glance went past the Centaurian and fixed on the man and woman kneeling in the sunken area of the room below.

They sat before an immense canvas, the woman's hands on the man's shoulders, her eyes closed, her head forward and touching the back of her partner's. He held a paint trowel delicately; its tip rested on the surface of the canvas, at the end of a long stroke of purple. Neither the man nor the woman moved as Kilgarin and the others entered. Both were as motionless as stone.

"Quiet," J'kar whispered. His eyes were bright, flickering briefly over Kilgarin, the girl, and the two Physicals with them. "Watch: Hand and Eye."

Kilgarin squatted beside the red-haired girl who'd been their guide. She rested on her haunches, arms folded across her knees, and chin set in the crossing of her arms. Seeing her posture, Kilgarin smiled. Raymond started to speak, but the Cook silenced him, gestured for the Physical to take a seat beside Kilgarin on the ledge surrounding the sunken area. Looking confused, Raymond did so.

"Watch," J'kar said, softly.

And slowly, the man began to paint.

His hand moved up, bringing the trowel with it, in a long arc that eventually bisected the original slash of purple. As the trowel moved, the man's thumb lightly pressed the control set into the handle, and the color released through the trowel's single aperture began to change: first the purple, gently melting into blue, then to green, finally to yellow. The man's hand trembled with the effort of maintaining the stroke. Gradually a shape began to take form on the canvas, shadows bringing out the highlights of the figure, adding depth to the background, perspective and tone with a minimum of detail. Not once did the trowel leave the surface of the canvas. Twice the man paused and the woman behind him moaned, almost inaudibly. The man's hand would then shiver, a muscle would jump in his forearm, and the painting would begin once more. A single stroke, swinging around and back and around the canvas again until a picture formed. A scene in a field, someone kneeling on a mound of earth and grass, shoulders thrown back, head tilted to a golden sky. The light in the picture was harsh at first, but as the painting progressed the glow became muted, gentle. Kilgarin realized that the woman was speaking. Her voice was too low for the words to be understood, but the syllables seemed to fall in a formal meter. He listened, drawing his attention from the canvas with an effort. The woman's words were modulated into a continuous moan—what was said, Kilgarin understood at last, was not important.

They watched for two hours.

When it was completed, the painting was filled with bright colors, each color developing out of some darker shade, building on each other for the total effect. Kilgarin would not have been able to fully describe the picture if he had not seen it forming, for the painting now bore no resemblance to a man in a field, kneeling or otherwise. It merely *felt* like a man in a field. It *felt* like someone raising his head to the sky, rising out of earth, reaching—Kilgarin couldn't have explained why he felt the way he did looking at the painting. He simply knew the feeling was not an accident; it was an effect sought and achieved by the painting's creators.

By the Hand and Eye.

In the room at the end of the hall, seated under the single window, J'kar explained to Raymond what had happened between the two painters.

"By selves, not good, one good sense, good feeling, other hands steady, strong. Neither paint by selves; together they paint, he holds, she guides. Sensitive, her; he's Physical. Hey, what's their names, Olivia?"

The red-haired girl handed J'kar a tray she'd filled with food, and as he accepted it, she said, "I'm not sure what his name is, but she calls herself Ruth. She came here about a year ago, with another Hand. I don't remember his name either, but he was a nice man. You would have liked him, J'kar; he looked a little like you, only his hair was black and longer than yours." She touched the Centaurian's red mane, smiling at him.

"Are they always like this?" Raymond asked. "In contact with each other, mindlocked?"

"No. Kidding? Burn out faster, much faster. No. Only when painting, safe only then. Need each other for painting, need mindlock then, not before, not after."

"Are they lovers?" The young Physical pulled a length of warm meat from the stew he was sharing with the Cook, and dabbed it in the jelly set on the floor next to him.

"Lovers? Yes, no. Together, yes," J'kar said. "Close like lovers, but maybe not so deep. Ask them, if care."

"Do you know who designed this kind of art, Kilgarin?" Olivia asked the Cork. He glanced up from his own bowl of stew; he hadn't been listening to the conversation. He found talk about mindlinks disturbing at times, especially in public. Seeing she'd gained his attention, the red-haired girl went on, "J'kar. He did it on earth, a long time ago. Didn't you, J'kar?"

The Centaurian nodded, grinning shyly. The girl ran her hand over his hair, returning his smile. "He couldn't keep it up though," she said finally. "Things happened. His father went into bankruptcy on Centauri, with Contracts still outstanding. J'kar was forced to take over the Contracts; he had his choice of service, of course, so he chose the mindships over the colonial processing plants. That was a long time ago, wasn't it, J'kar?"

"Long, Olivia," J'kar said.

"I knew him then, Kilgarin. I was just a girl, only about—what, three or four years old?—but I knew him. My mother and he were Hand and Eye for those first paintings. It started a whole school, with J'kar its leading exponent and its sharpest critic. When he left, it all fell apart. No one could guide us, tell us what to do. People stopped coming to the shows, without J'kar to lend them authority, and pretty soon all the credit mother had saved was gone, and we had to leave. She Contracted out to the colonies. So did a few of the others. Groups of us ended up here and there, on planets like Helmswuld. We kept working. What else could we do?"

She flicked her green eyes toward Kilgarin. He shrugged, uneasily.

"I never thought we'd see J'kar again," Olivia said, "until two days ago, when he walked into a pub a few blocks from here. There aren't many men in the Outworlds with hair like that. It's a dying gene. He'd changed, but I'd expected that. I really did, J'kar; mother told me to, she knew what the Contracts would do to you. She said you wouldn't be the same. She was wrong."

"Kristin," J'kar said.

"She's dead now," Olivia told Kilgarin. "Four years ago, in a Company plant."

"Here?" the Cook asked.

"I don't know where. The Company wouldn't tell me."

Raymond said quietly, looking at J'kar, "He and your mother must have been very close."

She smiled. "He's my father," she said.

Kilgarin blinked down at the half-eaten bowl of stew resting in his lap. He'd lost what little appetite he'd had. He didn't feel well, and he knew why. "J'kar, I'll talk to you later," he said, and rose to his feet unsteadily, catching himself with a hand to the concrete wall. He managed to cross the room and escape to the outside with a minimum of difficulty. He paused just beyond the arch and listened for a moment to make certain none of his shipmates was about to follow. He heard Raymond ask the Cook what was wrong, and he heard part of the Cook's reply, and then he turned and went down the stairs to the street and out into the setting night.

Toward morning he wandered back to the city from the outlying suburbs. He hadn't answered any of the questions he'd felt within him, but he had, at least, subdued them.

The sky was splintering with dawn when he returned to the port, found the apartment where he'd left J'kar and the others, and rolled into one of the blanketed corners to sleep.

The girl named Olivia woke him and gave him some food. As he ate she asked him about the worlds he'd visited and the people he'd seen. He found that conversation was difficult, but out of gratitude for the food she'd prepared for him, he told her the things she wanted to hear, in short sentences that conveyed his objective meaning and little of his own experience. Toward the end of the meal she sensed his reticence and abandoned the questioning, launching into a monologue that Kilgarin listened to with half-interest. She went with him to the street, still talking, and together they walked the few blocks to the port, where the *Charter* was ready to lift from the planet. In answer to an early question of his, she'd told him that J'kar and the other two crew members had gone ahead shortly after dawn.

She told him about a show she was planning with other of the artists in Wylder, a major display of their best work, and she revealed that she hoped to organize a sojourn to one of the major colonies with the proceeds from the local exhibition. Kilgarin expressed polite enthusiasm. She continued to talk until they reached the port terminal, where they parted. Before he entered the building, she touched his arm and leaned up to kiss him. Kilgarin was startled.

"What was that for?" he asked.

She smiled at him, her eyebrows rising. "Don't be threatened," she said. "I just want you to know I like you."

He stared at her. Her smile faded, and she shook her head, once.

"You must be an awfully lonely man," she said.

His last view of her was as she swung away from the transparent doors of the terminal entrance and strode down the street to a squat port bus waiting at the corner, her hair trailing out behind, her hips rising and falling as she stalked, her shoulders straight. He watched her until she climbed inside the bus. Then he entered the port and headed for the *Charter*.

A crowd was gathered around the lower exit port of the ship, men and women dressed in maintenance overalls leaning against one another, shifting and pressing to obtain a better view. Kilgarin pushed through the crowd, sensing the anxiety and distaste that played through the Physicals gathered there. He pushed out the sensations and shoved through into a clearing, which centered on the end of the cargo ramp. He recognized three of the Physicals standing guard over a large plastic container set on end at the ramp base. He asked the closest Physical what had happened. The man eyed him, noting the Sensitive's blue uniform and the officer's patch on Kilgarin's right shoulder, and decided to answer.

"Bit of fight in the control room. Man's dead, t'other's in with the medic. All over now, I imagine."

"Who's dead?" Kilgarin asked.

"Physical from maintenance. Started screaming at the girl in charge of Communications when she wouldn't put through a message, went right off his head. She tried to report him, he attacked her, there you go—" the Physical indicated the container. "Blew out his brain, from what I hear. Mess, it was. Fool didn't have a chance."

Kilgarin recognized the repressed anger in the Physical's tone; behind it were the same emotions he'd sensed in the colonists of Elysson. Kilgarin had been awaiting an outbreak of resentment since the journey began; now that it had come he found himself unprepared for the reality. He glanced from the plastic container to the Physicals guarding it.

"Is she all right? Ryork, the Communications agent?"

"Imagine so," the Physical said. "Check for yourself, Fellow."

"I will," Kilgarin replied. He moved around the guard and hurried up the ramp into the ship.

Another crowd—smaller than the one around the dead man's coffin—blocked the entrance to the medic's office. Shouldering his way through, Kilgarin managed to get near the speaker grill beside the door. The third time he pressed the call button, a voice answered. "Medic's busy. Talk when we can."

"This is James Kilgarin, medic. I'm Cork on this ship. Let me in."

After a minute's wait, Kilgarin was able to slip through a partly opened door into the cramped medical quarters. The medic faced him, flushed a deep red, annoyed at having his orders superseded. "She's inside if you want to see her," the thin-faced man said. "Not conscious."

"I won't be a moment."

Her face was badly bruised, one lump under her eye swelled to the size of Kilgarin's thumb and discolored an ugly purple. Part of her face was bandaged, cloth covering her neck and jaw. Kilgarin looked a question at the medic, who'd followed him to the table in the nook. "Broken," the medic answered. "Almost crushed her windpipe."

"Ryork?" Kilgarin whispered it, bending near the Communications agent's uncovered ear. The impressions he received from her mind were chaotic, without form or design. He said her name again, hoping to spark some level of her brain into response, but there was nothing. Nothing for him to latch onto, no path to follow into her mind, where he could—what? Kilgarin had no idea what he intended to do, but it was hardly important. He could do nothing.

"Is she a friend?" the medic asked him when Kilgarin straightened.

"No," Kilgarin said. "Not really." He lifted his eyes from the Elyssonian's unconscious form. "I just know her."

"So?"

"She reminds me of someone. It happened to her too, in a way."

"Here? On the *Charter*?"

Kilgarin stirred. He blinked at the medic. The man's features were pinched in a disapproving frown. "Not here," Kilgarin said. "On another ship, the *Drowner*. It was a long time ago." He shook his head angrily. "And dammit, it's not important now."

Kilgarin felt the medic's eyes on him as he left, but at the moment the Cork couldn't have cared less.

Ryork died the hour before the *Charter* was due to lift from Helmswuld; her pet disappeared at the same time, out of the Communications agent's cabin, where it'd been put while the Elyssonian was in the medic's office. Kilgarin never found out what happened to the small animal. Kilgarin didn't attend the funeral; he couldn't help thinking that if the woman had been allowed in the Company hospital that had taken Gunyon, she'd be alive. But regulations forbade it. So instead of attending the funeral later that evening he found an automated pub in the port terminal and was drinking there when the Captain entered.

"Mind if I sit?" the older man asked Kilgarin, sliding onto the bench across from the Cork. Kilgarin shrugged, watching as the Captain punched a drink combination into the console section of the tabletop.

"You weren't at the funeral either, Captain?"

"I made an appearance," he said, loosening the collar of his jump suit. "Business called me back to the port, I'm afraid. Cargo manifest needed adjustment before the port officials would sign out the ship. We're carrying a full load now, you know."

"Are we?"

"Yes," the Captain said, mistaking Kilgarin's tone. "First time since I took over the captaincy. We almost ran full out of Endrim, but not quite. Bad weather there a few years ago, and we're feeling the effects with this year's trade. Not much liquor. On the other hand, Helmswuld had a fine crop last year. One of the more exotic natural narcotics. Ferments nicely in wine, from what I hear."

"Captain, may I ask you a personal question?"

The older man frowned. His drink appeared, and he sipped at it before answering. "What is it, Kilgarin?"

"Does Ryork's death bother you in any way?"

"What do you mean?" Lines of concentration furrowed the other man's brow.

"Are you sorry she's dead?"

"Sorry? She was a good officer, a good agent. Of course I'm sorry."

Kilgarin drank, set his mug down gently. "Sir? Did you ever speak to her? Did you know anything about her?"

"Not very much, no. The private lives of my officers are their concern, not mine."

"I'm glad to hear that, Captain," Kilgarin said. He got to his feet, tossed a standard chit on the table by his empty glass. "I'd hate to think you'd known her, and felt the way you do."

Kilgarin managed to avoid Marka on the run along the Arm, making a point to leave the ship early whenever the *Charter* touched port, keeping to the less-frequented areas of the mindship whenever it was in drive. During this same period the tension aboard the psi vessel rose to an unbelievable peak, building on the deaths of both the Physical and Ryork; Kilgarin found himself under constant pressure to relieve the straining emotions of the crew. This delicate balance was maintained for almost ten days, through six stops at various minor colonies, but on the eleventh day after the *Charter* left Helmswuld, Kilgarin was cornered by Marka in the processing area of the hydroponics garden. She'd lost what little weight she'd gained during the early days of the voyage, her face was pale, the lines under her eyes pronounced, and when she grabbed at his tunic and spun him around, her hands trembled—slightly.

"Where in hell have *you* been?" she shouted. "I haven't seen you in almost two weeks."

"I've been avoiding you," Kilgarin said.

She opened her mouth. She closed it. "Thanks for telling me," she said. "Now try why. What have I done to you, Kilgarin? Tell me *what I've done.*"

"You were crowding me," Kilgarin said, "just like before. I don't want that, Marka. I thought that was clear."

Muscles worked in her jaw. She looked away from him. There were eight planters in the room, shallow trays connected by wires and cables to the main processing bank in the floor beneath the platforms. She ran a hand along the rim of the glass-enclosed tray nearest her. "You're really holding that over me, what I did that night you found out about your brother. Aren't you? You never mentioned it, but you hate me for leaving you alone. That's what it's been all along, isn't it?" Her hand stopped moving on the rim. "Listen, I'm sorry I did that, OK?" She looked at him. "Is that what you wanted to hear?"

"You don't understand at all," Kilgarin said.

She let her hand fall to her side. "Is it what happened before? When you found me with that man? Tell me, Kilgarin. I want to understand."

"I've already told you."

"About us getting closer? I can't believe that. There has to be something I haven't done, or something I did do—there has to be *something,* Killy. I won't believe you just don't *want* me." She was becoming hysterical. Her hands went toward Kilgarin's jump suit; he eased aside.

"Believe what you want to, Marka. I've told you what I felt."

She brought her hands up and held them clenched before her. The knuckles whitened, the fingers mottling from the pressure. Her hands trembled. "Tell me, Kilgarin, please," she said, "Please, I *want* to understand. What you're saying *just doesn't make any sense!"*

"It makes plenty of sense," Kilgarin said, "to me."

When the *Charter* landed on an Outworld planet named Denford, Kilgarin went down on the first shuttle boat with the Captain and Wells, accompanied by the Cook. He waited beside the craft while the Captain signed the release papers for the first batch of cargo, and he helped with the unloading, guiding the automatic handlers into place around the open hatch and supervising as the machines emptied the hold of liquor and placed it on the patch of plastisteel that was Denford's only landing pad. The rest of the port area was equally small; there was only one building, which was little more than a shack.

The unloading completed, the Captain dismissed the three shipmates, and Kilgarin and the Cook, with Wells filling out the three-man flier they borrowed from the port agent, set off on a tour of the planet's southern hemisphere.

Denford was a lower-class planet, with a few local industries, which produced novelty items that had little practical importance; these were exported in return for the necessities of life, graciously provided by the Company. There was a tape that came with the flier, supplied by the port's information bureau, that described these industries in detail. The tape also gave geographical data, which the three shipmates ignored. They agreed that they preferred to meet the planet fresh, imagining themselves the settlers who had first colonized the world a hundred years before. They could have been at that, for much of the planet was virgin country.

Like most of the worlds opened up in the past hundred and fifty years by the discovery of the mind-drive, Denford was still only subtly invaded by man. Unlike earth and Centauri, two of the more cultivated worlds, the Outworlds still had many rough edges, such as climate, air quality and pressure, and general disposition—which was normally antihuman. On the whole man settled on worlds that approximated earth conditions to a fair degree; Denford was one of the few exceptions, and because of its abnormality it survived as a colonial base. On Denford, gravity was one-fourth again earth normal; air pressure was a bit greater than sea level on Endrim; climate was generally wet and cold; and the planet's electromagnetic field was twice as strong as it should have been.

Because of that powerful electromagnetic field, almost all of the materials used by the colony had to be plain plastic, instead of the usual plastisteel compound. Kilgarin had no clear idea of what effect this EM peculiarity had on Denford's industry; he only knew it was a considerable effect, allowing the colonists to make novelty items that would have been impossible to realize under normal conditions.

He also knew the field had a considerable effect on psi powers, as all EM fields had; he could already feel the effect taking hold of him, in the form of a mild headache. The headache would grow, Kilgarin knew, and as it did, his resistance to psychic probing would become weaker, as would the resistance of the other two men in the flier with him. Kilgarin knew this, because he knew about the field; and so did the Cook, because Kilgarin had told him.

Wells did not know. As far as the Engineer was concerned, the three of them were touring. Kilgarin and the Cook knew otherwise.

Most of the planet's surface was barren, sparsely covered with a layer of unhealthy weed the Cook identified as a form of grass. There were no trees or large plants of any kind; in the distance the hills were a naked brown tipped with white.

As he brought the flier closer to the foothills—cursing the flier's antimatter power source, which was apparently running low, making steering difficult—Kilgarin saw that the ravines were bright with water. The plains below the foothills were also well irrigated, a fact that made Kilgarin wonder about the poorly growing weeds. He realized it was an effect of the planet's magnetic field. Probably the field screened the full effect of the local sun during the spring months, collecting the radiation in the ionosphere until late summer, when the energy was finally released or filtered through, melting the snow and ice formed during the long winters—and thus creating the rivers and lakes. Kilgarin hoped Wells wouldn't work this out on his own, and so arrive at a realization of the planet's field. Kilgarin didn't see how the Engineer could, but the anticipation of finally probing the man's mind was making Kilgarin tense and nervous. He wished the magnetic field would have the same effect on implanted mindblocks, so that he might probe the Captain's mind and solve the mystery at once; but such an easy solution wasn't to be. Angrily, he turned his attention from his thoughts to the land beneath the flier.

An hour out of the port, they reached the upper hills of what the maps named the Southern Range. Kilgarin guided the flier to a landing on a shallow slope, setting the three-man craft down at a cant. Wells and the Cook climbed out ahead of Kilgarin, the Engineer moving downslope and finding a promontory that overlooked a wide valley. "Hey, Kilgarin, not much like home, huh? This is one sick planet. Look at that, dead grass, plants no taller than a man's knee"—Wells waved his hand, taking in the spotted vegetation below—"not fit for animals, never mind us. Cold as hell, too. Hey," he said, laughing, "did you hear that? Cold as hell."

Kilgarin came up to the Cook. The small gray man was sitting on his haunches near the front of the flier, watching Wells. "This better be worth it, Killy," the Cook said. "My head hurts like a demon."

"It's worth it," Kilgarin told him. He called out to the Engineer, "You want to do some climbing? There's enough of a path over this way."

After a moment's discussion it was decided that the Cook would stay with the craft and prepare the day's meal, while Kilgarin and Wells followed the cut of a ravine to the top of the mountain, in search of a high altitude plant the touring tape claimed grew wild in the Southern Range. Wells agreed vigorously, which disturbed Kilgarin; the large man hadn't yet given any sign he was suffering the same headache effect that plagued Kilgarin and the Cook.

The slope was uneven, composed mostly of a fine soil that slid away under the boots of Kilgarin had worn specially for the expedition. There were few large rocks, and those were spaced awkwardly for climbing. The two men progressed slowly, pausing frequently to catch their breath, which was easier in the higher altitude.

"Not much like Wellington, huh?" said Wells during one of the pauses.

Kilgarin shook his head. "You do much climbing back there?" he asked.

"No. Left Crispin when I was a kid, not more than ten, I guess. My father couldn't take the land. He hired himself out as a medic for the Company, and my mother took me back to the lowlands to wait for him to fill his Contract. Not many hills down there. Not much going for it, besides the weather."

"Guess not," Kilgarin said. He was from the lowlands of Wellington himself.

Another moment passed, and they began climbing again. Kilgarin's head was clearing with the crispness of the mountain air, and after another few meters had crawled under them, he tried a probe on Wells, who was climbing above him.

He encountered the block at once, a hard shell enclosing the substance of Wells's subconscious mind. To Kilgarin the shell was vaguely spherical, pulsating with a silver glow, and the area around it was murky, the thoughts of the Engineer's conscious mind sheering from the hidden portion of his brain. Once more Kilgarin realized Wells was not aware of the mindblock; if it was a defense against Kilgarin, it was probably more efficient than the Engineer would have wanted, for not only did it prevent the Cork from seeing the secrets within, it prevented Wells from seeing them also.

Gently at first, Kilgarin pressed against the barrier. He felt the resistance, power being summoned by the block from other sources in the mind. But the block acted sluggishly, and the power came too slowly, and Kilgarin, sensing this, took the opportunity and *thrust.*

The shell shattered, the mindblock collapsed, and in the same instant the Engineer screamed.

It happened quickly. Almost too quickly.

One moment the two men were climbing, the Engineer drawing himself up with a hand clasped tightly to the jutting edge of a huge stone. Kilgarin waited below him, balanced on another rock, leaning against the slope, his hands flat on the stone facing him.

The next moment Wells cried out and released his grip on the ledge. Kilgarin felt the large man's bulk sliding past him, and instinctively his hand shot out, his body turning to slam into the Engineer's and break the falling man's momentum.

Both men tumbled from the slope, Kilgarin locking his arms around Wells, trying to pull the Engineer's head against his shoulder to protect him as they fell. Wells kept screaming. In Kilgarin's mind the screams had an echo, and it was all he could do to keep from blacking out.

He half saw the ground canting wildly about them, first on the left and then on the right. His leg struck rock; he stumbled and felt stone rip through his jacket; he ploughed through loose dirt, waiting for the inevitable boulder to smash up into them, crushing ribs and snapping their spines. Somehow he lost his grip on Wells. The two Sensitives fell free of each other, continuing their plummet downslope.

When Kilgarin came to, the Cook was bending over him.

"You OK, Kilgarin? What happened? He try to kill you or something?"

The Cork elbowed himself into a sitting position. He saw Wells lying with his head propped on an aid kit, a few meters away. "Is he all right?" Kilgarin asked. The Cook nodded, and Kilgarin sighed gratefully. *"I nearly killed him,"* the Cork said. "See if you can get him awake. I want to talk to him now."

"It was on Centauri," Wells said, "back in '28. I was a Corps Engineer then, working on one of the barrack planets, Tarweal Base. I was with the militia, fixing things, jimmied special project devices, like that. It was the kind of thing I enjoyed doing; I didn't even feel like part of the militia. All that was somebody else's job. We'd heard about the revolutionaries on Centauri; some of them had even come to Tarweal to talk to us, but none of us paid it any attention. People were always talking against the Company. We did it ourselves. Nothing new; nothing to get excited about.

"Nothing, that is, until the rebels tried to take over Centauri port."

Kilgarin watched the Engineer sip at the coffee the Cook had made for him. The big man held the cup in two large hands that were marked with the white lines of calluses. The Cook sat next to Kilgarin, listening. Kilgarin wanted it that way, for the Cook to hear it directly from Wells. It was not a story the Cork cared to repeat.

"We were called up pretty quick," Wells said. "Same day they took the port over. The Company officers must have been figuring on trouble for months, which was why they had all the soldiers there to move down to the planet fast. We went down in eight ships, each about the size of the *Charter*. I found myself going with them, carrying a weapon like all the others. I'd been trained for it, I knew how to use the damned thing, but I never thought I'd need to. Even then I didn't really believe I'd be part of the attack.

"We hit them after dawn. Two ships to each of the major cities, three to Centauri port itself, one to the suburb. I was in the last ship. We came out in patrols of ten. They put me in charge of a patrol and told me to sweep the area, look for any natives on the street, that sort of thing. They called them natives, not colonists. We looked. There wasn't anyone in sight.

"I reported in. My commanding officer told me to take my team into an apartment building overlooking the central plaza. There'd been sniping in the area, he said, six of our men were down, he said, and he thought the sniper might be hiding in one of the apartments. We went up."

Kilgarin poured Wells another cup of coffee.

"Three men in my patrol were Outworlders. The Outworlders were different then, in a lot of ways. The Company hadn't pressured them yet and they still felt secure being colonists; they liked it. To them the revolutionaries were madmen. Mad dogs. That's what Barker called them. Barker was my right-hand man. I wasn't too familiar with the militia—they'd put me in charge of the patrol because of my rank; Corps Engineers were full staff sergeants in those days—so I was dependent on Barker for tactics.

"He heard gunshots—he said he did—from a room at

the end of a hall in one of the buildings. I asked him what we should do. He told me to go in with him and Fitzhugh, one of the other Outworlders, and keep the other members of the patrol as backup. So I did.

"Barker went in first, firing his weapon in an arc spray. He'd told me to lock my rifle in the same position; he said it was the most effective setting. I did. I came in behind him, spraying the side of the room he'd missed. Fitzhugh was behind me.

"You can guess what we found."

"No snipers," Kilgarin said.

Wells stared into his coffee. "An old lady and an old guy, some kids. The parents of the kids were in the next room, doing the sniping. We got them too, but we got the kids first."

"What happened then?" the Cook asked quietly.

"We went back outside and the commander assigned us another building, and we did the same thing there. For three months we did that. When it was over, I quit, joined up with one of the traders the Company owned, and for eight years I shipped back and forth along the Arm, didn't once head back to Centauri. Around '36 I quit those ships and went on a binge until my credit ran out, which took about two years.

"Finally I forgot everything. It was the only thing I could do. Even the ship's Corks couldn't help me. I forgot it all, and I've been able to live with myself these past seven years . . ."

". . . until now," Kilgarin finished for him. "I'm sorry, Wells. I misunderstood."

"Sure," Wells said.

A little later the Cook whispered to Kilgarin, "What are you going to do for him?"

"He isn't the man I want," Kilgarin said. "What am I supposed to do?"

"You know," the Cook said. "Fix his mind."

Kilgarin glanced at Wells, sitting apart from the two other men, nursing his cold cup of coffee. The Cork nodded. "You're right," he said. "That much, at least."

"Hey, Kilgarin. Are we going to do any climbing or not?"

"It's getting late, Wells," the Cork said. "The Captain said the ship's lifting at 2100."

"Outside air agrees with you," the Cook added, helping the Engineer to his feet.

"Sure," Wells said. "How long have I been asleep, anyway?"

Kilgarin shrugged. "Long enough," he said.

He accepted the Cook's offer of a beer when they returned to the ship, following the small man into the almost fully deserted lounge and taking a seat on the counter near the food console. As it had the first day he stepped aboard the *Charter*, the psychic aura of the vessel—centered here in the lounge—threatened to overwhelm Kilgarin. His increased Sensitivity to the aura was due partially, he knew, to the recent unpleasantness with Wells, but there were other factors at work also. Marka was near, Kilgarin sensed, and her presence made him uneasy. More, the tension in the crew had doubled since Ryork's death. That and other pressures he couldn't discern gave the ship's atmosphere an almost physical weight. Kilgarin tried to shut out the emotions, but found that his training as a Cork wouldn't let him; he was forced to act as a valve to those minds around him, and for the first time since the incident aboard the *Drowner*, Kilgarin doubted his ability to handle the pressure.

"Make that two shots of absinthe," he told the Cook. The small man blinked, but made the necessary adjustments and handed the stein to the Cork. Kilgarin drank, said, "What now, Cook? If it isn't Wells, who's responsible for the Captain's block, who is it?"

The Cook's expression became puzzled. "Anyone at all," he replied. He eyed Kilgarin's stein. "Another one?"

"Only one shot this time."

"Right."

Kilgarin closed his eyes. He felt weary, weaker than he'd been in many years.

"Hey, Killy," the Cook said softly.

He uncovered his eyes. The Cook was looking past his shoulder, at someone who'd entered the lounge. Kilgarin swiveled around and saw Raymond and Marka sliding into a booth under a blank display screen. Raymond was speaking to Marka, but at that distance Kilgarin was unable to hear the young Physical's words, and was unwilling to probe his mind. He returned his attention to the Cook, who was punching an order into the console.

"Marka's been pretty upset lately," the Cook said.

"Who told you that?"

"Raymond. And even if he hadn't, I've still got *some* senses left. Enough to tell about a thing like that."

Kilgarin said nothing. The Cook removed two glasses from the console, each brimming with beer, and set them on a tray. He pushed the tray toward Kilgarin. "Take that to them, would you? Their usual."

"And if I don't?"

"Then I will, and I'll tell them you wanted to speak with them. Just do it, will you please, Kilgarin?"

Reluctantly Kilgarin took up the tray and carried it to the booth. He sat down opposite the two Physicals and raised his own glass in a toast. Neither of them followed. He drank it anyway.

"It's my turn not to want to see you, Kilgarin," Marka said.

"It wasn't my idea to come over here," he answered.

"Then make it your idea to leave."

"OK," Kilgarin said. He got up and started toward the door. He was stopped by Raymond's hand on his shoulder. Kilgarin tried to shrug off the Physical's grip, but the young man only tightened his hold and moved around in front of the Cork.

"Can I talk with you a minute, Killy?" Raymond asked.

"Your hand's in the way, Fellow."

Raymond dropped his hand, curled it into a fist, and stuffed it and the other one into the loose pockets of his jump suit. Kilgarin realized that the young man had lost most of the extra weight he'd had when the Cork first met him.

"Listen," Raymond said, "I feel bad about what's been happening with all of us. I really hate to see us breaking up like this. The way we came together and all, it seems a shame—" He stopped, started again more slowly. "I don't understand what's wrong, and I hoped we could talk about it so maybe we could work something out. If that's OK with you."

"I'm going for a walk," Kilgarin said. "Come along, if you like."

He waited while Raymond went back to speak with Marka, and when the young Physical returned Kilgarin struck off at a full stride. It was an effort for Raymond to keep up with him, but not as great an effort as it once might have been. Kilgarin headed up a ramp that during Drive would become a curving wall. Raymond trotted alongside him, huffing to stay within talking distance.

"What happened with Wells today?" Raymond asked between breaths. Kilgarin told him and Raymond asked a few questions, which Kilgarin answered with a minimum of detail. Finally, Raymond asked: "Killy, are we friends?"

"We're friends," Kilgarin said.

"Is the way you're acting because of what you're trying to find out about your brother?"

"How am I acting?"

"Kilgarin, please. You know what I'm talking about. You're treating all of us as though *we* were the ones who destroyed Marc—at least that's the way it seems. Avoiding us, being brusque, cold . . . if we've done something to hurt you, don't you think we should know about it?"

"You've done nothing you couldn't help doing," Kilgarin said.

"That's very clear," Raymond said bitterly.

"Look," Kilgarin said, over his shoulder, "I did not ask *any* of you to come with me. I'm not taking that responsibility. You're all trying to make me out as some sort of freak because I don't want to get involved in *your* problems. Marka wants me to love her; J'kar wants me to save him from Ty'ger; you want me to be your friend. All I want is to be left alone, and to be given the *minimum* help I ask for—and maybe that's where I made my mistake, in asking any of you for help. That was weak of me. I apologize. I don't like people to need me, I don't like to need people, and is that *simple enough for you?*" He was shouting, he realized. He calmed himself and continued walking. "I'm sorry, Raymond, but that's it."

"Guess I'm sorry too, Kilgarin. For you, not with you."

Kilgarin stopped to stare at Raymond, but the Physical had already turned and was walking down the hall, back toward the lounge. The Cork shook his head and walked on.

Chapter Eight

Ninth month, twenty-ninth day, anno Domini 3146

Rumors about the Outworld insurrection dominated the conversation aboard the *Charter* during the next few days of drive. Kilgarin paid little attention to it, concentrating for the most part on maintaining the shaky equilibrium of the crew. Ryork's death—and the death of the Physical who killed her—had caused more of a disturbance than even Kilgarin had anticipated at first. As the days passed, reaction set in, and the resulting pressure grew more and more dangerous. Resentment was building in the Sensitives, mirroring a similar resentment in the Physicals. Kilgarin found it more and more difficult to soothe the tendency toward violence present in the crew. On the fourth day out from Denford he decided to go to the Captain.

It was his third visit to the Captain's private quarters, and the room was still as bare as it'd been the first time he'd seen it, save for the addition of a tiny figurine set on the display console near the bed. The Captain noticed Kilgarin glance toward the statue as the Cork entered, and he smiled, motioning Kilgarin closer. "I found it on Rylon," the Captain said, "in one of the antique shops on the second level. I believe it's third-century Centaurian, but Wells doesn't think so. He says he's never seen anything like it."

"Captain, I wanted to talk to you about the crew."

The older man broke his attention away from the figurine, turning to regard Kilgarin with a frown. "Yes? What's the problem?"

Kilgarin told him. The Captain listened without expression as the Cork offered his opinion of the nature of the ship's distress and its probable outcome. When Kilgarin was finished, the Captain looked up at him, unsmiling.

"I've been told to expect it," the older man said. "The Company has been having trouble all across the Arm, and of course there was that business on Elysson. The Outworld colonies, some of them, are in open rebellion . . . and it seems to be spreading to the mindships. I should have realized Ryork's killing was a part of it, but there's been so much to think about. . . ." His gaze drifted back to the figurine. "You do understand that, don't you, Kilgarin?"

Kilgarin shrugged. "I don't think she was killed as part of a plot, Captain, but it doesn't matter. What should we do?"

"We'll be reaching our last port in this sector within the next two days. Planet named Maylind. After that we head down to Centauri. I think we can hold out that long."

"Yes, Captain," Kilgarin said. He turned to go, peered once more at the figurine, a delicate sculpting in blue stone of a man cradling a child. He caught a final glimpse of the Captain raising his hand toward the statue, and then Kilgarin moved down the corridor to the outside door, the wall cutting off his view.

The Captain was wrong. The problems didn't hold until the ship reached Centauri. They didn't hold until the *Charter* touched its final colonial port. Trouble broke out almost at once, that evening in the mess, and most of the ship's Sensitives were fortunate to survive.

Kilgarin came to the lounge late; he often arrived after the other Sensitives because he wanted to avoid the added pressures of a crowded mess hall when he was Corking during mind-drive. Entering the low-ceilinged chamber, he could feel the tension as an almost tangible barrier separating him from the men and women in the benches and booths lining the walls. Hostile stares greeted him, which Kilgarin ignored—he knew the difference between expressed dislike and hidden hate, the latter more dangerous because it allowed no release. Kilgarin, as Cork, was poignantly aware of the crew's need for release, and so in a way he welcomed the glares.

He picked up a tray from the counter, accepted a beer from a sullen Physical who'd clipped her hair too close to her scalp, and struck across the room, looking for the

Cook. The small man would be off duty and was probably enjoying his dinner in a booth far from the food console.

Someone jostled Kilgarin. He stumbled, tripped over a foot he hadn't seen a moment before, and sprawled on a table, his tray skidding out of his hands and splashing beer and fortified meat-product on three Physical women. The men with the women came to their feet and lunged for the Cork. Kilgarin almost blacked out under the onslaught of their hate. Before he could move they were on him.

Hands locked on his elbows, snapping his arms back and restraining him. A fist planted itself in his stomach. Another flicked against his jaw. A third connected with his cheek. It was then that Kilgarin began to move.

Jerking from the man who held him, Kilgarin butted his head into the face of the Physical before him. As that man crumpled, the Cork swung around and brought the edge of his palm up, striking the second Physical hovering beside him. The heel of his hand struck the man's nose, shattering cartilage and shoving the splinters into the man's brain. Spinning, completing his turn, Kilgarin kneed the Physical who'd held him and carried through by doubling his fists and slamming them down on the man's neck as the Physical bent in agony.

Kilgarin stepped back, aware of the emotions firing the room around him.

Hate, pure and stark. And fear, and anger, and concern. He was unable to pick out the individual feelings: there was too much, all of it mixed together in one gestalt—violence. Violence was going to happen, and quickly.

"Killy, over here"—the voice cried out to him from the left; Kilgarin whirled—"get over *here.*"

Past the faces of the men and women nearest him, Kilgarin saw the Cook, and with him, Ty'ger and Luanne. The Cook was waving, his features twisted with worry and terror. The small man was close to panicking, Kilgarin realized, and also realized with a start that so was *he.*

Around him the room was in stasis. Physicals stared, not quite comprehending what had happened. Everyone in the lounge was caught in the paralysis of the moment, that peculiar inability of those involved in an instant of decision to accept the decision and act. Kilgarin took advantage of the moment to run down the aisle toward his three friends. Midway to them, he was attacked.

A bare-chested Physical in shorts that only partially covered a heavy paunch hit Kilgarin with a body block.

The Cork careened into two Outworld women who caught him and tried to lock him in a stranglehold. Kilgarin twisted. The thinner of the two Physicals lifted over his shoulder and landed on the back of the still-pitching bare-chested man. Leaning into the motion, Kilgarin continued to turn, managed a grip on the leg of the woman still gripping his neck frantically and heaved her over his head. She fell onto a table a meter away.

"Watch your back, Kilgarin," the Cook's voice said beside Kilgarin. The Cork didn't bother to acknowledge the warning; instead he ducked and sensed a tray sail over his head. "What in hell did you do to these people?" the Cook asked him, gasping. Out of the corner of his eye Kilgarin saw the small gray man wrestling down a Physical half again as tall as he was.

"Nothing," Kilgarin replied to the Cook's question. He stepped between the small man and his assailant, snapped the edge of his hand down on the neck of the Physical. "It's been in the wind, waiting to break," Kilgarin said. "If I had a moment to think I might"—he slipped out of the path of a black-bearded Physical charging at him with a knife—"be able to do something about it. Don't have time. Only react." He tripped the knife wielder. The man fell, the knife clattered across the floor, and Kilgarin jerked his foot in a kick that assured no further threats from that Physical's direction.

"We'd better get out of here," the Cook said.

Kilgarin swore. "I've been trying."

Ty'ger called to them. Not far away, the Sensitive was under siege by two youngish Physicals in the mottled jump suits of the hydroponics attendants. "Head this way," the Centaurian shouted. "Exit's here, under the mural."

Near Ty'ger's table the girl Luanne swung her fists in blows that seemed more mechanical than human. She was under Ty'ger's direction; Kilgarin could tell. It was there in her movements, graceful yet unnatural. More graceful than the situation deserved, Kilgarin thought. He grabbed the Cook's arm and pulled him out of a circle of Sensitives and Physicals already locked in combat.

"Ty'ger's holding a way out for us," Kilgarin told the Cook, dragging him past men and women who slipped forward and back, bodies blocking the full view of the battle that had sprung up. Kilgarin sensed the hatred about him. Spontaneous, it came from a variety of sources, not all of them rooted in the class rivalry between Physical and Sensitive. It was that rivalry that had provided the tinder, but it was the combination of Ryork's death and the incident on Elysson that had provided the spark. Now the ship was afire—and Kilgarin couldn't find the strength or concentration to dowse the flames.

Ahead, Ty'ger was waving. Kilgarin waved back.

"Move, Cook," Kilgarin called. "Outside, maybe we can—"

He saw it happen and he tried to stop it as it happened, but already it was too late. The girl was dead.

There was a gracefulness to her death, as there'd been a gracefulness to her fight. Arms lifted over her head she seemed to writhe as though on fire, making the silver jutting from her rib cage move in a slow figure eight. At the center of the figure eight a circle of red spread out until it touched the underside of her left breast and extended a curving tail across her stomach. Her mouth worked and her eyes pinched shut, and at the end of her arms her hands spasmed into fists as she writhed, more slowly now. Gradually her arms relaxed and her hands came down, hovering for a moment around the handle of the knife protruding from her chest. Then her hands fell, and the girl was dead. Slumping to the floor, she was dead. Luanne was dead.

The Physical who'd killed her danced back from her body clumsily.

Ty'ger screamed and turned, and sprang in the same motion.

Kilgarin watched. Consciously this time, he did nothing.

When it was over, Kilgarin caught Ty'ger's neck and pulled the Centaurian to his feet. Ty'ger's hands were stiff; he held his fingers splayed as though his hands were unclean. He stared at them dumbly as Kilgarin shook him, said, "We've got to go, Ty'ger. Come on."

Ty'ger glanced up. His eyes were unfocused. Kilgarin knew what the Centaurian was seeing: the inside of Luanne's mind, frozen at the instant of her death.

"We have to go," the Cork said quietly. Ty'ger rose.

Outside the lounge Kilgarin and the Cook shut and locked the door behind them. The Cook worked the complicated punch-and-spin mechanism. His hands trembled as he fumbled at the controls. From within the sounds of struggle continued without abatement.

"There's nothing you can do for him," Kilgarin told the Cook. "You don't understand what he feels, what's happened to him."

"Maybe I do, a bit," the Cook said. He ran a hand through what remained of his hair, blinking at the display screen set over their booth, shifted his gaze to take in the rest of the recreation room. Ty'ger sat on a chair with padded armrests and back support; he lolled in it, unconscious. The Cook sighed, looking at the Centaurian. "Will you be OK with him here? I want to have a talk with the Captain."

"Why?" Kilgarin asked. "Things are quieter now. I've seen to that, now that I've had a chance to think."

"You can't keep Corking this ship alone, Kilgarin. You shouldn't have needed time to concentrate; you should have been ready to Cork immediately. The strain's telling on you, Killy. I'm going to ask the Captain to find another Cork to work with you when we reach Maylind."

"Don't do it, Cook," Kilgarin said evenly. "I don't need any help."

"The hell you don't."

"I said *I don't need any help.*" The Cork's voice went very soft. "Is that clear? I can handle this. I can handle it myself."

Mind-drive:

Kilgarin stands apart from the ship, in the Back Region. Here and there in the structure of the psi field he can see ripples of discontent. The emotions that destroy, the frustrations that will betray first the other members of the crew, and then ultimately, the self. There are madmen aboard the *Charter*, and their madness is visible in the lines of the mindship net. There are angry men aboard the *Charter*, and their anger, too, is visible.

Gently, Kilgarin touches. Mental fingers soothe, remove anger, relieve—for a moment—madness.

In a chamber near the Engineer's room a woman cries hysterically. Kilgarin reaches into her mind and sees the anguish that has grown from concern: she'd feared for her lover's life, now lost in an argument with another member of the crew. He sees also how the anguish is mixed with self-loathing: she'd seduced the other crew member; she'd been bored with her lover. In her mind the two were connected, though in reality they are not. He removes the self-loathing and leaves the anguish. The woman cries, but no longer does she think of hanging herself from the bulkhead. She stops twisting the rope in her hands.

He finds a group of Physicals leaving the lounge, stumbling in a daze. The force of their combined will is weaker than it should be, and Kilgarin sees why: when he touched them before, immediately after the fight in the mess hall, he'd been more brutal than necessary—he'd cut through their souls. Now they are empty, their emotions drained, and they themselves like husks. Gently he works to correct this. A push there; here, a guiding pressure. At first slowly, and then more quickly, he moves among them, returning lost motivation. He keeps the tension light, however, not allowing it to build anew. It does not take long.

Finished, he turns to other souls within the ship.

For many minutes he works, Corking the minds of the mindship field. He avoids the mind closest to him for as long as possible; it is not a task he relishes. Finally all else that can be done now is done, and he turns at last to Ty'ger.

Ty'ger's mental beacon is the strongest among the lights of the mind-drive, yet now the beacon is off shift, directed inward rather than out. Kilgarin digs deeply into the Centaurian's soul. He sees the Sensitive's despair. He sees the love—flawed, it is true, but love nonetheless—Ty'ger had felt for the girl Luanne. He sees the involvement of the Centaurian with the young Physical's life. The moments of intimacy shared, the thoughts held in common. He sees in it his own involvement with Lucille, and this realization upsets him. Kilgarin withdraws from the Centaurian's mind and readjusts the thin man's emotions from without. It is more difficult and the product is imperfect, but Kilgarin feels no desire to go further.

Leaving Ty'ger, he continues through the mind-field netting the ship. The evening lengthens before him.

He'd seen this kind of game before, but was unfamiliar with the *Charter*'s version of it, and so he remained in the recreation room after Ty'ger left, and sat in front of a console that connected with two display screens set equidistant on either side of the central console board.

On the left screen green mingled with blue. On the right, red with yellow. By adjusting tabs on the console, Kilgarin found he could direct the colors from one screen to seep into the other. If the adjustments were delicate enough, an optical effect would be created that would seem to bring a third set of colors into being directly before him. The third set of colors was an illusion, and its effectiveness depended on the deftness of the hands operating the controls. Kilgarin enjoyed the calming pastels he created in the center "display." Images came and went, sounds faded to a background whisper, and everything around him vanished—except the screen.

He came to abruptly when a hand brushed his shoulder. He was halfway off the console stool before he recognized the man above him. He sank back wearily. "You still don't understand Sensitives, do you, Raymond?" Kilgarin said. "When I'm Corking, I'm on the edge of my life. Don't ever cut into that, not if you want me to say sane."

"I'm sorry, Kilgarin. I just wanted to . . . well, apologize."

"Apologize for what?" the Cork asked.

"The way I behaved the other day," Raymond said uneasily. "I keep forgetting you've been under a strain, with your brother and . . . you see, I've got brothers and sisters too, and I know how I'd be if one of them died like Marc did. We're not so different, you and I. At first I thought we were, and it made me feel important knowing you—but I guess I expected too much. I'm sorry." He shrugged. "I know better now."

"How do you know better?" Kilgarin asked. He swung around, putting his back to the display screens.

"What you said about keeping to yourself. That's the way I've always been, only with me it's because no one would bother to pay Raymond Velacorte any attention. You, you're from one of the colony worlds, and I know what the colonies can do to people. I know what they almost did to me, but I had a reason to stop it from happening: nobody *wanted* to need me, so I had to *make* them need me, somehow. You never had that to worry about; you're the sort of person a fellow thinks he can depend on. J'kar, Marka, me . . . we thought you could take care of us. Especially J'kar. He even gave you his Contract."

Kilgarin waited. Raymond cleared his throat before continuing.

"We were wrong, of course. You didn't want that, any more than any colonist does. It's the way we're bred. Independence first, last, and always." Raymond laughed without humor. "The pioneer spirit."

"Which means?"

"You don't want us on your back. OK, we'll keep our distance. But Kilgarin, will you help us with one thing? It's important, and you may be the only man on this ship who can do something. No exaggeration. You know the facts as well as I do."

"J'kar."

"That's right," said Raymond. "Ever since Ryork was killed J'kar has been sick with fear. He doesn't know what to do. He's afraid to ask you for help, after the last rebuke you gave him—the gentle letdown. But he needs you, Killy. Ty'ger might listen to you; you're both Sensitives, and from what the Cook's told me, you've locked, so you *must* be able to reach him somehow." He let out a sigh, injured eyes focusing on Kilgarin. "He'll kill J'kar if you don't stop him. He will, or the strain will. Please help us, Killy. Please?"

Kilgarin looked down at his hands. "You've said one thing that's come close to being true, Raymond. Ty'ger and I are both Sensitives, and we've locked. I've seen the inside of his soul and he's seen mine. Perhaps he isn't all a man should be, but he's closer to what I think is right than you can ever be. He doesn't ask anything of me; he goes his own way. We've had fights, but he hasn't pushed them. We're friends, but he doesn't infringe on our friendship. You do."

Kilgarin reached into his tunic and pulled out something that flickered in the display screen light. It was a Contract disk. He held it out to Raymond.

"Thanks for reminding me about J'kar's Contract," he said. "Here's the disk I had made for him. I never asked for it. He can have it, or you can hold it for him. As far as I'm concerned that tears it."

"You're killing him, you know," Raymond said tightly.

"I don't think so," Kilgarin answered. "Are you going to take this or not?"

Raymond plucked the disk from Kilgarin's hand and dropped it in his pocket. His mouth opened and he almost began to speak; then he stopped; his eyes became hard; he turned and left.

Expressionless, Kilgarin returned his gaze to the game. Fingers pressed tabs, and an image formed slowly in the air before his eyes.

It was red. The warm color of blood.

Passing the custom stalls on Maylind after receiving his clearance, Kilgarin almost ran into several other people from the *Charter* crew. He stepped back under the awning of an open bar and watched Marka and Raymond walk by in a group of Physicals, and felt relieved when neither of his two former companions noticed him. J'kar, he saw, was still having his disk checked; the Centaurian stood with his arms folded nervously, his back to Kilgarin as he answered the port official's probing questions. Taking advantage of the opportunity, Kilgarin went around the stalls and through a push door, into the terminal proper.

Walking the length of the terminal, through a crowd of short, stubby people he decided were Maylindian colonists, Kilgarin passed merchant shops offering clothes in the current Outworld style: severe jackets cut at the waist, loose pants without pockets and blouses that looked as though they'd fit like a second skin. The colors were dark, not a red or an orange visible. The only concession to brightness Kilgarin saw was a white blouse in the display screen of a store that, unlike the other merchants, who advertised in the port but had their shops elsewhere, boasted a retail outlet on the main floor of the terminal. On impulse Kilgarin stopped and picked out one of the white shirts in the largest size the shopkeeper could find. He also bought a pair of slacks and a jacket—the former in the smallest size available. He tried the outfit on in the shop fresher. The pants were still loose, but the shirt fit nicely, showing a handsome bit of cloth at the wrists and neck. The shopkeeper clucked his disapproval when Kilgarin reappeared.

"It's your credit," the man said, "but I think you look awful. Sensitive?" he asked, indicating the blue uniform Kilgarin was stuffing in the disposal unit. Kilgarin grunted assent. "Staying long?" the shopkeeper asked.

"And if I am?"

"Not much work for Sensitives on Maylind," the shopkeeper said. "We've been having a bit of trouble with non-Physicals looking for port jobs. Company won't hire them. Factories have their own crews from Out-system, and farmers won't touch a Sensitive with a pole. So it's either your pension or the dole. Too many people without work; people in the city have begun thinking . . . you know?"

"Thanks for the advice," Kilgarin said. He paid and left.

In contrast to most colonial worlds, the central city of Maylind, Farway, was a subtle mixing of architectural styles. Normally the first independent government of a colony chose the style in which the capital would be built, as the Independence government had chosen Spanish Colonial on Endrim. Some ports were baroque, some Gothic, others Greek Modern; many had developed their own styles, differing from those imported from earth. The Maylindian port of Farway, however, had settled on a blending of several milieus. The streets were narrow and winding in the earth European manner, but the buildings rose to several dozen stories, creating a dense effect Kilgarin found disturbing. The buildings themselves were a peculiar combination of Romanesque and twentieth-century modern: slabs of stone and steel rising monolithically into the yellow afternoon sky. Few windows broke the walls of the towers, which Kilgarin supposed was due to either a lack of industry or resources—it had developed that on some planets, silica and limestone were extremely rare and difficult to obtain, thus limiting the availability of glass. Kilgarin found the blank effect of the unrelieved tower walls oppressive. He wondered how the absence of windows would affect the people who were forced to live and work in those buildings; even a starship had viewports and display screens. Kilgarin supposed the buildings of Farway had similar screens to provide a view of either the city or, more likely, the surrounding countryside. Though he realized the irony of the emotion in a spacer, Kilgarin thought it was an unsatisfactory way to live.

The streets were active, more or less. Children ran in and out of alleys, an occasional animal looked up out of the gutter, men and women bustled on mysterious errands. Kilgarin weaved through the light crowd with relative ease and soon found his way to a park located near the north gate of the city. Buying a bottle of local wine from a park vendor, he strolled along the grass-lined paths, looking for a spot to sit and drink. He found a place on a knoll overlooking a blue lake. Few pedestrians came near the lake, though an infrequent flier would cross its surface as a shortcut from one end of the park to another. Kilgarin settled down and watched the ripples which accompanied the passage of each flier. He wanted a few moments to think and decide what next to do.

One thing was clear. To date his efforts to learn the Captain's motive in killing Marc Kilgarin had been in vain. Wells had been a blind alley; unfortunately, Kilgarin could sense no other alleys to follow. He knew no more now than he did when he first met the man.

No—that wasn't true. Certain things were now obvious: the Captain's competence in a crisis situation and his corresponding incompetence in handling interpersonal affairs, such as the pressures on a mindship crew. In some way, Kilgarin knew this inability of the Captain tied in to the man's treatment of the Cork's brother, but until he was able to probe the Captain's mind, Kilgarin was helpless to discover *how*.

The question remained: what to do next? Kilgarin disliked the thought of a direct confrontation with the Captain. He'd avoided it because he felt the possible benefits were outweighed by the definite danger of permanently alienating the Captain. Now he wondered if he had any other choice.

He hadn't heard the Maylindian approaching and was startled when the squat man lowered himself and asked, "You going to hold that or drink it, buck?"

Kilgarin jerked around. "What?"

"I asked if you were going to drink it, that bottle you got. If not, I'll be glad to take it off your hands."

The Cork flustered. "I'm drinking it," he said. The Maylindian frowned with thick black eyebrows, scratched at a dangling moustache, and said nothing. Feeling increasingly uncomfortable, Kilgarin said, "Do you want a drink? Is that it?"

The other man lifted narrow shoulders. "I'd like one, 'less you prefer drinking alone."

"It doesn't matter," Kilgarin said. "Here." He handed the bottle over and stared as the Maylindian ripped out the plastic stopping and upended the bottle in his mouth with a single flicking motion. After several swallows, the stranger returned the bottle, sighing.

"Not as good as what we used to have," he said, "but serves the purpose fine. You're not from around here, are you? Noticed the way you dress, not many people dress like that in Farway."

"I'm off the *Charter*," Kilgarin said.

"Heard another ship landed. Haven't had too many out this way, last month or so. Trouble in the colonies; guess it's slowing up trade. Getting harder to find good liquor every day. Your ship bringing any?"

"Some absinthe from Endrim."

"Now *that's* drinking. Say, my name's Hans Reedy. Used to be a Physical myself, till I dropped ship here in Farway. Pension's kept me in bed and board, but not much left over for drinking, which is why I bothered you, you seeming friendly and all. Want to thank you for that, by the way."

"Forget it. My name's Kilgarin, James Kilgarin. Out of Wellington."

"Have a hand, Jamie."

"Call me Kilgarin." They shook; Reedy's palm was moist in the Cork's hand.

"Now," the squat man said, "how about another hit of that wine?"

Kilgarin had no idea why he concealed his Sensitivity from Reedy; it just seemed to happen—the man assumed Kilgarin was another Physical, and at first Kilgarin didn't think to set him right. By the time it became apparent that the two men would be spending more than a few casual moments together, Kilgarin had already learned enough about Reedy's attitudes to know what he could expect if he revealed his true position.

"Those Sensitives," Reedy had said when they first started drinking, "you see them everywhere, and you know what? They've always got credit, even the pensioned ones. I'm dying of thirst and those Sneeks are taking baths in absinthe. It's true. Company keeps them fed like they were made of limestone or something."

"They need them for the ships, don't they?"

"They need *us* too, but you don't see Physicals getting six-year Contracts. Term Contracts, that's all, and not even full insurance. I get a leg broke, I get my pension, nothing else. A Sensitive goes stupid in his head, he gets a pension and enough insurance credit to live on for ten, fifteen years. What kind of fair is that?"

"If he breaks a Contract, he's in as bad shape as you are. And insurance credit doesn't help a man if he's insane."

"Hey, what do you care about those Sneeks, anyway? They're stiffing you as much as they're stiffing me."

"I thought you were being too simple about it, that's all."

"Hell, what's so complex about being robbed?"

Part of what kept Kilgarin from telling Reedy the truth was his desire to learn more about the Outworld situation. He had a growing suspicion that his trouble with the Captain was tied to the rebellion brewing in the colonies, and he wanted to learn as much about the rebellion as he could. At least, he *thought* that was his reason.

He and Reedy had a meal in a dome tavern on the far end of the lake. Kilgarin paid. Reedy led him to a seat near a clear plastic wall, the only one Kilgarin had seen so far in Farway, and insisted Kilgarin take the outer seat. Kilgarin found himself eating on a transparent platform six meters off the lake's surface. Reedy explained that the tavern was usually frequented only by Company factory employees. "They're the only ones can afford it," he said.

While they ate, Kilgarin and the Physical talked.

"Now what we've been planning, some of the others and me"—Reedy paused and scratched at his moustache—"well—how long have you been in the Outworlds, Kilgarin?"

"Six years. Since I left Wellington."

"Then you know how the colonists are?"

"They seem tough. A bit hard."

"That's the word, Kilgarin. I'm from earth myself, from North America, province called Canamer, and that's pretty hard land—but these Outworlders, they beat anything I ever saw at home. They have this plan, they want their *own* system—you see? They figure the Sneeks and the Company have done enough to them, to us, to everyone. You see that?"

"I understand what you're saying," Kilgarin said. He forked greens into his mouth from the plate before him, chewed. He preferred the ship's algae product to natural-grown greens, but sometimes enjoyed the variation.

"You do? Good. Maybe you'd like to meet some of the men hey?"

"Sure."

"You're OK, Kilgarin." Reedy nodded thoughtfully. "Yeah, you'll meet them tonight."

"You didn't just come over to me at random, did you?" Kilgarin asked. Reedy shook his head, laughing.

"I saw you, I knew what kind of guy you are. The way you were holding that bottle you looked like the last guy in the world. You know? Sure. People get pushed around, they get confused, don't know what they're going to do . . . they look like you did. I saw you, I knew where your mind was, and I figured you and I'd have the same things in common. Figured you'd want to meet the others. Like that." He snapped his fingers.

"Like that," Kilgarin said, and thought: *That's the way it is to be a Physical. You can never know for certain where you stand. You're always guessing and depending on body language. Just as I'm guessing about the Captain.*

He joined Reedy in his laugh. For Kilgarin the laugh was bitter.

"Hey, what's wrong?"

"I thought I saw—would you wait here a moment?"

"Sure. I'll be inside. You want me to order you a beer too, Kilgarin?"

"Do that," Kilgarin said. He left Reedy and crossed the street down which they'd been walking, dodged a groundcar that bleered! at him as he waved it aside, and trotted to the corner.

The street beyond was busy with people, but nowhere did he see the two men he'd glimpsed a moment before.

Reluctantly he recrossed the street and joined Reedy in the bar the Physical had indicated. Reedy gave him the beer he'd ordered for Kilgarin, and the bartender handed the Cork the tab.

"What was that all about, anyway?" Reedy asked him.

Kilgarin looked for the bartender, who'd taken his credit chit.

"Just two men who shouldn't be together," he said. "Two former friends of mine."

Reedy looked confused, then shrugged. "Your business," he said. Draining his glass, he added, "Another beer?"

Twilight turned the Maylindian sky a mellow orange and traced the clouds with tinted gold along their western edge. Repeatedly Kilgarin's gaze went to the part of the sky visible between the high buildings, and repeatedly he had to force his attention back to the ground, and the route Reedy was taking through the alleys of Farway.

Even the most modern cities had their slums, an area where the poor and disadvantaged collected in communal misery, and Farway was no exception. The streets Reedy led Kilgarin along were dark, the pavements cracked and worn: it was the oldest section of the city, and though it wasn't in the same state of disrepair as its counterpart in Endrim, the area gave off the same aura of weariness and apathy. Kilgarin wondered why Reedy's friends found it necessary to meet in a ghetto, and then decided that many—if not all—of them were probably from the ghetto area. Crippled Physicals, pensioned crew, colonists who'd emigrated to Maylind to find a job and found instead that all the jobs were spoken for—these would be the revolutionaries, Kilgarin was sure. He sympathized with the Outworlders in principle, though he found the application of the principle distasteful: he couldn't blame the Sensitives for the Company's oppression, and he didn't think this was solely because he was a Sensitive himself.

"We've got a place in the basement of a confab," Reedy said. "Belongs to Conners. He rents it on the side."

Kilgarin said nothing. He followed the Physical up a flight of steps to a wide court. Several buildings larger than any Kilgarin had seen in Farway faced the court, their lobbies brightly lit in contrast to their upper stories. Reedy skirted the edge of the court, slipped down a passage between buildings, and halted in front of a plastisteel door. Kilgarin watched as the squat man put his palm against a checkplate beside the jamb. The plate glowed and the door cycled open. Reedy shook his hand, laughing wryly as he gestured Kilgarin inside. "Always burns a bit," he said.

Another flight of stairs led downward, around a corner to a second door. Reedy pressed a call tab and the speaker grill asked his name. He gave it, the door opened, and Kilgarin followed him in.

Kilgarin's first impression of Conners was amazement at the man's size. Conners hulked at least two and a half meters tall, with shoulders half again as broad as a normal man's, hands that were each as massive as both of Kilgarin's, and arms that dangled to Conners's mid-thigh. After size what impressed Kilgarin was Conners's face: the revolutionary's features were ascetic, aquiline—completely self-possessed. He greeted Kilgarin with a grim nod and indicated that he and Reedy were to take seats with the others.

"We were talking about this ship of yours, Kilgarin," Conners said after Reedy had introduced Kilgarin and explained the Cork's background. "From what we hear, she's a hate ship. Is that so?"

"That's what she's been called," Kilgarin said.

"A man we have in the port tells us there was trouble aboard the *Charter* two days ago, before she landed on Maylind."

Kilgarin related the incident. Conners inclined his head as he listened, his eyes shifting as he took in the expressions of the other men and women in the room. When Kilgarin finished, Conners said, "It's happened all across the Arm, then. Thank god. If what we're planning is only local to Maylind, we'd be dead. But if the Company can be kept busy jumping from outbreak to outbreak, we *may* have a chance after all."

"That's a little much to hope for, Franklyn," a squarish man on a bench not far from Kilgarin said. "I think we'd do best to work with whatever we can expect to encounter here, and not depend on outside influences to save our outstretched necks."

"Of course, Orlando," Conners said wearily. "We've been through that, and we've made our decision." To Kilgarin: "I'm sorry if we seem a bit disorganized, but, as usually happens in groups like ours, though we all agree on ends, we don't all agree on means. Some of us, including Orlando, opt for violent revolution; others, for what they call educational evolution—showing the Company our wants and needs, in effect educating them to our condition. Recently our more patient colleagues decided to abandon us as hotheads, and for the past few days we've been trying to finalize a course of action. We haven't yet all agreed on what to do. When you've been a member of our group a little longer, you'll be allowed to assist in our plans—but for now, I think, we'd simply like to learn a little more about you."

"Precisely," said a woman behind Conners. "Tell us about yourself."

Kilgarin did, omitting all reference to his Sensitivity. Conners listened without expression, while those around the group's leader showed varying degrees of interest. Least attentive was Reedy, who wandered over to a table stocked with bottles and casks of wine and beer, and after opening an ale for himself, the Physical got one for Kilgarin, handing it to the Cork as he regained his seat beside him. Kilgarin nursed the bottle, using it to cover what he felt must be the obvious trembling in his hand's. He didn't like the emotions he felt surrounding him; if the men and women in the room discovered he was not a Physical, he would be dead inside of a minute.

Finishing his story, glad for the verbal ability he'd always possessed and taken for granted, Kilgarin paused for a long swallow of ale. He closed his eyes as he did, and shut his mind to the feelings of those around him. If the reaction to his story was negative, Kilgarin preferred not to know until action was taken. There was, after all, little he could do. He was on their ground.

Conners cleared his throat. He glanced at the woman behind him. Kilgarin opened his eyes. The woman's face was hard, her eyes unreadable, but she inclined her head in a curt nod, and when Conners turned back to Kilgarin he was smiling. "Well," Conners said, extending his hand, "you're in."

Kilgarin laughed and grasped the outstretched hand.

"Essentially what we want to do is this," Conners said, resting an arm around Kilgarin's shoulder and pointing at a spot on the diagram on the table before them. "The main processing plants for the Company are here, sixteen levels below ground in the third building of this complex. That's where they refine the hide, press it, add the preservatives to the juices; it's where they make the milk. If there's any single place on Maylind which is paramount to the Company's operations on this planet, that's it."

"I'm not sure I understand," Kilgarin said. "What's this 'milk'?"

The woman who'd spoken earlier answered Kilgarin's question. "You know what Yrrl Root is? You've drunk absithe? You've eaten Brex? Bloodmilk is the same kind of thing, a narcotic. If you're not an addict of the drink, you probably have never heard of it. Its highly specialized."

"And makes quite a profit for the Company," Orlando added.

"I can imagine," Kilgarin said, peering at the diagram more closely. "Cutting down on their production will probably hurt them badly."

"Not just cutting down, Kilgarin," Conners said. "We intend to cut it off completely."

"By destroying the plant?"

"By destroying the plant," Conners agreed.

Kilgarin sighed. "That's a bit ambitious."

"We don't have the patience for anything less ambitious," the woman said quietly. "We've been pushed to extremes."

"Do you honestly think this is the answer?" Kilgarin looked around at them. Reedy, he saw, was drunk; the man's head rested on his folded arms, his mouth fluttering in a snore. "I've worked on the rim for six years, and there've always been plans to cut off the Company. Do you know why none of them have worked? Because the people behind them have always ignored the economics of the situation's existence. This colony stays alive because of this—what do you call it, 'bloodmilk'? Wipe that out and you wipe yourselves out, never mind the Company."

"That's a simplistic attitude, Kilgarin," Orlando said. "Admittedly, there's a risk involved—"

"Risk is the least of your worries. Understand, I'm not saying anything against your revolution. But try to go about it realistically. Ask yourselves this: is Maylind self-supporting? Do you need Company products to survive? Are your farming tools home produced? Listen, I was on a world where every piece of machinery was rented from the Company—and none of it was self-replicating or repairing. Do you understand what that meant? The planet *needed* Company engineers to fix the crop harvesters, the planters, the processing machines—and all of the repair equipment was kept off planet. Ditto the men to repair them. The result: effective slavery."

"You're not telling us anything new," Conners said. "We're aware of the situation here. That's what we're trying to change."

"But don't you see you can't go about it violently? If you do, you'll only be hurting yourselves. I want change as much as you do, perhaps more: I work on a mindship. I have to live with the Company daily. I've suffered at their hands, their collective hands—so listen to me when I tell you, *this is not the way.*"

He paused for a moment and looked at the colonists standing around the table. They were watching him intently. Orlando was frowning; the woman smiling wryly. Conners, again, was expressionless.

Shaking himself, Kilgarin let out a sigh, relaxing. "First of all, you have to make Maylind self-supporting. Revolutions on alien planets are not like the revolutions we read about that happened on earth. Earth is basically friendly to man. Most other planets aren't. The Company helps keep your colony alive. Before you can get rid of the Company you have to tame this world . . . completely."

He glanced up. "Do you understand that?"

The woman's laugh was harsh, bitter. She glared at Conners, her smile vanishing. "Well? Are you going to answer him? Are you going to tell him what we've been through?" When Conners said nothing, she screeched, *"Are you going to tell him?"*

Conners started and shifted his gaze from Kilgarin to the woman. "If that's the way he feels, Grenna, there's nothing I can tell him." His attention returned to Kilgarin. "You say you want change, Kilgarin, but you refuse to accept the risk of change. I was going to ask you to help in our efforts, but now I think it's best simply to ask you to leave . . . and to think about what's been said here. I think, in some way you're not even aware of, you're tied to the Company. Possibly you're right in your beliefs. We may be risking too much. But that's something only we can decide, because only we've lived through the oppression from *this* perspective. For you, the solution may be different. Perhaps. I won't pretend to have all the answers . . . and neither should you.

"Reedy will take you back to the port. Grenna, wake him up and set the two of them on their way."

This was done. At the door, Conners gripped Kilgarin's shoulder and leaned close to him. "I want you to know you came very close to being killed. It's only because I believe you meant well that you're leaving here alive." His hand dropped, and he said, "Don't make me regret it, Kilgarin."

Calmer now—strangely calm, he thought—Kilgarin said, "It's your affair, Conners. I hope you're doing the right thing."

"So do I," Conners said, studying him.

Kilgarin went out the door, Reedy at his side.

The port area was splashed with light from the spots to aid the repair crews working on the ships being readied for lift-off. Harsh shadows stalked the field as Kilgarin left the terminal and struck out in the direction of the *Charter*, which occupied a pad apart from the other ships many of which had been on Maylind for several weeks—near an unloading conveyor.

There was no one visible around the ship; the pad was deserted, silent but for the continuous hum of the equipment working to unload the *Charter*'s hold and replace its contents with a shipment—Kilgarin supposed—of bloodmilk. Kilgarin wondered where the watch crew was. Procedure demanded a three-man team on hand during all trade operations, including cargo transfer. The team's absence was ominous.

He took the ramp up to the air lock in three bounds, entered the ship, and called for the watch officer. No one answered.

The halls were empty. So were both the recreation room and the cafeteria lounge. There was not a sound other than the whisper of the ship's LS system and the hum of the unloading equipment. He probed—no one was board. He was alone.

Back on the ramp he looked around the field and saw a port mechanic sitting on a pile of crates not too far away. Kilgarin hurried in that direction.

"The *Charter?* You mean that Sneek ship on pad twelve? Yeah, I saw it, you don't need to point it out. Sure must have been an hour ago, some sort of commotion. Only about fifteen people there, I guess, everybody else in town, but those fifteen, they lit out like a fire was after them. How'd I know where they went? I'm just waiting for my relief, Fellow."

He found them on a side street on the fringe of Farway's Sensitive District. The psi blast was "audible" from a mile away, the mingled emotions of the *Charter*'s crew acting as a beacon to guide him against his will. And it was against his will. Kilgarin didn't want to see what he knew he'd find when he reached the crowd, but he had no choice. Like a moth to flame, he was drawn to his doom.

He was dead: Kilgarin saw that immediately. There'd been no doubt in the Cork's mind, ever since he'd missed the man's presence when he scanned the crowd. He'd hoped there'd be some other explanation, that perhaps the Centaurian was unconscious or in a coma—anything but the finality of death. Until the last possible moment Kilgarin refused to accept the reality of what had happened. He knew that if he did, he'd be forced to accept culpability as well.

The two of them were in the center of the crowd, one kneeling over the other, his hands bloody, his jump suit soiled with garbage from the gutter in which they'd fought. The crew members parted as Kilgarin pressed against them, until he stepped into the circle occupied by Ty'ger and J'kar. Kilgarin looked at the dead man and felt a sting of agony. The Centaurian's neck was mottled, the skin pierced by the white edge of a broken bone. His eyes were open and staring, already glazing, already dull. Kilgarin knelt and closed them. The other kneeling man stirred, but said nothing.

"You should have helped J'kar when we asked you to," a voice said behind Kilgarin. "This wouldn't have happened, if you—"

"Shut up," Kilgarin said. He didn't need to look to know it was Raymond who'd spoken. "I know it," the Cork said, "I know it, I know it."

He searched the eyes of the Centaurian with the bloody hands, and asked him, "Will you forgive me?"

There was no light of understanding in the other man's eyes. His mind was gone, Kilgarin knew; the Cork's question had been rhetorical.

J'kar would never answer.

Chapter Nine

Tenth month, second day, anno Domini 3146

"Ty'ger never had a chance, not really," Raymond said. "J'kar was twice his size, half again as strong. He may have been frightened by Ty'ger, but in a struggle J'kar had to win. Ty'ger pushed him, and pushed him, until all J'kar could do was defend himself . . . even then, I don't think he intended to . . . it just happened. Now he's cracked up, broken completely, finished. He's ruined, Kilgarin. How does that make you feel?"

They were outside the clinic where they'd left the shattered Centaurian. Kilgarin had said nothing since that moment in the alleyway several hours before; he'd listened, accepting Raymond's verbal attack, not letting it touch him. Now he roused himself to ask, "When did it happen? How? I thought J'kar was avoiding Ty'ger, but I saw the two of them walking together this afternoon . . . or thought I did. I didn't believe it . . . "

"Ty'ger came to J'kar an hour before we all left the ship. He told him he wanted to end the feud. He said he'd been wrong to blame J'kar for what happened to his family. I was there, and I thought Ty'ger was sincere . . . but I'm not a Sensitive, I couldn't know." He glanced at Kilgarin coldly. "Neither could J'kar. He wanted so badly to see an end to the trouble, he bought Ty'ger's story. He didn't have a choice, did he?"

Kilgarin was silent. He'd closed himself from the Physical's emotional attack hours before; the verbal assault meant nothing. Kilgarin felt isolated, filled with emotions he couldn't comprehend. He wanted time to think. He needed time.

Finally he said, "I am sorry, you know."

Raymond stared at him. "That's fine, Kilgarin," he said. "That's just fine."

As though that was what he'd been waiting to say all the time the two of them had stood outside the clinic, Raymond sighed and moved away. Kilgarin covered his eyes and listened to the sound of the young man's footsteps fading into the night. Soon the sound was gone and Kilgarin was alone.

Once he found the pub he became drunk very quickly. Bloodmilk didn't taste as bitter as he expected it to; it was sweet and rather syrupy, like a kind of honey he'd tasted once when he visited earth. The bartender advised him to go slowly, but Kilgarin paid little attention.

He passed out after his third drink.

When he woke he went in search of Reedy, and found the squat Physical in the park, eating crackers out of a paper bag and sitting on a bench not far from the spot where he'd introduced himself to Kilgarin. Reedy looked up as Kilgarin approached, stared, swallowed, and got to his feet, dropping the paper bag and wiping his hands on the sides of his pants.

"Kilgarin, hey, we were hoping you'd show up again." He grinned, offering Kilgarin his hand. The Cork took it and pressed it briefly. Reedy's smile waned. "Hey, you OK? You look like you've been drinking."

"I have," Kilgarin said.

"Well, we all get a little now and then, right? Listen, what made you change your mind? Seeing things Conners's way after all?"

"Not exactly," Kilgarin said. Reedy's face puckered into a frown, but the little man pried no further.

Conners, on the other hand, apparently felt no need to be delicate. He was frankly suspicious of Kilgarin's change of heart, and said as much when Reedy brought the Cork before him. The three of them stood in the anteroom of a factory located in the central industrial area, an outlet for the processing plant where Conners worked. The large man's face and hands were smudged with grease and sweat, and Kilgarin found his appearance disturbing and, in a way, intimidating.

"You expect me to believe you've turned around completely in your thinking?" Conners asked. He peered at the Cork intently. "Why, Kilgarin? Why should I accept that?"

"That's not what I said," Kilgarin replied.

"Last night you thought we were committing suicide. Now—?"

"Last night I was sure of myself. Since then I've had to question some of my reasons for doing things . . . for thinking things."

"And you've decided you were wrong?"

"No," Kilgarin said. "I've decided my reasons were wrong."

Forehead wrinkling, Conners said, "Give me that again, Kilgarin?"

"Listen. On a planet called Endrim, I own a bordello. I turn a nice trade; or at least I expect to when I get back. It's occurred to me that maybe I was trying to protect my interests in the Company economy when I told you that what you were planning was a mistake. If that's true, it isn't fair to me, or to you. A man shouldn't let something like that affect his moral judgment. That's why I'm here. I have to help you, to find out if some of my other ideas were wrong also. Mostly I'm here to get a handle on myself before my ship lifts for Centauri. I have to decide if I want to be on it when it does."

Conners rubbed a grease-darkened hand along his jaw thoughtfully. "Strange thinking, Kilgarin. Most people settle for a code they can apply to everything. You seem to want something to fit every situation as it comes up. Just be careful you don't ask others to be as hard on themselves as you are. You'll be disappointed. You might also be killed." He regarded Kilgarin a moment, then asked, "What brought on the self-doubt?"

"I let a man be killed, and I let another man destroy himself. I got drunk. It made me think."

"I imagine it would," Conners said. He grunted. "I should throw you out of here, and Reedy with you"—the squat man cringed—"but I've a feeling *that* would be a mistake. I don't quite know what to do with you, Kilgarin . . . but I'll think of something."

He strode away, and Kilgarin realized that he and Reedy were dismissed. Looking down at the Physical, Kilgarin said, "Come on, friend. I'll buy you a drink."

Reedy was talkative until he had his second absinthe and beer; then he became silent, speaking only now and then to ask Kilgarin a question. The Cork, on the other hand, became more verbose as the afternoon wore on. He preferred absinthe's familiar sweetness to the milk he had the night before, and was working two drinks to the Physical's one before a full hour had passed. Eventually he told Reedy about Marka, and what had transpired on the *Charter* between them.

"If you felt that way about her, why'd you let her go?" Reedy asked him at one point. Kilgarin stirred the bit of plastic that bobbed in his glass, and lifted his eyes to take in the midafternoon shadows filling the open-air tavern bar.

"If I knew the answer to that, maybe I wouldn't have pushed her," Kilgarin said.

"Do you want to know?"

"I'm not sure," Kilgarin replied. "I have to give it time. I'm beginning to understand things about myself I never thought about before."

"Things are coming up fast, aren't they?" Reedy asked sympathetically.

"A bit too fast," Kilgarin said.

Another time Reedy prodded Kilgarin in the ribs with a bony elbow, ending a joke that had reminded the Cork painfully of Lucille. "Imagine getting burned by two men at once," the Physical said. "Wouldn't want to be that girl for anyone's credit."

"Neither would I," Kilgarin said.

On their way back to Conners's basement apartment, Kilgarin and Reedy paused at the port on Kilgarin's insistence. The terminal was empty—it was almost midnight—and the gates leading to the pad area were closed. Kilgarin didn't go near the gates, however. He stopped by a wall-sized window that showed the six ships that were in port, five in-system shuttles and one starship: the *Charter*. Kilgarin couldn't tell whether the *Charter*'s cargo doors were open or not, but he supposed they weren't—no spotlights were directed on the ship to aid in the loading and unloading. At this time of night, despite the brilliant starlight from the galactic spiral filling the sky, spots would be necessary if any work was to be done.

The ship would be leaving in the morning, then.

Next to him, Reedy asked, "You want anything here?"

"Perhaps," Kilgarin said, "but not now."

The Physical checked his watch, replaced the pendant in its case. "We'd better hurry," he said. "Conners wants to be started before 0200."

Kilgarin nodded and they continued on their way.

"You and Reedy are going to stay here on watch," Conners told Kilgarin. "Orlando, Grenna, Halford, and I will go down there together. If we're gone for more than fifteen minutes—fifteen minutes *exactly,* Reedy—get out of here. The antimatter mines will go off automatically, taking most of this building with them. You know what to do if anyone shows up before then. Are your weapons in order? Kilgarin, you're sure you don't want one?"

"I'm not sure of anything," Kilgarin said. "You'd better keep your pistol."

The large man shrugged. Light from the processing plant's lobby played off the pillars surrounding the group, casting shadows that hid features and expressions. "I hope you know what you're doing," Conners said. He eyed the cask of wine under Kilgarin's arm. "Grenna, Orlando, you come with me. Halford, three meters behind. Wish us luck, Kilgarin."

"Luck," Kilgarin said. Reedy echoed it. The two men watched as Conners and the rest slipped through the open doorway into the lobby proper, each of the rebels carefully stepping over the Company guard who was lying unconscious outside the door arch.

"Nervous?" Reedy asked.

"A little," Kilgarin admitted. He glanced at the building above them. Several of the windows were lit, sparkling in the darkness and acting as a set of spotlights pinpointing the Company's wealth and the planet's priorities: no other building in Farway had as much glass for simple decoration. No other agency could afford to import it.

"Do you think they'll make it?" Reedy asked.

"They're trying," Kilgarin said. "That's all that matters."

And wasn't that the difference between these men and the crew of the mindship? These colonists were prepared to take their lives into their own hands, while the crew allowed themselves to drift from incident to incident, without goal or direction. For Kilgarin, that latter course had become suddenly intolerable.

Yet as he thought this, Kilgarin sent his mind probing outward through the darkness ahead, into the bright light of the lobby. He "felt" the light as an ethereal obstruction, something he was forced to push aside in order to reach the object of his probe. Gently, he touched his goal. He sifted through the layers of his subject's forebrain and passed into the subconscious, where he could watch without disturbing. Conners was unaware of Kilgarin's presence, and that was precisely how Kilgarin wanted things to remain.

The view through Conners's eyes was distorted, as vision always was for Kilgarin when he took on another man's perceptions. Here and there the tones of the colors were slightly off, the textures on some objects too refined, on others too vague, the depth perception extended too far—or not extended enough. Sound also was a difficulty, coming at a different pitch. Conners's whispered instructions to the other members of his team were harsh to Kilgarin's mental ear; at first, the Cork could barely understand the words. He heard them as though through a filter, as they echoed in the large man's mind.

According to the plan Kilgarin had lifted from his host's memory, each of the four rebels carried a supply of industrial-quality antimatter, in shaped charges designed by Conners and Orlando. In his capacity as an engineer at the plant that processed the AM for fliers, Conners had been able to obtain enough of the material to destroy thirty cubic meters of the narcotics plant—enough to kill the Company operation on Maylind for at least six months, till replacement machinery could be built and imported from other of the colony planets. Six months was long enough, by Conners's figuring, for the rebels to completely undermine the strength of the Company colonial government. As the large man kept reminding himself, a government that starved its constituents could not long remain in power. It was Conners's plan to instigate that "starving," which would be chiefly a reduction in Maylindian luxury.

Through the leader's eyes, Kilgarin saw a flight of stairs leading to the subbasements. Conners and Grenna jogged down the steps, while Halford and Orlando went to investigate another passage indicated on the blueprints Conners's agents had stolen.

In the stairwell, only every third glowplate was lit, and as a result the stairs were shadowed with crisscrossings of gray and black, where the glow filtered through the stair railings and onto the lower walls. Kilgarin felt himself pitching forward as Conners took the steps three at a time. At last a door loomed; he saw Conners's hand slap an entrance plate on the wall next to it. The door slid open and Conners and Grenna slipped inside.

The processing room was immense—at least, that small part of it that was visible. Kilgarin knew, from Conners's memory, that this was only a portion of the entire factory, and even at that, the chamber was impressive. Walls stretched into an arch far overhead, joining over an array of catwalks that held Kilgarin in fascination when Conners glanced upward. Here and there spotlights were set into the bottoms of the walkways, each light directed in such a manner as to light a block of the deck below. Kilgarin counted quickly before Conners turned away. Sixteen spots. The architect had been a master: the room was at least two hundred meters square, and that the designer had managed to illuminate that much floor space with so little in the way of lights and reflectors was a feat Kilgarin could respect. Conners, he knew, would not understand this. With a start which broke his contact with the rebel, Kilgarin realized that J'kar *would* have understood—even in his former state of near-madness—and what was more, would have commented on it in a way that would have made it something both he and Kilgarin could share.

He shook himself, and found that he was crouched beside Reedy next to a pillar on the plaza outside the glass-walled lobby.

"Are you OK?" the small man was asking him. Kilgarin nodded. "You looked bad there a moment," Reedy said. "I wanted to be sure you weren't sick or anything."

"I'm fine," Kilgarin said. He returned to his place in Conners's soul.

The large man and Grenna had walked several meters into the chamber, and Conners was directing her toward a massive machine set in the center of the wide space beyond the archway, connected to several wide tubes of plastisteel. Without a word the woman slid into kneeling position under one of the polished cables. Conners strode around the processing unit and found another bulky machine against the far wall. He too bent and unstrapped the pack he carried on his shoulder. Several items were inside, neatly arranged. Conners removed them and placed them in order on the floor before the machine. The only thing Kilgarin recognized was the cube of an AM power pack.

"Open up that cask," Kilgarin said to Reedy. The Physical complied, snapping off the top and offering Kilgarin the first swallow. The Cork took it and drank for a long half-minute. Reedy's face went from polite interest to concern to outright dismay. Kilgarin didn't seem to notice.

Six minutes later the packs were set and the rebels were on their way back to the lobby. Kilgarin had made spot checks with the other two members of the team, Halford and Orlando, and had found them performing similar duties in another section of the plant. Each rebel in both teams worked with a mechanical precision Kilgarin didn't understand, even when he witnessed it from within their leader. It seemed as though they'd disconnected their minds and were acting on reflex, letting training assume control of their bodies for the time it took to plant the makeshift bombs. Now that the operation was completed, however, personality was returning to the teammates, and two of them—Orlando and Conners—were eager to escape. Kilgarin sympathized. The empathetic tension he'd experienced during the bomb placement was too strong for his strained nerves. He wanted the evening to be over.

In a minute, it almost was.

Conners and Grenna were on the staircase when the Company guards hit Orlando and Halford. Kilgarin heard the weapon fire from two sets of ears: his own and Conners's. Instantly he drove more deeply into the large man's mind, sending directions to the motor control of Conner's brain, making the man's hand snap up, latch onto Grenna's wrist, and literally drag the woman upward, four steps at a time.

"Conners, what is it?" she shouted at him, "What's wrong?"

Conners didn't answer. His personality was in a state of shock, stunned at seeing his body act without his instructions. He watched from a corner of his mind as his body launched itself for the door to the lobby, struck and went through, rolling to the floor automatically, and pulled Grenna down with it, thus ducking the burst of weapon fire that tore off the top half of the swinging door. Conners watched, amazed, as his body came to its knees and threw itself with a kick across two meters of space to land heavily against a Company guard holding a rifle. He gaped within his mind as his body fought a battle without his active control.

Kilgarin, however, realized that something was wrong. Though moving more rapidly than it could have done under Conners's direction, the rebel body was still reacting sluggishly to Kilgarin's commands. It was not the smooth lock Kilgarin had felt with Raymond, nor was it the tense linking the Cork had experienced with Ty'ger—rather, it was painfully incomplete, as though Kilgarin's hands were holding Conners's and forcing them to move, instead of guiding them from within.

Something was wrong with the linking, and if Conners was to survive, Kilgarin had to discover where the wrongness lay and correct it quickly, before the moment was past.

Outside the lobby, Reedy was on his feet, clutching the wine cask to his body with trembling hands. "It's Conners, all right, Kilgarin. That's him on the floor. And Grenna too. They've got to get out of there, Kilgarin. The guards haven't gotten this far yet, maybe they can still escape. But they've got to get out of there."

Grenna was on her feet now, Kilgarin saw. He stared at the woman in the lobby.

"There's nothing we can do," Reedy said behind him. "There's nothing we can do."

Grenna did a dance. Like most colonists she'd been taught the art of self-defense at an early age, for use against the unknown dangers of a new world. Now she used it against the known dangers of an old one.

Her foot came up in an arc that ended in an attacking guard's jaw. The jaw splintered unter the skin; Kilgarin could see the shape go out of the man's face. Grenna carried through with the kick, ending the motion with a dip forward and back, straightened fingers of her hands poking into the soft material of another guard's chest. From this she moved into a balletlike motion Kilgarin couldn't follow. The motion ended and another man fell to the floor, squirming. Startled with the violence of the act, Kilgarin also squirmed—uneasily.

Conners was recovering from his leap, pushing himself off the body of the man he'd thrown to the floor and casting his glance about as though he were wondering what he was still doing in the plant lobby. Across from Conners a door opened and more guards stumbled into the hall. Grenna noticed them at the same moment as Conners, but Kilgarin saw the men just an instant before.

He eased into the rebel's brain.

Who is that? What are you doing to me?

Kilgarin ignored the question and swung Conners's body into action. A moment later, the question came again.

What are you doing to me? Who are you?

Reedy's hand touched Kilgarin's shoulder. "It's fifteen minutes," the small man said.

"So?" Kilgarin's eyes were unfocused. He couldn't see Reedy's face, but he could feel the Physical's hot breath on his neck.

"That's how long Conners said we were to wait. He said we were to get out if it was any longer. You heard him, Kilgarin. The packs are going off at any moment." The squat man's voice shattered and he choked into silence. Kilgarin ignored him, concentrating on developing the link with Conners's mind.

Something surged in the subconscious Kilgarin had invaded. A part of Conners was straining for dominance. Kilgarin sensed that the trouble was here: the core of the problem, the failure of the linking here, with Conners. He stepped back from the motor responses and centered his attention on that portion of Conners's brain that was fighting him. The Cork sensed disorientation and fear; to quell Conners's disturbance, Kilgarin opened his memory and allowed the Physical in. He expected the rebel's distress to fade, but instead the man's struggling increased.

What's wrong? Kilgarin asked. *I've given you all the information you need.*

Get out of my mind, Conners's mental voice came back: *Stop treating me like a Company* puppet, *dammit!*

Kilgarin dropped back, shocked. *A Company puppet?*

For god's sake, let me fight my own battles—the words tumbled in Kilgarin's mind, emotional, irrational—*get out of my mind—get out—get out—!*

For a moment Kilgarin debated doing this, then decided against it. There was too much at stake. He wanted to hurt the Company, and hurt it badly. Conners *had* to win, and Kilgarin would see to it that he did—for Kilgarin would be in control.

From that instant on, Conners's body began to crumble.

The legs went first. Kilgarin felt the knees buckling as he tried to drive Conners into two guards who'd arrived through an entrance at the rear of the lobby. Gravity seemed to jerk the Physical downward; it required all of Kilgarin's will to force Conners to remain standing, and he had barely enough strength left to bring the rebel's hand up in a sweep that intersected the guard's throat—with little effect. The guard stumbled back, coughing, and his companion slipped past him, grabbing Conners and heaving the rebel backward. Something caught Conners's heel, his legs collapsed, and the large man went down.

"Come on, Kilgarin, we've got to get out of here."

"Shut up, Reedy."

"You won't come, I'm going alone."

"Then go."

The small man's hand fell from Kilgarin's shoulder. Distantly the Cork heard Reedy's breathing become harsher as the Physical struggled with himself. Finally there were footsteps that faded, and Kilgarin knew he was alone in the plaza behind the pillar support.

The struggle in the lobby was almost finished. Grenna had been borne down by three guards, two holding her arms and a third clinging to her legs desperately. She was screaming and cursing in languages unfamiliar to Kilgarin. The sounds of scuffling in the stairwell Orlando and Halford had used were more sporadic now, and one or two of the uniformed Company men were making noises about helping their fellows finish with the last of the intruders. None of the guards were aware, apparently, that Conners and his fellow rebels had accomplished their mission. The guards thought they'd stopped the saboteurs as they were entering the building, and had no idea of the power packs planted in the sections below. Kilgarin tried once more to gain control of Conners's brain; the packs, he knew, were only a minute away from detonation.

And you can't stop them, Kilgarin. There's nothing you can do.

Kilgarin was as startled by the fact of Conners's speech as he was by the what the rebel said.

Why would I want to stop it?

You're a Sensitive, aren't you? A Company man.

They're not necessarily the same thing, Kilgarin told him.

Aren't they?

Kilgarin dismissed Conners's presence. He drove more deeply into the man's brain and found the motor controls, seized them with more energy than he'd ever expended before.

The guard holding Conners was taken by surprise when the seemingly unconscious man came suddenly awake. Conners's shoulder caught the guard under the jaw and the Company man fell back, stunned. Conners's body was on its feet and moving toward Grenna when the building around the two of them abruptly ceased to exist.

An antimatter implosion is unlike any reaction known to man. In the moment of meeting, when matter comes in contact with its structural and material opposite, mutual annihilation occurs—instantly. So complete is the destruction that even the energy produced by the reaction is consumed, in direct contradiction of physical law. Just where the energy and matter vanish to is a subject of intense speculation among researchers, but of little practical importance.

What is important is the effect of such consumption.

Upon the moment of antimatter/matter destruction, the magnetic and gravitational forces intersecting the implosion are warped and twisted out of shape, a vacuum is formed that requires filling, and much of the immediate vicinity collapses under the combined pressure of all that occurs. The amount of antimatter Conners used in the power packs could only have been measured molecularly, but the effect it produced was equivalent to the explosion of several thousand pounds of conventional nitroglycerin.

In a matter of seconds the processing plant was reduced to rubble and Kilgarin was flung against a solid stone wall—part of the pillar he'd been standing near the instant before. Quite probably it saved his life.

There was nothing to save Conners.

Gold was the most prominent color in the morning sky. It streaked the eastern clouds just as it'd gilded the western horizon the evening before. Kilgarin didn't notice the sky, however; he walked in a daze, drained of all emotion. He'd had revenge, a part of it at any rate, but it seemed to make no difference to the way he felt. He was empty.

Above him the sound of the Company fliers streaking toward the ruins of the processing plant was already growing dimmer. He wondered if the port authorities would think the explosion an accident, or if they'd place the blame properly, and so give reason to the rebels' sacrifice. He hoped they would. Perhaps it would help him live with the sickness inside him.

Ahead, the *Charter*'s lights glowed, signaling that lift-off was to be in one hour. Kilgarin hurried. He wanted very much to be on board when the *Charter* left Maylind.

He expected to find her in the recreation room, and when she wasn't there, he tried the lounge. The Cook was the only person in the cafeteria, however; he was sleeping with his head resting on his arms, an overturned stein of beer lying near his elbow on the grimy table. Kilgarin jogged the gray man's shoulder twice before the Cook stirred, mumbled something incoherent, and finally pulled himself erect, eyeing the Cork standing over him.

"We thought you weren't coming back."

"Where's Marka?" Kilgarin asked him.

The Cook came awake. "What do you want her for, hey? You've done enough to her, to everyone."

"I know that," Kilgarin said. "I want to tell her I'm sorry."

Peering at him with hard gray eyes, the Cook shook his head, slowly. "You're not, Kilgarin. You think you're sorry, but you're not. Full of ideas, but nothing for her. Why don't you look around you, Kilgarin? Why don't you look outside yourself?"

"Tell me, Cook. Where is she?"

The small man sighed. He made a decision, and his features grew hard. "Her room," he said. "The door's open, or was when we left."

"You and Raymond?"

"We were all upset. You can understand, after what happened to J'kar? We didn't like you very much then, Kilgarin. Marka liked you least."

"Then I've got to see her, tell her—"

"Tell her what, Kilgarin?" The Cook turned away. "Go ahead, talk to her. Go ahead."

For a moment as Kilgarin headed out of the door, the Cook turned toward him, his face softening, and he called after the receding Cork, "I'll be here, Kilgarin. You can come back here."

After going to Marka's room and seeing her sleeping, entwined, with the duty officer from the hydroponics garden, and seeing the credit chits lying in payment on the desk beside her bed, Kilgarin did go back to the lounge. He said nothing, and neither did the Cook.

A drink was already waiting.

Chapter Ten

Tenth month, fifth day, anno Domini 3146

Centauri was ten days' voyage ahead of them, a week if they strained the crew. The Captain seemed intent on doing just that, Kilgarin learned soon after the *Charter* left Maylind. Apparently the Company required the ship's presence on the colonial base, for it'd ordered the mindship's speedy return. Kilgarin felt that pressuring the crew was a mistake, and told the Captain as much, reminding the older man of what had occurred in the mess lounge little over a week before. "Our orders are clear, Kilgarin," the Captain replied. "This is, after all, a Company-owned vessel. Our first allegiance as ship officers is to the Company, not to the crew of this ship." To this Kilgarin said nothing.

As a footnote to his experience on Maylind, Kilgarin learned a few days after the *Charter* passed out of the planet's system that the government sponsored by the Company on the colony was on the verge of collapse, following the political uproar attendant on the processing plant's destruction. Kilgarin greeted the news with a disturbed satisfaction. He was not so much pleased as relieved that the rebels had achieved their purpose. This neutral reaction was a continuation of the emptiness he'd felt since leaving the ruins and returning to the *Charter*, and he dismissed it as simple depression. He didn't care to delve into its cause.

He didn't think about Marka at all.

During the early days of the run into Centauri, Kilgarin kept to his room and worked on his wooden figurines. The statuettes were coming along nicely and he hoped they would be finished by the time the mindship reached port. He wanted to sell them at one of the bazaars that crowded the central Centaurian city of New Saint Johannesburg. He had no clear idea of how to accomplish this, since in the past he'd always given the statues away to friends, but he knew he'd think of something when the time came.

As the days passed, however, he grew more and more aware of the tension in the Physical end of the ship, and this awareness began to distract him from his work. Always before he'd managed to maintain a separation between the work his mind performed and the operations that occupied his hands; now, however, he found himself making slips that couldn't be excused by simple clumsiness. His psychic world was beginning to intrude upon his real one. It was the first sign of a Sensitive breaking.

In an attempt to reinforce the separation he knew had to exist between himself and the crew, Kilgarin stopped going to the lounge, taking advantage of his position as Cork to have his meals served in his quarters. The second day of the new arrangement, the Cook arrived with Kilgarin's dinner. There were two servings on the tray, and the Cook stood against one wall and ate his serving with Kilgarin. When the two men had finished eating, the Cook asked the Cork what was wrong.

"Nothing," Kilgarin answered. "I just needed to get away."

"Too much pressure?"

"More than usual, but not too much."

"I've felt it too, Kilgarin. You sensed it the first day you stepped aboard. This is a hate ship, and the hate is building."

"I'm aware of that, Cook."

"The Outworlds. All this talk of revolution. It's set the men on edge."

"I know," Kilgarin said.

"Listen, despite everything, I don't want you to kill yourself, Killy. Tell the Captain you can't handle this alone. Tell him to assign one of the other Sensitives to help you. It's been done before, when a Cork wasn't foolish enough to think he could valve this kind of madness alone."

"I can do it myself," Kilgarin said. "I don't need the Captain's help."

"The Captain? Is it still him, Kilgarin?"

"Cook, when the *Charter* reaches Centauri the Company's going to break up the crew and send us off to other ships. That's what usually happens when a mindship gets as sick as this. If I ever want to find out why the Captain killed my brother, I'll have to find out now. In the next few days. That's why I can't start sharing my mind."

"Kilgarin, you're too damned independent . . . don't let it destroy you. You've let it go too far already."

"Thanks for the coffee, Cook."

The Cook left, taking the tray, and Kilgarin returned to his figurines. He cut his hand once. It took him several minutes to get the blood off the wood.

On the fourth day out from Maylind Kilgarin applied for permission to take up a post in the Control Room. The Captain agreed; Kilgarin found that the decision left him oddly suspended—in a way, he was no longer sure he *wanted* to probe the Captain's mind. He doubted his ability to survive the probe, on top of the regular pressures he encountered as Cork. Yet he knew it was something he had to do. The new urgency demanded it.

Also on the fourth day a man committed suicide in the Central Life Support Plant. Kilgarin had been aware of the Physical's depression but had neglected to soothe it, and so the boy—it wasn't fair to call him a man; he was hardly over eighteen—had become more and more despondent, until finally he'd taken his life. Kilgarin recalled something about a woman the youth had met on Maylind, some ship follower who'd given the boy a discount because of his age. More than this the Cork couldn't remember. The suicide was found in the Plant itself; somehow he'd contrived to shut off all LS controls for that section of the chamber, and it wasn't until late in the afternoon that a maintenance engineer had discovered the malfunction and reported it to the Captain. Kilgarin was present when they finally managed to unfreeze the lock mechanism on the Plant section. Inside the subzero chamber the boy's body was completely decompressed, blood crusted on his face and under his fingernails, stains marking his suit leggings where his body had completed the indignity he'd begun. Kilgarin wondered at his inability to feel remorse, and decided that it was better he couldn't; he wouldn't have known what to do with grief. There was very little of him left to deal with it.

He saw Raymond once in the hallway. The Cork was

returning to his cabin from the Control Room and he passed him in the corrior outside the lounge.

Almost, the Physical stopped. His eyes met Kilgarin's, and a question seemed to spark there for an instant. It must have been his imagination though, Kilgarin decided, for the spark died in the moment of visual contact between the two men. Just as well. Kilgarin had little to say.

"Kilgarin, do you see this?"

The Cork studied the abstraction portrayed on the screen near the Captain's Set. Rainbow lines radiated from a central boiling core of black. Though each of the men would see it in different terms when they stepped beyond the ship during mind-drive, here both the Captain and the Cork were provided with a common frame of reference for discussion.

"It's a Black Hole, sir," Kilgarin said. The Captain nodded, rubbing his fingers over his chin absently as he leaned forward, peering at the screen.

"We're headed on a course that will take us within several thousand parsecs," he said. "It's the only way we can reach Centauri within the next forty-eight hours. Going around would add a week or more to our ETA."

"Do you think it's wise to go that close, Captain?"

"We can use her gravitational pull for a boost. It could mean even more time saved."

"Are we sure we can use that trick in the Back Region?"

"Theoretically, Kilgarin, spacial conditions have equivalents in hyperspace. We already know that Black Holes extend their event horizons into the Back Region, that they exist as singularities both in normal space-time and in the distorted space-time in which mindships travel. My own experience with Black Holes has proven they present no insurmountable obstacles. A little caution is all that's necessary, and on this occasion we have ample time to prepare. We can *use* this Black Hole, Kilgarin."

"As you say, Captain."

It was near a Black Hole that Marc Kilgarin had died. The Cork thought this hole would serve his purpose perfectly. There could be no further delays.

He was in the lounge picking up a bottle of absinthe when the ship slipped once more into the Back Region. The Cook caught his hand as he turned away, stopping him.

"Be careful, Killy," the Cook said. "Don't kill yourself."

Disengaging his hand, Kilgarin moved away, walking unsteadily—almost as though against his will—toward the corridor. A Physical sitting on a bench not far from the food console glared at the passing Cork, spitting at him as Kilgarin left the room. The Cook's hand tightened around the neck of a bottle on the counter, and he brought it up, about to swing at the spitting Physical when something touched the Cook's mind, soothing the anger. He put the bottle down and poured himself a drink. The rage was almost gone.

The Cork was back at work.

Mind-drive:

Kilgarin rises from the ship, tensely extending his mind in a number of directions and encompassing the sphere of mental energy that powers the *Charter*. Colors swim within the sphere, jagged arrows of yellow and green, blue and fiery red, each an interpretation of his mind of the emotions expressed by the crew. Here, a man is filled with anger. There, a man is overcome with fear. Both emotions are removed by the Cork and fed into the stream of energy powering the *Charter*'s flight. Love goes also, as do envy, and lust, and greed, and pride, charity, and all the rest of the human emotions Kilgarin has come to know so intimately. All are fed to the Engineer, and all resume existence as power—nothing more.

Kilgarin searches and at last finds the Captain, who is only now drawing on the full strength of his Set, only now slipping into control.

Kilgarin decides that the final moment has come, that it is time to force himself into the Captain's brain. It is an invasion he's avoided as long as possible. Now there is no more time—no more room for avoidance.

His mind lunges forward.

He strikes the Captain's shell, pierces, bounces back. There is no opening. None, none at all.

As he draws within the security of his personality, Kilgarin feels a turmoil in the ship below. Within the mental sphere the colors are becoming agitated—yellows blend with reds, blues with greens, softer colors losing their strength as brighter, more antagonistic tones are produced. It's his fault, Kilgarin knows. His preoccupation with the Captain has caused him to turn from his duties as Cork. Quickly he moves among the souls represented in the sphere, touching, removing, soothing—easing the pain that is the cause of the antagonism. Yet as he moves among the minds, helping some, others break into rage. He turns to those, and the ones he has healed return to madness.

Suddenly Kilgarin finds himself turning from one man to another, spinning in his efforts to reach them all. Madness erupts around him: in one of the lifeboat pods, a man stabs a Sensitive with a plastisteel sliver ripped from a wall casing; in the lounge, two Physicals fall to the floor screaming, tearing at their faces and clothes; and in the corridor leading amidships a woman is raped by three Sensitives—and she herself is a Physical. Everywhere there is chaos. And abruptly, as he strains to his capacity in an effort to ease the insanity, Kilgarin *sees.*

Coming into view, an open wound in the flesh of space, the Black Hole.

"Kilgarin, are you all right?" The Captain's voice echoed in the Cork's ears and in his mind.

Fine, Captain. Just give me a moment.

"We don't *have* a moment, Kilgarin. The ship is pulling apart *now.*"

I'm trying, Captain. You have to understand, the pressures—

"Damn the pressures, Kilgarin." (In the Control Room, a hand grasped his arm and drew him to his feet. Vaguely, he was aware of the Captain bending over him, though his awareness was blurred, for his mind was beyond the mindship walls.) "Let me give you a shot."

No! (Kilgarin shoved the Captain's hands away and shook his head like a drunk man.) *I can handle this alone. You won't kill me like you killed my brother.*

"I see." (The Captain's physical voice was cold.) His mental voice carried no emotion. "Take hold of yourself then, Cork. We're about to pass the hole, and I don't want you cracking up and taking this ship with you. Understand?"

(Kilgarin settled into a cross-legged position at the foot of the Captain's Set, his eyes staring blankly ahead. The Captain snapped the plugs back into his body and returned to his trance. Outside the Control Room there were the sounds of a scuffle, blows, someone crying out. Inside the room there was silence.)

It is only four kilometers in diameter, but that small space contains the compressed matter of a star. So great are its gravitational forces no light can ever escape from its horizon, the speed of light insufficient to break the pull of the Black Hole's gravity. Tidal forces surrounding the hole are on the order of a nightmare—in an instant the pressure of those forces could reach the infinite. Any object passing within the farthest limit of the hole's event horizon would simply be flattened to the submolecular level. In the Back Region, the Black Hole appears as a puncture in space, surrounded by fragments of color whirlpooling toward its central maw.

The *Charter* among them.

Kilgarin feels his mind begin to scream. The madness in the psi vessel is reaching the breaking point. He knows he will not survive the dive past the Black Hole, and if the Cork does not survive—neither will the ship.

Images fly through his mind: Marka, lying in the arms of a stranger, not once before Kilgarin, but twice—aboard the *Charter*, and also three years earlier, on Endrim. The two images become one, a scene of betrayal. She'd made herself part of him, and then she'd torn that part free, leaving him wounded—leaving him on Endrim, forcing him to return to the *Drowner*, forcing him into the arms of Lucille.

Another image: Lucille abandoning him for Baeder, telling him that he asked too much of her, and gave too little in return. That image is only one of many—each of them an aspect of her mind, which he touched each day as he Corked aboard the *Drowner*. This image too fades into madness, and becomes one with the third:

Women: the women in his brothel, unthreatening in their expressed lack of need for anything but his credit. No dependence, only simple financial reward. Somehow, this is the most painful image of all.

He pushes the memories away and finds himself floundering in the insanity around him. Each soul demands his attention, each begs his understanding—each needs him. Slavering insanity, boiling him alive.

He screams.

Ahead of him, the Black Hole screams also.

In blind fear Kilgarin gropes for support, sensing himself swirling into a darkness from which he would never truly return. He gropes, and finds support beside him. In the Captain's mind. A mind open and ready to receive him.

Breaking, he enters, and this is what he learns: the Captain is a Sensitive.

The ship buckles underneath them, but now Kilgarin has the strength to resist the tide of emotion surging below. For several seconds he floats in confusion, stunned by what he's just learned. Then he moves among the men and women of the mindship *Charter*, releasing their tension and hatred, their fear and their despair. Strangely lightheaded, he finds his energy doubled; the energy of a second mind added to his own. For the moment he accepts the aid without question. There will be time for probing once the ship is free.

The hole looms closer. Flares of power lunge past the ship, strike it, guide it downward. The mindship resists. One side of the ship seethes in agony: two hundred minds shrieking in torment.

For an instant it seems as though they are lost.

Then the *Charter* slips away, passes the hole, and slides out into normal space.

Kilgarin woke to the sounds of heavy machinery, cranes and loading devices at work nearby. At first he was disoriented, but after a moment the harsh light grew softer to his eye, and the sounds less raucous, and he began to remember where he was. He sat up on the narrow cot, blinking in the diffused glow cast by Centauri's morning sun, and focused on the two men sitting on a bench opposite him. Both men were haggard, dark smudges under their eyes indicating that neither man had slept in recent hours. Kilgarin started to speak, but the Cook waved him into silence. "Plenty of time for you to talk, Killy. Just relax."

"The Captain . . . where. . . ?"

Raymond spoke up. "He's gone to New Saint Johannesburg, Kilgarin. He left right after the crew broke up. Whatever happened between the two of you seems to have upset him quite a bit."

"Let him rest," the Cook said. "We can talk, but don't push him for any answers. All right?" He waited for Raymond's nod before continuing. "The *Charter*'s finished, Kilgarin. You should know that. After you and the Captain managed to get us into Centauri, most of the crew deserted. There was some trouble at the port gates; some of the guards were killed. From what the port master tells me, the Company plans to decommission the *Charter* altogether, possibly turn her into a troop transport."

"They're going to need as many of those as they can find," Raymond said. "The Outworlds are in open rebellion. Looks like they're going to make it this time."

"Don't excite him with that kind of talk," the Cook said, harshly. He smiled at Kilgarin. "You've been out for thirty-six hours straight, Killy. Raymond and I have been with you most of that time. Medic says you're lucky you didn't break; he doesn't know what held you together. One thing's certain though, Fellow . . . no more Corking, if you want to stay alive."

Kilgarin nodded. He noticed that Raymond kept glancing at him and then away again. The Cook caught Kilgarin's look. "I guess you'd better tell him why you're here," the small man said to Raymond. The youth frowned.

"During those last few minutes, when you and the Captain were pulling us past the Hole . . ." He broke off and ran a hand uneasily over the bristle darkening his jaw. ". . . there was some sort of feedback. Some of us, those who knew you . . . we could see things in your mind . . . just glimpses, but enough to make us realize what you've been going through, even if you don't. I still think you've done some ugly things, Kilgarin, but I suppose I can't blame you for them as much as I could before." He paused, finishing with his jaw, and dropped his hand into lap, sighing. "That's it."

"Marka?" Kilgarin asked.

"It's over for the two of you," Raymond told him. "She's sorry for what she's done, but as she says, you didn't help her be what you wanted her to be. You simply expected it. For now, she's agreed to go with me to earth; we don't have any plans for anything serious, we're just companions for now . . . but I've a feeling it might work into something. I won't ask as much of her as you did."

Again, Kilgarin nodded. He knew what Raymond had said was true, and felt no anger because the young man had said it. "I was afraid of her," Kilgarin said. "Don't you be."

Raymond grinned. "That's a promise."

"Did you find out what you wanted to know, Kilgarin?" the Cook asked. He leaned forward eagerly, apparently ready to accept the Sensitive's returning health now that he had a question of his own. "About the Captain?"

"And about myself," Kilgarin said. "About us both."

"You must have frightened him," Raymond said. "You should have seen the expression on his face when he left the *Charter*—like someone who's seen his own ghost."

"He has," Kilgarin said.

Getting to his feet, Kilgarin braced himself on the Cook's shoulder and glanced around the small port office where he'd been recovering. His clothes were draped on the single chair, folded neatly. He wondered if Marka had been there after all, and decided not to ask. "Would you get my clothes?" he asked Raymond, pointing. "I've got an appointment in the city."

When he was dressed, he thanked them for staying with him. The Cook asked when he'd be back. "I'm not sure," Kilgarin told him. "I've got to find out what someone wants of me, first."

"Who's that?" Raymond asked.

"Myself," Kilgarin replied.

Epilogue: "Sensitive"

It was several hours before he discovered the tavern where the Captain was drinking. A small outdoor pub, it was in the Sensitive District of New Saint Johannesburg, an area slightly older than the rest of the city, not as well kept as some part of the metropolis, but not as badly kept as others. The pub was named Second Sun—after Beta Centauri, Kilgarin supposed—and was in a court beside a large apartment building. The attendant at the gate probed Kilgarin for identity, realized he was a Sensitive, and allowed him through. Past the grillwork gate that separated the lobby from the central part of the tavern, Kilgarin saw a familiar figure sitting hunched on a stool, sipping from a large stein filled with green liquid. Kilgarin recognized the Captain immediately, though the man was no longer dressed in Company official grays. The Captain's clothes were loose-fitting port tunic and trousers, the inexpensive disposables sold in most port terminals. Kilgarin guessed that the older man had changed clothes moments after debarking.

"I'm sorry, sir," he said.

The Captain showed no surprise at Kilgarin's approach. Instead he indicated the stool next to his with a motion of his chin. "Don't be sorry, Kilgarin. You only opened up my mind. I was the one who'd blocked it from my thoughts."

"I should have left it that way."

"How? By killing yourself? By ignoring what I did to your brother, just as I did? You couldn't have lived with yourself that way, Kilgarin."

"You did, Captain."

"I had a mindblock. I pushed everything out of my mind, my Sensitivity, what it did to my brother, what I did to yours . . . I shut it all away. But that's no way to live. Sooner or later it all comes crashing in. If it hadn't been you, it would have been someone else." He lifted his head, caught the bartender's eye, and ordered two more steins. When Kilgarin began to protest, the Captain waved his objections away. "Take it. Consider it a privilege. You'll be the last man to drink with me. The last man I'll ever toast."

"What, Captain—?"

"I'm finished, Kilgarin. I'm a dead man. I'm just getting my energy together to do the deed, but it's only a matter of time. Effectively, I died when you broke through my mindblock."

"Sir, you aren't being fair to yourself—"

"Really? Kilgarin, let me tell you what happened to me back there. Perhaps you don't understand. When I was a child, I was a Sensitive, a prepubertal freak . . . and the only Sensitive in my colony. I was persecuted by my peers, but that wasn't why I threw up the block. You see, when I was four years old our entire colony was wiped out by a plague, and everyone died except for me and a few others scattered over the planet . . . me, my brother, and another man were alone in the city, though. A desert city, on a desert world. You know that man, Ty'ger, that Sensitive your friend killed? You know how he constantly received every emotion around him? I was the opposite, Kilgarin. Everything I felt, I broadcast. Everything I saw, I broadcast again and again.

"Even the death of my parents.

"For two weeks while we waited for the rescue ships to reach us, I tortured my brother and that other poor survivor of our city with my memories of the plague. They couldn't sleep, but for waking with my dreams in their minds, my nightmares in their brains. I drove them insane, Kilgarin, like a child ceaselessly crying for its mother—and finally my brother killed himself and that other man, thinking the man was me. I wish it had been.

"Can you imagine the pain of that, Kilgarin? To drive your own flesh to madness and death? Even at four, I knew what I'd done. I couldn't accept it, so I shut it out. I shut it out so efficiently no psychic probe ever revealed any trace of latent Sensitivity. The power was tied to pain, Kilgarin, and by bringing the power back, you've brought back my nightmare as well."

"You were the one who brought your power back, Captain. To save the ship. Maybe to save me. You did it before, to an extent—that time we were hunting with Wells."

"That was subconscious; it never threatened the block, Kilgarin. Your presence was the catalyst. I could sense your desire to know why I'd brought your brother to his death, and it sparked a similar curiosity in me. I know now—we both know—I let your brother die because he was a substitute for my younger self, for the innocent boy I'd been when I—" The Captain broke off. "We've been through that. There's no point in letting this conversation continue."

He drank off the rest of his beer and absinthe, set the glass down, and got unsteadily to his feet. He started toward the gate, and Kilgarin stopped him before the older man had taken three paces.

"Captain, you're not seeing this properly at all," Kilgarin said. "Let me—"

"Get away from me, Kilgarin," the Captain said, jerking free of the ex-Cork's grip. He continued toward the door.

A moment passed while Kilgarin debated with himself. Then he made his decision and plunged into the Captain's mind. He found the core of the man's anger and self-loathing, the hatred consuming his soul. Deftly, Kilgarin's mental fingers plucked the pain away. He located the despair he'd seen reflected in the Captain's eyes, and he dissolved it with a touch of compassion. He moved through the older man's mind, shifting and rearranging perceptions and memories, putting them in order and perspective. Gradually the Captain's fires of self-hate dimmed, shrank, went out. With an almost audible mental sigh, the Captain stumbled and fell to the patio floor.

Kilgarin waved away the Sensitives who came to the Captain's aid, and bending over the elder man, he helped the Captain to his feet and guided him to a nearby table, where they could sit and talk in private.

"Most men have Sensitives to relieve them all their lives," Kilgarin said. "You had your guilt come on you all at once. You couldn't stand it. No man could." He watched the Captain from within and without, maintaining the mindlink he'd established with his former superior officer for the older man's safety.

"You should despise me," the Captain said.

"If you were better trained in your Sensitivity, you could look into my mind and see that I never could. Not anymore. Something changed inside me the same instant your block was dissolved. I realized something about myself, perhaps about the whole mindship system. I can't hate you for helping me see that."

"See what?" the older man asked. He watched as Kilgarin ordered them more drinks.

"I used people," Kilgarin said. "Part of it was because of the kind of colony I came from, a frontier world, a hard world where people have to be independent—or they die. A man on Wellington was considered weak if he needed people. I'm afraid I've suffered from that all my life. Whenever I began to think I needed someone, I'd break away from them and try to hurt them in some way. But it went deeper than that. This way of life, mindshipping . . . it trains you to think of people as objects, things to use for your own ends, just as we use them as fuel to power our ships."

"And I showed you this?" The Captain was clearly incredulous. His face, still pale and drawn from the shock of what he'd learned about himself, was creased with lines of confusion. Kilgarin smiled and pressed his hand on the other man's.

"Not directly. You just released me from the ship's pressures so that I could see it. For the past few weeks I've been coming closer and closer to understanding what's been wrong with my life. Did you know I used to own a brothel? What better way to use someone, how can you better show your disrespect for someone as a person—than by using her body to earn credit? And the way I tried to use Ty'ger and Raymond to learn about you, or the way I wanted to use Marka—or even those revolutionaries, I used them to get revenge on the Company—"

Kilgarin stopped speaking and shook his head. "That's all over," he said. "I'm finished as a Cork. I'm going to have to learn to live as a human being."

"We both are," the Captain said thoughtfully.

As the bartender brought them their steins, Kilgarin remembered the revolution, and another thought crossed his mind. "We *all* are," he said.

Something occurred between the Captain and the Cork at that moment. Their common realization brought them suddenly together, and their minds completed the link Kilgarin had begun. With a start Kilgarin realized that he was dependent on this man now, who knew him better than any other human had; and the Captain in turn was dependent on him. Each of them had a great deal to learn from the other. Each of them had something to give. And for the first time in his life Kilgarin found he coulo pletely trust the other mind linked to his own.

Teach me, each man said, *I have to grow*.

Kilgarin raised his glass as the Captain raised his. Th motions of each man were in counterpoint to the motions of the other. The mindlock was complete: total symbiosis.

Smiling, they drank.

Usman Aziz

THE MINDSHIP

was the break-through to the stars. In spite of work on Faster Than Light, hyperdrives, and such, it was the power of the mind that turned out to be the most certain directing force between the worlds. So the mindships came into being, driven forward by the lines of mental energy, directed by trained crews—and held together not by the navigator or the captain but by the man they called the cork.

He was just another man but he had the ability to siphon out the discords which could wreck a ship, to create the harmony without which starflight would be disastrous.

Kilgarin was such a "cork," but he had deliberately grounded himself until they forced him to take up the mental reins again. It was their risk and they should have known better—because Kilgarin had ulterior motives no ship's cork had a right to harbor.

MINDSHIP

is a brilliant new concept by one of the young rising lights of the science fiction cosmos.

A DAW BOOKS ORIGINAL

—NEVER
BEFORE IN PAPERBACK—